DRINKING
FROM THE FLAMES

"Open your eyes and stare into the Sun!" Moth opened his eyes and stared, trying not to flinch as the knife sawed back and forth across his throat. The Sun seared his soul, burning out his childhood; he could feel the child within him choking as it struggled to escape his throat, and then the knife cut into him and his childhood bubbled out of him, and he wept with relief.

"The child is dead. You are Sartor-ban-i-Tresh and you are reborn a child of the clay." The voice was still not that of the father he had known, but was no longer menacing.

"My truename is Sartor-ban-i-Tresh and I am a child of the clay,". . .

DRINK THE FIRE FROM THE FLAMES

Scott Baker

A Legend book
Published by Arrow Books Limited
62-65 Chandos Place, London WC2N 4NW

An imprint of Century Hutchinson Limited

London Melbourne Sydney Auckland
Johannesburg and agencies throughout
the world

First published in 1987 by Tor Books, USA
First published in Great Britain in 1988 by Legend

Printed and bound in Great Britain by
Anchor Brendon Limited, Tiptree, Essex

ISBN 0 09 962510 5

For Suzi, who has the courage to open my
eyes to the things I need to see

"The alchemist, like the smith, and like the potter before him, is a 'master of fire.' It is with fire that he controls the passage of matter from one state to another. The first potter who, with the aid of live embers, was successful in hardening those shapes which he had given to his clay, must have felt the intoxication of the demiurge: he had discovered a transmuting agent. That which took natural heat—from the sun or the bowels of the earth—so long to ripen, was transformed by fire at a speed hitherto undreamed of. This demiurgic enthusiasm springs from that obscure presentiment that the great secret lay in discovering how to 'perform' faster than Nature, in other words (since it is always necessary to talk in terms of the spiritual experience of primitive man) how, without peril, to interfere in the processes of the cosmic forces. Fire turned out to be the means by which man could 'execute' faster, but it could also do something other than what already existed in Nature. It was therefore the manifestation of a magico-religious power which could modify the world and which, consequently, did not belong to this world. This is why most primitive cultures look upon the specialist in the sacred—the shaman, the medicine man, the magician—as a 'master of fire.'"

Mircea Eliade, *The Forge and the Crucible*

ᚪᚬᚪ Chapter One ᚪᚬᚪ

In those days Ashlu was a land of mountains and deserts. A single great river, the Nacre, flowed from Lake Nal in the Lattan foothills to the Sea of Marshes. Men lived in the foothills and on the fertile plains surrounding them; men swarmed in the Nacre's broad valley and fertile delta; all else was desert of salt and sand, or so the men of Chal believed.

Chal, City of the Eighty-four Sils—the eighty-four priesthoods—was nineteen days by barge or coracle from the plains, but Kyborash, the colony Chal had planted on the ruins of conquered Drea-'Est, was almost on the edge of the plains, and it was to the Fair at Kyborash that the Nomads came to trade horses and rare dyestuffs. It was to Kyborash as well, where the clays, glazes, and woods for charcoals were all far finer than those to be found elsewhere in the Chaldan Empire, that the Ri Sil—the Potters' Sil—had come, forsaking its former home in the city of Chal itself.

Ri Tal was a Master Potter of the Ri Sil. He was a stout, strong, open-faced man with yellow-brown

1

skin and coarse brown hair. As a Master Potter, he
would never have left Kyborash had he not married
Kuan, the second daughter of Tas No Sil, the High
Smith, but by smith law a woman who married
outcaste had to spend the first year of her marriage
in ritual exile from the city of her birth. A Master
Potter had been needed to supervise the Sil's affairs
in Chal, and Kuan was beautiful, tall and full-
bodied yet supple, with the fire-red hair and black
eyes of the smiths; besides, the Sil Smith had
offered Ri Tal a truly magnificent brideprice for
what was, after all, only the outcaste marriage of a
second daughter, so Ri Tal had accepted exile
willingly.

In this, Sartor had smiled upon them. Some
seven months after their arrival in Chal, Kuan
blessed Ri Tal with a son, but the boy's eyes were
yellow, and had their child been born anywhere but
in Chal itself, the Warriors of the Hand and Voice
who had come to record its birth would have taken
it from them to be killed. Only the Kings of Chal
had yellow eyes, and King Asp made sure that no
child bearing the outward signs of royal birth grew
to challenge his rule. But the Warrior of the Voice
who examined the boy was an old man who had
served in the Palace for more than twenty-four
years; he had known Asp's father as well as Asp
himself, and it was clear to him as it could never
have been to some Warrior of the Voice who had
only seen King Asp rarely and from a distance, if at
all, that the strange sun-fire yellow of the boy's eyes
could never be mistaken for the royal amber of a
true King's eyes. So, in his mercy, he granted Ri Tal
and Kuan their son's life.

When he learned that his son was to live, Ri Tal contrived to extend his residence in Chal another year. The clay for the boy's thirteen baptisms had to come from the same earth, and it would have been folly unthinkable to subject an unnamed child to the rigors of the journey to Kyborash. Though Chal was only nine days downriver from Kyborash, the Nacre's powerful currents rendered traffic back up the river impossible, and the return trip took forty-three days by oxcart.

The first night of each full moon Ri Tal painted his son with wet clay and chanted ritual words over him. From each baptism the potter saved the clay with which he had anointed the boy's forehead. This Ri Tal placed in a cool, secret place, and there it was seen by no one but himself.

On the first night of the first full moon following the boy's one-year day, Ri Tal took the clay from its place of concealment and, covering it with the skin of a freshly killed male goat to keep the moonlight from defiling it, carried it into the room where he did what little working of the clay his administrative duties allowed him.

The room was in utter darkness, sealed from all light for two days, and no one but Ri Tal had been allowed to enter it. During that time he had consecrated the room and all it contained to Sartor many times; now, in the darkness, Ri Tal drew blood from his right arm with a knife of chipped stone. This blood he consecrated and kneaded into the clay; then, working by touch alone, he molded the clay around the stone blade and began the fashioning of the dolthe figurine in which his son's soul was to be embodied. It was a strange dolthe, its

shape revealed to him in a dream imperfectly
grasped; yet as he worked the clay he felt its
recalcitrance leave it and he knew that Sartor was
working through him.

He wrapped the finished dolthe in damp cloths to
keep the soul from drying too quickly and cracking,
then sealed the room behind him with his cylinder
seal.

He did not return again until the moon was full.
He uncovered the window—a narrow slit, set high
in the wall—then removed the cloths and for the
first time saw the shape his hands had molded.

The dolthe was strange, far stranger than he had
realized, a thing of curves and angles, hollows and
protuberances, yet it was beautiful and he could
feel its power. His son's soul was well embodied.

He thanked Sartor, then sealed the room again
and began gathering the woods with which to make
the charcoal he would need to fire the figurine. It
was no ordinary soul, and no ordinary mixture of
grasses, dung and oakwood would do. Ri Tal carefully collected acacia wood and the roots of the
hill-loving sari grasses; with these he mixed chips of
gummy sarbatu wood stored under hides since the
previous summer. The kiln had already been exor-
cised and consecrated to Sartor and to the nameless
Earth Mother. Ri Tal placed the wood in it and,
covering the kiln with a layer of earth, kindled the
wood by slow degrees until he had the charcoal he
desired.

This too he consecrated. Then he fired his son's
soul. Had the dolthe cracked in the firing his son
would have been condemned to life as a potter-
pariah, unable to work anything beyond baseware,

but Ri Tal was a Master Potter and not given to carelessness. Sartor favored him: the dolthe did not crack.

Taking the fired soul from the kiln, he realized that part of it had the shape of the great scarlet-winged moth found nowhere but in Kyborash.

His usename will be Moth, Ri Tal thought, well pleased. He painted the soul with glazes of his own discovery and fired it again. When he removed it from the kiln it was banded orange and purple, while a single knife-edged projection jutting from its side gleamed a metallic copper.

His truename will be Sartor-ban-i-Tresh, Sartor of the Setting Sun, Ri Tal thought, and again he was pleased: it was a name of good omen, for in Ashlu the setting sun was reckoned the beginning of the new day.

Ri Tal dictated a letter asking Ri Cer Sil's permission to return home, then arranged for the inscribed clay tablet's shipment to Kyborash.

While he awaited the Ri Sil's reply he fashioned Moth the glazed clay toys that only a potter's son might own, the tiny bowls and balls and manikins, the ceramic flutes that only potters were permitted to play, the tiny oxcart with its four wheels attached with leather thongs.

When Ri Larshu, his replacement, finally arrived on the barge from Kyborash two months later, Ri Tal spent seven impatient days instructing the man in the current state of affairs in Chal, in the subtleties of the ceramic trade with the cities of the Delta League, and in the various offerings to be given Sartor in each of Chal's many temples. Then he loaded his wife, child, and belongings aboard an oxcart, making sure Moth's dolthe was well hidden where it would be safe from harm, and set out for Kyborash. The journey was arduous, but no more so than was to be expected. Since all the peoples between Chal and Kyborash were subject to King Asp—and since the oxcart obviously contained little to attract brigands—they made the voyage without incident.

Ri Tal had never enjoyed his life as an administrator. He was anxious to return to Kyborash and to working the Earth Mother's clays.

In later years Moth remembered nothing of Chal, nor of the journey. His earliest memory was of playing in the dirt in front of his father's house in Kyborash.

He was a strong, even-tempered boy, with hair dappled the red of the metalsmiths and the black of his potter father. One eyebrow was red, the other black, while his skin was a deep brown. He spent the years before his initiation like any other master artisan's child, playing with his friends whenever he could steal time away from helping with the womanswork or weeding the vegetable gardens and the barley field.

✑ Chapter Two ✑

Moth's teeth were chattering. It was just after dawn on the morning of his seventh birthday, and he and his cousin Tramu were huddled together with two dozen other children looking at the body of a dead lion. The lion lay at the far end of one of the Temple barley fields, almost in the irrigation ditch; two black-fletched arrows protruded from its body and a third stuck out of its neck. The children had congregated silently, as if by instinct. None of them had thought to inform an adult.

The King! Moth thought, for lions were sacred and only King Asp was permitted to hunt them. Perhaps if I wait I'll see the King!

"What if it's just playing dead?" Rafti asked, breaking the silence. She was eight, the same age as Tramu, and her hair was as red as his, but she was still a child. Girls stayed children until they married. "Lions do that," she continued. "My father told me."

"It's dead," Tramu said. "Look at the arrows sticking out of it."

"Maybe it's just wounded and pretending to be dead until we get close to it," Rafti said, excited by the idea.

"No." Moth pointed at the carcass. "See? There are flies on its eyes."

"So?" Rafti demanded. "A lion pretended to be dead so it could kill King Vitrus. Father told me."

"Nobody cares what *your* father says," Dilea said. She was a weaver's daughter, and though younger than Moth was already a head taller than he was. "Everybody knows that story."

"Besides, that was for King Vitrus. For a King," Golgin said. He was round and fat, with protruding eyes and an incongruously long head. Moth hated him: he was a bully like his father, Snae Tka, the tax collector.

The last time Golgin's father had come to collect the summertax, he'd thrown down the jar of barley he was rummaging through, breaking it and spilling the precious grain, then grabbed Moth by the nose. His eyes staring from sunken sockets like the eyes of an ancient ferret—fierce, bright, hating—the tax collector had twisted the boy's nose and demanded the secret of Ri Tal's hidden wealth. Moth had known nothing, said nothing, though he had been unable to keep himself from crying.

"You don't have anything to worry about, Rafti," Golgin continued. "No lion's going to put up with flies in its eyes for anybody less than a King. Oh, for a beautiful princess, maybe—but not for a second-rate silversmith's ugly little daughter."

Rafti glared at Golgin and Moth thought she was going to spit on him, but an instant later she'd turned from the Snae's son to glare at *him*. It's not my fault, he wanted to say. Don't look at me like that, look at Golgin.

He said nothing.

"It's dead," Tramu said. "Let's go get a good look at it." He began walking across the field, the other children following hesitantly. Moth could see the black blood matting the honey-colored fur and silver mane. It was a big, big lion.

He ignored the commotion behind him until he felt his mother's all-too-familiar grip on his wrist.

"Moth!" She yanked at him. "Your father's furious. How could you have forgotten—oh!" She'd noticed the lion, stood staring openmouthed at it, her face gone old and grim.

Then: "Come along!"

"But, Mother, a lion, the King—the *King*, Mother!"

"Are you going to let a dead animal keep you from being sealed to the clay? What kind of son would your father think I'd borne him?"

"A good son, Mother."

She started firmly off along the path leading to the West Gate, her long muscular legs moving determinedly beneath her dress of scarlet linen. Moth looked wistfully back, but the children crowding around the lion hid it from his view.

He followed her, hurrying to keep up, through the city, down long dirty streets winding between close-packed buildings of sun-dried and kiln-dried bricks, out another gate. It was still very early and the day was not yet hot.

"But, Mother!" he cried, unable to restrain himself further. "But, Mother, the King!"

"Be quiet, son. Were you told that the King was

coming? No, if he came he came in secret, by night perhaps, and most likely he'll leave the same way. You won't get to see him this time."

"Why did he leave the lion there, Mother? It was such a fine lion."

"Lions are the King's business, not yours. Today is the most important day of your life; you should be thinking of the clay, and nothing but the clay. Not about lions."

"Yes, Mother. Is it the most important day for all my life, or just for all my life until now?"

"For all of your life."

They reached their house. It was a big house —only Ri Cer Sil, of all the potters, had a bigger house. Moth followed his mother in through the narrow doorslit. They passed through the ante-room and into the central courtyard, then on into a room whose second doorslit on the far side, always hidden by a curtain of densely woven gray wool, gave entrance to the potting compound behind the house. Neither Moth nor his mother had ever seen the compound.

But the familiar curtain was gone, replaced by a gaudy scarlet one from which hung dozens of tassels, each ending in a ceramic disk. Some of the disks were unglazed red, buff, tan, or white pottery; others were glazed; still others had been painted. It was hard to make out the painted designs in the dim light of the room.

From the compound came the sound of a ceramic flute.

"May you return to me alive and a potter," Moth's mother whispered to him. She kissed him, then blindfolded him with a strip of black linen wound seven times around his head.

"Mother?" Moth asked, suddenly afraid. There was no reply. He waited a moment, summoning up his courage, then pushed his way blindly past the hanging into the compound.

I must be brave, he told himself.

Once in the compound he stopped. "Father?" he asked. There was no answer. The music of the flute had ceased. He could feel the sun hot on his head, but he could see nothing. "Father?" he repeated.

Strong hands gripped his wrists, held them firm. "What is your name?" demanded a voice—his father's yet not his father's. The voice sounded harsh, cruel; it frightened him. He began to cry.

"Your name!" The voice not his father's was heavy with scorn.

"Moth," he ventured.

"No! That is only what people call you in the world outside. Here you can have no name but your truename. Tell me your name!"

"I don't know," Moth said, trying to stop crying.

"You are here today to learn your truename, if you have one. The name of your soul-in-clay. Without this name you are nothing, no one; you are only a hated outcast, accursed of Sartor. Do you understand what I am telling you?"

"Yes."

"Do you want this name, this precious name?"

"Yes," Moth sobbed.

The hands released his wrists. "Open your hands!" the fierce voice commanded. Something was pressed into his right hand.

"Do you know what this is?" the voice not his father's demanded.

Moth shook his head.

"Answer!"

"No."

"Feel it with your other hand. Do you know what it is now?"

"A toy cart."

"Whose toy cart?"

"Mine?"

"Yes. Do the other children envy you your toy cart?"

"Yes."

"Kneel." Moth knelt. "Place your cart in front of you on the ground. Open your hand again." Something cold and hard was pressed into Moth's hand. "Grip it tight. Do you know what it is?"

"A stone?"

"Yes. A stone born of the womb of the Earth Mother. Now, repeat after me: 'I take this stone—'"

Moth repeated, "I take this stone—

"—from the Earth Mother—

"—and with it I destroy—

"—this, my favorite toy—

"—of my childhood—"

"'—that I may die to childhood—'" the voice intoned.

Die? But— Falteringly: "—that I may die to childhood—

"—and be reborn—

"—a child of the clay."

"Good. Raise the stone over your head and call on Sartor for strength."

"Sartor," Moth whispered.

"Louder!"

"Sartor!" Moth cried.

"Take the stone and smash your toy. Destroy it utterly, that you may destroy your childhood."

Moth hit the toy cart. He groped for the fragments, hit them again and again and again, until his arm ached and the cart had been broken into pieces smaller than the fingernail on the little finger of his left hand.

At last the voice said, "Enough!" and the stone was taken from his hand.

"Repeat after me: 'I die to childhood.'"

"I die to childhood."

A hand grasped his left shoulder. He could smell hot breath on the back of his neck. Something sharp was pressed against his throat. He gasped.

"Do not move."

Moth struggled vainly to still his trembling.

"Do you feel death at your throat?" the voice not his father's demanded.

"Yes," he whispered.

"Know that this is a krisse, a knife-of-the-earth, and that it will drink your blood whether you be reborn or not. If you are truly dead to childhood, the knife will cut the dead child from your throat and free you of it; but if you are in truth still a child, the knife will cut you into little pieces, for it is a knife that hates childhood.

"Close your eyes!"

Moth's eyes were already closed but he tried to squeeze them more tightly shut. The hand released its hold on his shoulder, lifted the blindfold from his face, grasped his chin and pulled his head back.

"Open your eyes and stare into the Sun!" Moth opened his eyes and stared, trying not to flinch as the knife sawed back and forth across his throat. The Sun seared his soul, burning out his childhood; he could feel the child within him choking as it struggled to escape his throat, and then the knife cut into him and his childhood bubbled out of him, and he wept with relief.

"The child is dead. You are Sartor-ban-i-Tresh and you are reborn a child of the clay." The voice was still not that of the father he had known, but it was no longer menacing.

"My truename is Sartor-ban-i-Tresh and I am a child of the clay." He was gasping for breath.

"Now bend forward, Sartor-ban-i-Tresh, that your face may rest against the Earth Mother, so She may drink of your throat's blood, for this is not only your birthday but your betrothal, man to earth, potter to clay, and your bride must drink of your life. Take your hand, knead the blood-damp earth with your fingers. Now take a single pinch of the earth you have watered and swallow it, saying, 'I, Sartor-ban-i-Tresh, accept the Earth Mother as my bride.'"

"I, Sartor-ban-i-Tresh, accept the Earth Mother as my bride." The earth tasted warm, salty, gritty.

"Close your eyes. Stand. Now walk forward."

Moth hesitantly pushed first his right, then his left foot forward, paused, took another step—

"Stop." The voice was behind him now. "Open your eyes, looking neither right nor left."

He opened his eyes, blinked. He was facing the outer wall. There was a niche in the wall level with his waist, and in this recess seven bowls rested, each containing a different wet, glistening substance. A large openmouthed water jug rested on the ground just right of the niche.

"These are the seven clays. Remember them: the white, the tan, the gray, the red, the brown, the yellow, and the brownblack. Repeat after me: 'O Sartor, I ask Your permission that I may touch these Your clays.'"

"O Sartor, I ask Your permission that I may touch these Your clays," Moth repeated.

"Now, take up the brownblack, holding its wet, cool body in your hands. Knead it, squeeze it, stroke it, mold it—but gently, very gently: you are introducing yourself to the brownblack and you must take care not to frighten it. Yet you are also the betrothed of the Earth Mother and the clays must learn to obey you as children obey their fathers.

"Replace the brownblack and wash your hands, for certain of these clays do not like each other's touch. Now, take up the yellow—the False Emperor, as it is called, for its color does not endure the flames. . . ."

When Moth had familiarized himself with each clay in turn, he was again blindfolded. The voice —and by now it had become the voice of his father, joyous only, no longer menacing or awesome —said, "Remember, Sartor-ban-i-Tresh, that your truename is your ultimate secret, to be revealed only to others of our Sil and not to be spoken at all unless you are in a potting compound or in search of clay. At all other times and to all other people —to your mother, your cousin, even your wife when you take one—you must remain Moth. Do you understand?"

"Yes."

Moth was led forward and shoved through the
doorslit. His mother removed the blindfold and
wept for joy. He had not seen the compound—only
the niche and the blazing sun—and he had not yet
set eyes upon the figure who must have been, yet
had been somehow more than, his father.

He did not tell his mother that the child for
whose return she rejoiced was dead.

He fell asleep early, only to be awakened in the
middle of the night by the sound of his mother
whispering to his father, "Tal, they found a dead
lion today."

"They *found* it, Kuan?"

"Yes. There were three arrows sticking out of it.
Tal, those were not King Asp's arrows."

"You're sure?"

"I've seen the arrows my father makes for him.
They have reed shafts and are fletched with yellow
feathers. The arrows in the lion were blackwood
fletched with black."

"Whose, then? Some warrior's?"

"No warrior of Chal or the Empire. They were
Nomad arrows."

"You're sure?"

"Yes. Turshi, perhaps. I helped Father fletch
some arrows for a Turshi once, and they were
almost exactly the same."

There was a long silence. Then she was lying to
me, Moth thought. It was the first time he knew of
that his mother had ever lied to him.

"Do you think there will be a war?" Ri Tal asked.

"I don't know, husband. Why ask me?"

"Kuan, I stay in my compound, I work with my
pots—I know nothing of these things. I do not

want to know. But sometimes . . ."

"Sometimes one needs to know."

"Yes, Kuan, your father might know."

"He wouldn't tell me anything. He takes his responsibilities as the King's Weaponsmith even more seriously than you do yours as a potter. But Tas Et has also been doing some work for the Palace. Maybe he's told Pyota something."

"Ask her. I'll bury the spare grain. Far away from the house, where Snae Tka won't think to look for it."

"Couldn't you just put it inside the compound?"

"No. It's against Sil law."

"Still—"

"No."

Moth fell asleep wondering what a war would be like, and why his mother had lied to him about it. But the next morning all Kyborash was talking about the King's secret visit.

Soon all the other children had forgotten the lion.

◆◆◆ Chapter Three ◆◆◆

Moth's eighth birthday was only six days away, but despite the obvious momentousness of the occasion Kuan refused to relieve him of his usual duties. He had no choice but to spend the morning helping her weed the gardens where garlic, onions and leeks, mint and saffron, coriander, rue, thyme, gourds, and multicolored melons grew in their separate patches.

His back ached from working hunched over. The date palms and apricot trees provided some shade, but not enough, and it was a hot, hot day, so he was only too happy when Kuan sent him to work in the family barley field. There, naked except for a necklace of azure-glazed cylindrical beads, a blade of chipped flint in his hand, he waded knee-deep through the muddy water of the irrigation ditches, cutting back the bright blue reeds that threatened to choke the channels. It was a day like any other.

But the next day the Sil Astrologer proclaimed the beginning of the Spring Inundation, and Kuan let Moth join his friends on the bank of the river—though she did not neglect to inform him that he would have to work twice as hard later to make up for the work he was missing.

Moth made his way to the river and climbed the high bank of piled earth that kept the river from washing out and drowning the city.

"Already up three bodylengths," Yeshun said. Moth looked down at the swollen, silt-laden waters. He could actually see the water level slowly creeping higher.

"Maybe the banks won't be high enough this year," Rafti suggested. "Maybe we'll have a flood."

"I'd like to see a flood," Shuner, Yeshun's brother, said.

"That's stupid," Golgin said. "The river could still rise another eight or nine bodylengths without overflowing."

"What if it rises twelve?" Rafti asked. "Or thirty-six?"

"There hasn't been a flood for . . . for I don't know how long," Golgin said.

"You don't?" Multas asked. Her father was a Warrior of the Voice.

"No."

"It was in King Chargon's time," Multas said. "But that was just a little flood."

"Maybe this time it'll be a big flood," Moth said.

"There won't be *any* flood," Golgin insisted.

"Probably not," Multas agreed.

"Would you like to hear about King Beduis and the great flood that drowned the world?" Alrabanas asked. His father was one of the city's most renowned sellers of songs.

"Yes," Moth said.

"I've heard it," Golgin said.

"So?" Tramu demanded. "We all have, but I'd like to hear it again."

"So long as you promise not to try to sing it," Rafti finished.

They all listened as Alrabanas told of the gods' anger against all mankind and of how King Beduis had sacrificed his son to Sartor so that Sartor would chain the gods' flood demon, Bvaicara, between the Nacre's banks.

"You'll make an excellent seller of songs," Yeshun told Alrabanas, and Moth nodded.

"If you ever learn to sing," Rafti said, but when Alrabanas's face fell she quickly added, "since you already tell them so well," and he looked happy again.

But the river stayed within its banks. So Kel Vaq Sil, the High Astrologer, dug the first channel in each bank; others soon followed his example, and the waters flowed out to drown the fields and cover them with new, rich soil.

Then the breaches were closed and the waters subsided, leaving the fields glistening expanses of rich yellow mud. But the heartiest weeds still poked up through the thin layer of new soil while other weeds waited unharmed just beneath the surface, so shod oxen were let loose to trample the ground, stamping out the weeds and leveling the surface.

While this was going on in the Temple fields, Moth was working with his family in their own small field. The Siltemple had awarded Ri Tal a certain amount of barley seed, and the Potters' Sil had granted him a certain amount more; in preparation for the sowing, Ri Tal guided their ox through the field while Moth and Kuan followed in his wake breaking up clods of earth with handleless stone pickaxes. Then the three together further smoothed the earth with a heavy wooden drag.

But before Ri Tal had a chance to till his field he was called away, leaving the task to his wife and son while he, like every man of Kyborash not of the Higher Mysteries, spent three days laboring in the Temple fields.

While he was gone Moth wore his beads and was head of the household. The previous year he'd told his mother that, since he was the head of the family, it would be demeaning for him to share in work fit only for women and children, and for three days he had done nothing. Kuan plowed the field with the shukil and bardin plows, harrowed and raked it three times, attached the seeding-funnel to the bardin plow and sowed the barley seed, then went over the ground a last time with a pickaxe to pulverize the clods the plowing and seeding had turned up. The memory of his father's return, however, was enough to keep Moth from repeating the experience this year.

While Moth and Kuan worked down by the river, on the opposite shore Ri Tal was working naked alongside coppersmiths and weavers, barbers and traders, stone carvers, field slaves, chisel workers, entrail readers, leather workers, and potterpariahs, for in the Temple fields all distinction of rank was set aside and all men worked for the Warriors of the Hand and Voice.

But at the end of the third day Ri Tal returned home to reclaim the beads his son had worn in his absence. Kuan applied a poultice of river mud, beer, ground turtle shells, and tanglethorn sap to the whip marks on her husband's back, and while he lay on his belly letting the remedy soothe him she prepared a special dinner—spiced fish, melons, fig and clam pastries, and palm wine instead of the customary flatbread, onions, and barley beer.

"Eat well," Ri Tal told Moth. "You will have to fast tomorrow."

"Because it's my birthday?" Moth asked. But his father just smiled.

After they finished eating Ri Tal took Moth into the potting compound and daubed him with the seven clays, then taught him the rituals for propitiating the clay spirits.

Moth was not allowed to sleep that night. His father watched over him as again and again he prostrated himself and prayed, "Sartor, All-Highest, Bountiful Creator of All the Gods and Men, I, Sartor-ban-i-Tresh, beg of You Your aid. Lend me Your strength, O Greatest of the Gods. Lend me Your wisdom, O Creator of All Things."

It was not a long prayer, but as the night wore on Moth found it increasingly difficult to keep the words straight. The moon was not quite full; in the half-light he could see his father's stern face watching him as he stumbled through the litany.

Three times he began to doze, only to be slapped awake.

The night was almost gone before Ri Tal said, "Enough." He handed Moth a necklace from which hung seven crude disks of unglazed but fired clay. Moth put it around his neck. His father motioned him to follow, and led the way out of the compound, through the house, and into the street.

Dawn found them far from Kyborash. They

worked their way upriver, paralleling the Nacre but avoiding as best they could the marshy lowlands adjacent to it. Sometimes they followed paths; sometimes they made their way through brush or forded streams. Once they had to detour around a small lake.

The valley grew narrower, the ground steeper. In late midmorning they came to a place where the valley walls closed in on them, forming a narrow gorge through which the Nacre rushed and foamed. Moth had never seen anything like it.

There was a guardhouse there, manned by the first human beings Moth had seen since leaving Kyborash. He recognized none of the warriors.

Ri Tal spoke to a black-bearded man wearing a copper breastplate and a conical helmet. A coin changed hands and they were allowed to pass.

Moth followed his father up the narrow, cliff-hugging trail. The rock beneath his feet was sometimes damp, even green with slime; he had only to look down to see the waters fighting with the rocks below.

At intervals tiny streamfalls on their way down to the river crossed the path. The first three Moth and Ri Tal encountered were small enough for Moth to leap without trouble and Ri Tal ignored them completely. He stopped at the fourth.

"We'll climb here," he said, pointing to a faint trail that descended from the heights parallel to the stream. It was the first time he'd spoken directly to Moth since they'd left the compound.

Ri Tal began to climb, Moth following. The going grew rapidly steeper and Moth found himself scrambling for finger- and toeholds on almost vertical cliffsides. He was afraid to look down. His father sent a constant rain of pebbles and dirt showering down on him from above; to his right the stream fell through countless tiny cascades that spattered him with cold spray and turned the dust on his face to mud. The mud ran into his eyes, blinding him and forcing him to let go with one hand for a breathless instant to wipe it away.

Ri Tal maintained a steady pace upward. Moth followed as best he could, but he lagged farther and farther behind.

At last he came out of a particularly difficult climb—the cascade to his right falling free for more than a dozen bodylengths before it crashed onto the rocks below; his father so far above him that he was invisible—to find himself on the edge of a broad, grassy field.

He scrambled up onto it, stood looking around, panting and smiling, then let out a sigh. He was on a plateau, a giant ledge large enough to hold half of Kyborash. The hard part was over.

Grass and tiny red conical wildflowers were everywhere; the stream they had been following was flanked by shrubs and small bushes. Moth's eyes followed the stream back to a distant wall of black rock that stretched upward to the clouds.

Moth and Ri Tal sat and rested awhile, then followed the stream inward. The ground was nearly level, the going easy despite the bushes. The air smelled good. Moth felt happy.

"Spring is the best time to find fresh clay," Ri Tal said. "The stream spirits reveal it to us."

The stream forked. They followed the right fork until Ri Tal stopped and pointed to one of the banks. "There. See that reddish, crumbly-looking soil? That's clay. The stream used to flow *there*"—he pointed again—"but when it changed its banks it cut away the soil sheltering the clay. The same thing happens every spring."

"What do we do now, Father?" Moth asked.

"Do you remember the rituals?"

"I think so."

"Don't 'think so.' Are you certain?"

Moth ran over the words and gestures again in his mind. "Yes."

"Good. Repeat the prayer to Sartor seven times, then give thanks to the spirit of the stream for revealing the clay."

Moth repeated the prayer seven times without stumbling over any of the words, then knelt by the stream and crossed his arms on his breast, left over right. "Hear me, Unslith, Stream-spirit," he intoned, then hesitated a moment before continuing, "I, Sartor-ban-i-Tresh, thank you in the name of Sartor All-Highest for revealing to me this clay. Accept of me my life's water as proof of my gratitude."

Opening his hands in the Gesture of Submission, he spat into the stream.

"Now ask the spirit of the clay for permission to dig."

Moth prostrated himself seven times. "Spirit of the Clay, Lithmar, Child of the Earth Mother, I, Sartor-ban-i-Tresh, beg you in the name of Sartor All-Highest to bestow upon me a portion of your body. I pledge that I will leave enough of your substance with which to regenerate yourself anew in the Earth Mother's womb. I pledge this to you in the name of the Earth Mother, my betrothed, and in the name of Sartor All-Highest."

Ri Tal took two tightly woven cloth sacks, a shallow white bowl, and a trowel of fire-hardened blackwood from his belt pouch.

"Remove the top layer of soil to a depth of two handswidths over an area an armslength in diameter," he said. "Then dig a small amount of clay from the center of the area you have excavated and place it in the bowl. Take care that none of the clay falls from the trowel onto the ground."

When Moth was finished Ri Tal took water from the stream in his cupped hands, thanking the stream-spirit as he did so, and moistened the blob of reddish clay.

"We must allow it to dry," he told Moth, and sat staring patiently at the red mud until it was dry again.

"Do you see that, Sartor-ban-i-Tresh?" he asked, indicating a thin white scum that had formed on the blob of clay. Moth nodded. "That means the spirits have declared that this clay is not for our use. We must return it to the soil, and ask the spirit's pardon."

They went back the way they had come until they reached the place where the stream forked. This time they took the other fork.

"Is that clay?" Moth asked almost immediately, pointing.

"Yes. Very good."

No scum formed when they wetted the clay. "The spirits have granted us their permission to use this clay," Ri Tal said, "but it still may not be to our purposes. Watch what I do."

He dug a small mass of clay from the excavated area and, moistening it again with water from the stream, kneaded it until it was all of a uniform consistency. Then he made from it a rope of clay as thick as his little finger and three times the length of Moth's thumb. Placing the clay in the bowl, he bent it into a ring, calling on Sartor in a low voice while he worked.

"It did not crack," he told Moth presently. "Clay that cracks is not to be taken. But this is excellent; we will bring some of it back with us."

He turned back to the bed of clay and prostrated himself seven times, praising the spirit's generosity, then used the blackwood trowel to dig more clay from the bed, taking care that each spadeful went directly into one of the cloth sacks.

"You must never remove more clay from the ground than you can carry," he told Moth. "And once the bag has been lifted free of the ground, you must make sure it does not touch the earth again until you are within a potting compound."

"Why?"

"The Earth Mother has lost Her child; the spirit its mother. If you reunite them, even for an instant, they will have to undergo the pain of separation all over again, and they will be angry with you. Do you understand?"

"Yes." Ri Tal handed Moth one of the sacks. It was very light.

"This is too little, Father," he said. "I'm strong; I can carry a lot more."

"Straight down the side of a cliff?"

"Yes."

"Good. You will have a chance to prove it when

we go after the mountain clays. But not today. You may have your grandfather's shoulders, but we're still a long way from Kyborash, and your sack will feel much heavier before we get there."

When the walls of Kyborash finally came into view, Moth said triumphantly, "I could have carried more. A lot more."

"Of course you could," Ri Tal said. "But there was no need, and only a fool would risk the Earth Mother's wrath without cause. Besides, you're tired enough as it is, aren't you?"

Moth had to admit that he was somewhat tired.

"Well, you're not done yet. We have to prepare the clay when we get back to the compound."

After welcoming the spirit of the clay to the compound's sacred precincts, Ri Tal taught Moth how to tread the clay and mix sand and wood ashes into it so as to give it the proper plasticity. But Ri Tal chanted the rituals for each stage of the process himself, for which Moth was grateful: he was too tired to learn any more prayers or rites.

When the clay was ready, Ri Tal had Moth bury it in a shallow pit and cover it with a thin layer of soil. And from that day on, whenever Ri Tal went in search of clay, Moth accompanied him.

❧ Chapter Four ❧

"Is anyone home?"

"Come in, Tramu!" Kuan called, looking up from her cheese-making. Moth's ten-year-old cousin ran in, came to a halt, and stood impatiently shifting his weight from one foot to the other. A year older than Moth, he was a handswidth taller as well, with the flame-red hair, black eyes, and broad shoulders of Tas Et, his father. He was the only child of Kuan's sister, Pyota.

"Sartor guide you, aunt. Where's Moth? Can I have some cheese?"

"No. It's not dry yet. Moth's with his father."

"Doing what?"

"Something for the Festival. Shouldn't you be helping Tas Et?"

"No, he's with Grandfather. That's why I'm here—Grandfather said to tell you we're all invited to his house for dinner tomorrow night."

"When?"

"Just after sunset."

"Run back and tell him we'll be there."

"Is Moth going to be busy all day?"

"All day."

"I've never seen a Seven-Year Festival."

"They've never had one here before."

"I want to see the King. Do you think I'll get to see him, aunt?"

"I hope so. Now—"

"Is Moth going to be busy all day tomorrow, too?"

"Yes. Now, go tell your grandfather we're coming."

"Yes, aunt. Sartor guide you."

"And you, nephew." But Tramu was already gone.

The next evening Moth and his parents rubbed their hair glossy with scented sesame oil and Kuan plaited Ri Tal's beard into two long braids. Both Moth and Ri Tal wore their finest siltunics of scarlet wool over linen undertunics, but Ri Tal had draped a short cloak of coarse white wool over his, and in his right hand he carried the ornately carved staff of a Master Potter. Kuan had emphasized her eyes with malachite and wore a necklace of blue faience, white quartz, and silver beads; her long dress of red linen left her right breast bare, proclaiming her initiation into the Women's Mystery.

Moth was very proud of the way they all looked, though embarrassed that he had as yet no staff of his own.

Outside, Ri Tal handed Moth the lamp and fastened the door to the doorpost with a cord, then dabbed a little clay on the knot and rolled it with his seal to invoke the law's protection for his home and property.

Tas No Sil's house was within the city's walls. All

the lesser gates were closed a daysixth before sunset, so they had to make their way to the South Gate. There they were forced to wait while the gate guard, a surly-faced Warrior of the Hand wearing a beautifully worked copper breastplate over a faded blue siltunic, argued fees with a slave trader just arrived from Lalacioon with twenty-four male slaves.

When Ri Tal's turn came he gave the warrior his cylinder seal. The warrior scowled, pressed it into a table of damp clay, then compared the mark it made with those on another tablet. Finding the corresponding mark, he rolled Ri Tal's cylinder in the impression to make sure the match was true.

"Two aubers," he said.

"That's too much," Ri Tal said. "One."

"Two this time, one the next." The guard had a strange accent, at the same time growling and gliding.

"How do I know you'll be here?"

"You don't."

Ri Tal handed the guard the stamped lead coins with poor grace. The warrior peered at them, thrust one back.

"Give me another. This one's got clipped edges."

Ri Tal found another coin, handed it over. The guard studied it, nodded, and finally opened the gate.

The wall was five bodylengths thick, the gate passage narrow. Six archers watched them from above as they entered. Ri Tal and his family waited until the guard had secured the outer gate behind them, then followed him to the inner gate. When that, too, had been secured behind them, they

made their way through the twisting streets to Tas
No Sil's house.

"Two aubers!" Ri Tal said as soon as they were
out of earshot. "Scandalous!"

Tas No Sil was wealthy. His house was two
stories high and rich with the scent of spices; even
the lamp outside his door burned perfumed sesame
oil. Carya, a former slave whom the High Smith
had taken to wife in the second-class marriage after
his first wife's death, met them at the door and
conducted them through the anteroom into the
courtyard, where the Sil Smith and Tramu's family
awaited them.

Everyone kissed everyone else. Pyota wore a
scent that Moth disliked and her husband's beard
always made him sneeze, but Tas No Sil had a rich
old man's smell that he liked.

Tas No Sil waved them to cushions. A seller
of songs—not Alrabanas's father, to Moth's
disappointment—entered and sang to them while
Carya served them. The food was excellent; there
were both lamb and fish, and they had molded
cheeses and honeyed sweets for dessert.

It was impolite to leave anything on your tray.
Moth demonstrated impeccable manners.

"The gate guard demanded two aubers," Ri Tal
was saying as Carya handed Moth a goblet of
yellow palm wine. "'Two this time, one the next'
—as if I couldn't tell from his accent that he was
just here from Bigandzin for the Festival!"

"You didn't recognize him?" Tas Et asked.

"No." Ri Tal shook his head.

"He was wearing one of your breastplates,
though," Kuan told Tas Et. Ri Tal looked surprised.

"It had a serpent coiled around an axe on the chest."

"Was he a tall man, with a sneer on his face all the time?" Tas Et asked.

"You know him, then?" Ri Tal said.

"Yes. Syrr Avyyrno. I had the misfortune to arm him. I hope you did nothing to offend him overmuch?"

"No. . . . I told him two aubers was too much, but I ended up paying him. He wouldn't take one of my coins, though—said it was debased and made me give him another."

"The man's worse than vicious, he's stupid," Tas Et said. "His father probably fought against King Vitrus. He may call himself a Warrior of the Hand of Sartor now, but—"

"But he doesn't understand that that means he is a priest as well as a warrior, and that every man initiated into a Sil is as much a priest as he is, and so just as worthy of respect," Moth's grandfather finished for him. "I, too, know the man. And I, for one, would be happier if the Warriors of the Voice did not choose such men for the Syrr Sil."

"Or at least kept them in their half-barbarian little cities instead of bringing them here," Pyota said.

"Still, the Syrr Sil honors them by bringing them to the Festival," Tas No Sil said. "So perhaps even Syrr Avyyrno will leave here a more willing servant of Sartor than he was before. Yet . . . But no matter. Moth, Tramu, can you both be trusted to keep a secret?"

"Yes," Moth said.

"Of course," Tramu said.

"Will you swear on your honor as Sil-initiated men that nothing told you here tonight will be repeated?"

They nodded.

"Then repeat after me: 'I swear on my truename, with Sartor and my Sil in witness, that I will keep secret those things told me here tonight.'"

Moth and Tramu repeated the oath.

"Good. We were speaking of honor, and both my sons-in-law are to be honored this Festival. Ri Tal?"

Moth's father looked both shy and proud. "Ri Cer Sil has given me permission to tell you that he has chosen me to make the King's coffin. Three days from now I go to the Fair to obtain what I need."

It was the ultimate honor a potter could be granted. Did that mean that Ri Tal was going to be the next Sil Potter? Moth opened his mouth to ask, but before he could say anything Tramu asked, "What kinds of things?"

"Jewels, feathers, some sky metal if there is any to be had. Things like that."

"Can I go with you? Please, uncle?" Tramu asked.

"The Nomads are too dangerous—" Ri Tal began.

"My grandson is a smith," Tas No Sil interrupted, "and no longer a child. Besides, the danger is slight. Fair law will protect them."

"Can I go, too?" Moth asked.

"I haven't said Tramu could go yet." Ri Tal looked at Kuan.

"Let them go," Kuan said.

Ri Tal sighed. "All right. Since you're all in

agreement. But only if both of you promise to do exactly what I tell you."

"And promise *not* to do anything he doesn't specifically tell you you *can* do," Kuan added.

"Yes." Ri Tal looked solemnly at them. "The Fair has its own laws and dangers; if you violate Fair law there will be nothing any of us can do to help you."

"Can I go, Father?" Tramu asked.

"Shouldn't you have asked me before you asked your uncle?" Tas Et's voice was severe but he was smiling.

"Yes, Father. I'm sorry, Father. Can I go anyway? Please? I promise I'll ask you first next time."

"All right, since Ri Tal has already agreed." He looked at Ri Tal and said solemnly, "It is a great honor, brother, and I am sure it is only the first of many more. I am glad for you."

Moth's head was spinning with excitement. He took another sip of wine and held his goblet out to Carya.

"And now I, too, have an announcement," Tas No Sil said. "This year I have asked Tas Et to forge the Dying and Reborn Sword for the King in my stead."

"A truly great honor indeed, brother," Ri Tal told Tas Et. "You must be proud."

"I am very proud, brother."

"As he should be, and as I am of him." Tas No Sil turned to Tas Et. "You bear a great responsibility now, son-in-law. Yet it is only right that I relinquish my part in the renewal of all things to you, not merely because you are my son-in-law, though you are a fine son-in-law, and not merely because I love you, though I do, but because save myself there is no smith of the Empire to equal you, and I am old while you are yet young. My days are passing; yours have just begun."

"I would not care to match my strength against yours, Father," Tas Et said.

"No? You are being too kind to an old man. Though for all that I might surprise you. I might indeed." He paused.

"You all know," he said suddenly, "how it saddened me that Ligue bore me no sons, and despite the love I bore her I reproached her for it often. Yet were she alive today"—he spat on the earthen floor, that the Earth Mother would convey the water of his life to his wife where she lay buried beneath the house—"I would forgive her gladly, for the sons my daughters have brought me are as pleasing to me as any who might have sprung from my loins.

"And my grandsons—Moth, Tramu, if only Ligue could have lived to see you! Tramu, you already have the strength of a man of the forge, and your cleverness never ceases to amaze me. And you, Moth—you too are clever beyond your years, and your father tells me that Sartor has destined you to become a potter like no other."

Moth stared at his father, surprised. He wished he'd drunk less wine.

But Tas No Sil was not finished. "The two of you are still young, but I am no dotard. Indeed, my health is excellent. I will live to see you both men of renown."

"But the young are often careless, no matter how great the futures for which they may be destined," Pyota said. "Remember your oaths: no one must learn where the sword is being forged until after the Festival."

"Why?" Moth asked.

"In Chal," Tas No Sil explained, "the Sil has a special forge, well hidden and even better guarded, where the sword can be readied in perfect safety. But here in Kyborash we have no such place, and no time to prepare one."

"My forge is beyond the city walls, where the sword will be harder to protect unless we keep it a secret," Tas Et said.

"Why not use Father's forge?" Kuan suggested. "The sword would be safe there."

"My hammer would not be happy away from my forge," Tas Et said, and Moth realized that he was being allowed to hear things usually not spoken of before anyone not a smith. It made him feel warm and trusted.

Neither Moth nor Tramu slept well the night before the Fair, though Tramu had spent the day in his father's forge and Moth had worked hard in the barley field. The night was endless; Moth lay on his pallet waiting for a dawn that he knew was only moments away but that never came, until suddenly Tramu was shaking him awake.

"Get up! Do you want to miss the Fair?"

Dawn had not yet broken. A tallow lamp flickered yellow in the center of the room. Moth dressed hurriedly in his finest clothes. Tramu was already dressed: his siltunic was red and gold, and a silver soul with the sun disk on it in red copper hung from his twin amulet chains.

Ri Tal picked up the lamp. They all followed him

outside. The sky was dark, moonless, but the sounds of a crowd reached them even before the narrow street they were following twisted one last time and debouched into the Avenue of King Delanipal the Conqueror, the broad thoroughfare the Chaldans had built to link the inner city they had constructed in the ruined heart of fallen Drea-'Est with the world outside the city walls. Long before they reached the gate they could hear onagers and oxen complaining, the many-tongued babble of the crowd, and the shouts of men trying to make themselves heard over the confusion.

It was not yet fully light, but Ri Tal extinguished the lamp. On the far side of the Great Square Moth could make out oxcarts and pack onagers and a few, very few, four-wheeled horse-drawn Chaldan battle chariots. The infant sun's weak rays glinted off the burnished metal shields on the chariots' sides.

The square swarmed with men. Slaves staggered by carrying loads heavier than themselves; one had collapsed under his burden and was being kicked by his master, a Chaldan freeman hardly better dressed than the slave himself. There were traders from all the cities of the Empire in green siltunics, carrying their jackdaw-headed staffs, some accompanied by scribes in gray wool with the yellow eye of the King emblazoned on their chests. There were merchants from the cities of the Delta League, some sent by their home cities, others representing powerful individuals or guilds; and Deltan artisans with their heads wound about with the lengths of multicolored cloth whose designs proclaimed their various crafts. And there were tall men in flowing

white robes who kept the lower halves of their faces
hidden behind bright silk and who had something
strange about their eyes; they sat aloof above the
crowd in their ornate oxcarts and spoke to no one.

"Our shrine's in the Warriors' Wall," Ri Tal told
Tramu. "Yours is over in the King's Wall, isn't it?"

Tramu nodded.

"We'll meet you by the cage. Try not to take any
more time than your rites require."

"Of course not, uncle." Tramu darted away.

After prostrating themselves thirty-six times to
the image of Sartor-of-the-Potters Moth and his
father left the Ri Shrine, Ri Tal giving the Warrior
of the Voice who was in charge the proper coin on
the way out. They made their way through the
crowd to the cage. For once it was empty, but Moth
could see the madmen it usually imprisoned huddled together nearby. Naked, branded, and fettered, some drooling, others gibbering or whining
or clutching fearfully at themselves, they were
given wide breadth by everyone but their keeper as
they waited to set off for the Fair. For reasons
known only to themselves the Nomads sometimes
paid high prices for such men and women, and the
cities were only too glad to be rid of them.

The crowd sound lapped at Moth like a greasy
sea, abruptly terrifying. He sensed dead truths,
putrefying falsehoods, all around him; he was
awash in greedy speculations and seductions, anec-
dotes in which the speakers boasted of how they
had successfully cheated, humiliated, threatened,
or beaten someone. A man—

No! There was only the murmur of voices, none
clear. Yet the greasy swell reached out to caress

him, drown him in the ugly herd-noise, make him a part of it.

His thoughts frightened him. Everything's all right, he told himself, edging away from the cage, closer to his father. Father's right here and Tramu will be back in a moment. Everything is just as it should be. I was just thinking a bit strangely —maybe I'm not really awake yet; everybody knows how strange dreams are.

I was dreaming, but I have to wake up now.

He stared around, at the crowd and then up at the godhouse of enameled blue brick atop the ziggurat that linked the Siltemple and the King's Palace.

But he couldn't make himself forget the madmen. Any one of them could have been the uncle he had never met, whom he would never even have known had existed if Tramu hadn't told him. Ri Sul, his father's younger brother, stoned to death under the careful supervision of Lapp Wur, the city's exorcist.

He could picture it, the man he somehow knew looked more like him than like his father huddled with his bound hands in front of his face, the stones flying as Lapp Wur kept up his steady stream of talk, like a merchant trying to sell overripe melons: "Careful, my lady, don't miss him. That's right— Take careful aim. You only get one chance at him today, and he's clever, he'll try to dodge you— You see? But perhaps you'd care to try your luck tomorrow. And you, sir! Would you care to try? Hit him and you injure the demon within, perhaps even kill it. Demons always fear a man who's killed one of their kind. If we kill enough of them here in

Kyborash, maybe the rest will leave us in peace. No? But, sir—!"

Ri Tal was staring at the cage, his face set and hard. That's why Father's here, Moth suddenly realized. To remind himself to be careful with us, that he could lose us like he lost his brother.

"Look at all the warriors!" Tramu said, startling Moth. "I've never seen this many all together."

Moth felt grateful to have something else with which to occupy his thoughts. And, indeed, there were already a great number of warriors in the square, and more emerging from the Palace of Warriors all the time. Most were peltasts, lightly armed fighting men carrying bows and spears, daggers and slings; their shields were flimsy wicker affairs and they wore heavy leather helmets and clothing. Among the peltasts there were a number of heavily armed warriors, each followed by his shield bearers. Each heavily armed warrior carried a long sword (the Chaldans wore theirs hanging from the waist while the Deltan warriors had theirs slung across their backs), and each had a dagger as well as a sword. Their polished silver, copper, and gold breastplates shone in the stark morning light; their eyes were impassive beneath their conical helmets; their laughter was overloud; and when Ri Tal stumbled against a heavily armed Chaldan warrior, the man hit him an open-handed blow that sent him sprawling into a Warrior of the Voice.

"My humble apologies, sirs—" Ri Tal began, only to stop short. The heavily armed warrior was Syrr Avyyrno. "Sir, I'm sorry, I—"

"Forget it, potter. You're not worth wasting my time on."

Syrr Avyyrno turned to his shield bearer, a handsome, strong-looking man of about fifteen who was carrying a shield of copper over wood. "Next time some mud-handed fool gets in my way, just take care of him for me. It'll give you something to do."

"Sure," the shield bearer said, grinning. Moth glanced at Tramu, saw the shame, the contempt, the sense of betrayal on his face as he looked up at Ri Tal.

Tas Et would never have let anyone humiliate him like that. But Tas Et was a weaponsmith, the King's Weaponsmith. Ri Tal was only a potter. It wasn't his fault he couldn't do anything.

"It was an accident, I assure you, Reverence," Ri Tal was telling the Warrior of the Voice. "I meant no disrespect—"

"Be quiet," the old Syrr said, not unkindly, and Moth was thankful when Ri Tal fell silent. "You did me no harm. But you do not have the mark of the Fair on you."

"We have only just arrived, Reverence. I am Ri Tal, Master Potter."

Ri Tal leaned close, whispered something into the old warrior's ear.

"Very good," the old Syrr said, seeming impressed, and Moth felt a little better. The warrior took Ri Tal's cylinder seal in his hand and inspected it, nodded, and handed it back. "But who are these?" He looked down at Moth and Tramu, and though he was smiling, Moth was afraid he'd say they had to stay behind.

"My son and nephew. They've both been initiated. I'll keep a close watch on them."

"See that you do." The Warrior of the Voice took

three small clay amulets from a basket he carried. The amulets were stamped with cuneiform characters and strung on leather thongs. "Put these around your necks," he said. "They will prove that you are at the Fair lawfully, though you won't be protected by Fair law until you've been accepted by the Judge. Until then, stay with your fellows."

"Thank you, Reverence," Ri Tal said. The Warrior of the Voice turned away.

"Why do we need to be protected?" Tramu asked. "We won't see any Nomads until we get there, will we?"

"Possibly not, but the Deltans we're traveling with hate us more than any Nomad ever could."

"Why?" Tramu asked. "Because King Asp keeps conquering more of their cities?"

"Yes," Ri Tal said. "But they have to go all the way back through the Empire on their way down to the Delta, so I don't think you'll really have anything to worry about from them."

They made their way through the crowd to the oxcarts on the far side of the square without finding the man Ri Tal was looking for. He plunged back into the crowd, but though he moved with the confidence of a man whose goal is in sight, Moth soon realized they were just drifting aimlessly through the crowd—drifting energetically enough, to be sure, but randomly.

Maybe that warrior was right to think Father is a fool, he thought, ashamed again, and angry at himself for being ashamed of his father when he should have been proud of him.

At last Ri Tal called out, "Sklar Ton!" He was answered by a short, stout man in a dirty green siltunic who wore his hair fantastically long, his single gray-brown braid falling almost to his waist.

"It helps me with the Nomads," he told Moth when he noticed him staring at the braid. "Among them, only slaves cut their hair. It makes me feel a bit foolish here among civilized men, though." He beamed at Moth and Tramu.

Sklar Ton's oxcart was small but filled to overflowing with trade goods, and there were four heavily laden pack onagers tied to the back. When at last the caravan started moving it moved slowly, to accommodate those traveling on foot. Moth, Tramu, and Ri Tal had no trouble keeping abreast of the trader's cart.

☙ Chapter Five ❧

The procession made its way along the Avenue of King Delanipal the Conqueror and out the West Gate, then across the Warriors' Bridge and onto the little-used East Road. They moved slowly, the men and animals ahead kicking up so much dust that Moth often found it hard to breathe. The day was getting hotter and he was beginning to sweat in his heavy, unaccustomed formal clothes. He did not like this journey, so different from the trips he had taken with his father; he was bored and unhappy despite the promise of the Fair.

Whenever Ri Tal took him in search of clay, they never strayed far from water and always tried to walk as silently as possible, just as they never took more clay than they needed. For they came to beg gifts of the Earth Mother and it would not have been right, as Ri Tal had explained, to disturb the music the winds and the birds, the trees and the cicadas and the frogs made in honor of Her—no, not even to startle the black wattle lizard into stilling his desolate croaking, for hideous though his song was to human ears, the lizard was singing

45

to the Earth Mother and She accepted his song and found it beautiful because he sang it to Her.

But now there was nothing but the sound of shuffling men and animals, the hot sun growing hotter, and the dust that clogged Moth's eyes and nostrils. Warriors and merchants were continually passing them on errands to the front or back of the caravan, but they had all begun to look the same to Moth, and he had lost interest in them.

"You'll see," Tramu said. "The Nomads look different."

"Different in what way?" Moth asked. "Anyway, how would you know?"

"He's right, though," Sklar Ton said, glancing down at them from his seat on the oxcart. "They don't look at all like us. They wear leather clothes and tattoo themselves all over their bodies and faces. If you look closely at their hands, you'll see that they're missing joints on their fingers. That's because they sacrifice their fingers to their gods for luck in the hunt and in battle. Some of their hunters keep just enough fingers to pull their bows, though the warriors need more fingers to grip their axes.

"But they're still a lot more like us than those are—" He pointed to an oxcart up ahead, in which Moth could see four of the white-robed figures he'd noticed earlier. "You see those? They're Royal Eunuchs."

"What's a eunuch?" Tramu asked.

"Neither a man nor a woman," Ri Tal said. Moth hadn't realized he'd been listening. "No sex at all."

"Right," Sklar Ton said. "They're taken away from their parents and castrated when they're babies—and their parents are the kings and queens of some of the greatest cities of the Delta. They're strange, very strange, and—wait, there's one turning this way. Look at his eyes. . . ."

Moth felt a shock as the great, round, pink eyes in the dark face met his, studying him for an instant before they flicked away, indifferent.

"You see those pink eyes?" Sklar Ton continued. "And that pretty piece of silk over the bottom of its face? That's to hide its mouth. They're toothless, people say, though I've never met a man who could swear to having seen one unmasked—and there are rumors about that, too. They say that if you see one of the Pink-Eyed—that's what most people call them, though their real name is the Royal Eunuchs —anyway, they say that if you see one of them with its face uncovered, you're dead. Whether by magic or simple murder is a point I've heard debated, though everyone agrees that you'll be dead in any case."

Moth, staring at the white-robed figure, felt a trace of uneasiness, nothing more.

Riding four to a cart, their slim bodies concealed by flowing robes, their toothless mouths hidden behind bright silk masks, the twelve Royal Eunuchs (who termed themselves simply Taryaa, the Chosen, after the fashion of their kind) studied the men of the caravan with the detached fascination they always accorded breeders. Though none of the twelve was above sixteen years of age, the other travelers took them for adults—and rightly so, for though these individual eunuchs would most likely be culled and killed during the two life-stages

separating them from their full maturity, yet they
were all among the few of their kind whose perfection of Loiia, Undeviating Skillful Accord, had
enabled them to survive the choices of the previous
life-stages. And such perfection of Loiia required
competence beyond any known to all but a few of
the cleverest individuals not of their kind, an
ability to adapt any situation in which one of the
Chosen found itself toward the skillful attainment
of the absolutely inflexible goals devised in the
forgotten past by individuals the only records of
whose existence were written in the eunuchs' minds
and flesh.

In the cart ahead of Sklar Ton's, the Nameless
One (for who could choose a name before knowing,
before becoming, the self to be named?) had
glanced at the three walking in the dust and had
known:

That the man was a potter. Even without the
scarlet siltunic and ceramic beads, the Nameless
One would have recognized him for what he was:
his pots had shaped him even as he shaped them.
And his staff betrayed him a Master.

That the younger boy was his son, though the
mismatched eyebrows, dappled hair, and broad
shoulders shouted his smith's blood. His eyes were
yellow, but not the royal amber: they indicated
nothing beyond mixed blood.

That the larger boy was a pure-blooded smith's
son. His hair, his stature, the cast of his features,
the arrogance with which he walked, all proclaimed
his identity, and the copper sun on his neck-soul
revealed that his father was a weaponsmith.

That the boys were related, probably cousins.

The shapes of their ears and skulls, certain proportions, similarities in facial expression, posture, and ways of moving, all betrayed shared ancestry.

So the man was a Master Potter connected by blood with the most honored of the artisans' Sils. Which confirmed what his presence in the Fair caravan in the company of a Sklar had already indicated: he was no ordinary potter, here on no trivial mission.

With the Seven-Year Festival so close, that mission was obvious: he was either the King's Coffinmaker, or sent by the Ri Sil to buy what the coffinmaker would need.

"There are two children here," the Nameless One told the three other Taryaa riding with it, gesturing back at Moth and Tramu. Its stance, the rhythm and cadence of its speech, the almost imperceptible movements of its eyes, proclaimed that its thoughts and intentions were in accord with That Which Must Be.

It grasped their concord as they grasped its intent.

Children were unguarded, curious. Much could be learned from a child.

Done with a child.

Chapter Six

"Hey, Sklar Ton, you heard about the omens?" a peltast with a leaf-shaped scar on his left cheek yelled up at the trader.

"Not yet. Anything special?"

"Special? No, I wouldn't say special. I sort of like the word grim. Yes, I'd say the omens are pretty grim."

"You wouldn't care to be more specific? That is, if you really know something."

"Listen. The Sil Astrologer warned King Asp that today was impossible for the Fair—at least, that's the word that's been going around—but those damn swamplanders said they couldn't start any other time because of their big thing in Dastar, you know, the Masquerade Carnival. I can see their point—me, I'd give almost anything to be there, five days with nothing to do but eat free food and drink good wine, and you can have any woman you want, doesn't matter whether they're married or not."

"I've been to Dastar," Sklar Ton said. "What about the omens?"

"Syrr Gratni was doing the sacrificing—you know him?"

"No."

"He knows what he's doing. Anyway, the first goat's liver was missing a lobe. He couldn't understand what that meant, so he tried sacrificing a second one. But there was something wrong with that one's liver too, I don't remember what—"

"You're sure he knows what he's doing?"

"Of course I'm sure!"

"Go on."

"Syrr Gratni was upset. He told me this was the first time in twenty-four years that he hadn't been able to interpret a goat's liver."

"So you don't know what the omens meant?"

"Not those omens, no. But we were all a little worried by then, so we hired an entrail reader to sacrifice an ox."

"Expensive."

"Very."

"What did you learn?"

"The entrail reader said the guts were very peculiar and that he didn't completely understand them—"

"Did you get your money back?"

"No. We tried, but he said that he'd learned more than enough for what we'd paid him."

"Well?"

"He said that something terrible is going to happen because of something that will happen at the Fair. Not *at* the Fair, but *because of* the Fair. So if I were you, I wouldn't cheat anybody too badly this time."

"I've never cheated anybody," Sklar Ton said.

"Hah."

"Well—should a foreigner wish to cheat himself, I see no harm in accommodating his foolishness, true, but the blame is on his head, not mine."

The peltast shook his head. "Watch yourself, trader."

"You, too," Sklar Ton said. The peltast shambled on past them.

"That's a prophecy?" Sklar Ton asked Ri Tal. "You get this many people together, three groups of enemies, and somebody's going to get hurt. You don't need ox guts to know that much."

"Still . . ." Ri Tal looked worried.

"How much farther, Master Trader?" Tramu asked.

"Not far. Are you tired?"

"You *look* tired, cousin," Moth said solicitously, delighted to discover that his long trips with his father had given him a kind of endurance that his otherwise stronger cousin lacked.

"He just wants to see the Fair," Sklar Ton said. "Don't worry, Tramu. It'll be worth waiting for."

"I don't like it," Ri Tal said after they'd walked a bit farther.

"Don't like what, Father?" Moth asked. Something in Ri Tal's voice put him on edge.

"The omens. And the fact that Kel Vaq Sil warned the King against holding the Fair today."

"Astrologers!" Sklar Ton said. *"I* say we're lucky to have a King who knows better than to let some *astrologer* tell him what to do."

"But the heavens reveal Sartor's will," Ri Tal objected.

"Perhaps, but—" The trader caught himself,

thought for a moment. "Look, Ri Tal, I know
you're an intelligent man—but you've spent your
whole life shut up in a potting compound and
you've never had much chance to see the world.
Am I right?"

"Not at all! I spent two years handling the Sil's
affairs in Chal."

"Don't get offended. Please. I don't mean to
sound like I think you're some sort of child; I know
you're remarkably well informed for an artisan, but
even so . . ."

He fell silent again. Moth's eye was caught by a
shield bearer hurrying toward the front of the
caravan with a copper-plated shield. It might have
been the boy Syrr Avyyrno had told to take care of
people like Ri Tal for him.

"Listen, Ri Tal, when a man from, say, Dastar
—a squalid, unfriendly city if there ever was one,
despite their famous five days of fun—when a man
from Dastar comes to Chal to buy your pots— No,
let's go back even further. Remember, this man has
to get the permission of a Warrior of the Voice
before he can even talk to you, and remember also
that, like every other man of Dastar, he worships
Triple-headed Eido, and thinks Sartor is a demon.

"Now, assume this Eido worshiper is talking
with that Warrior of the Voice. Does he scorn
Sartor? Does he denounce King Asp as the crazed
follower of a minor demon? Of course not! Rather,
he requests to be allowed to make a small offering
to Sartor. And if he's at all clever, he keeps up that
pretence with you and with every other Chaldan he
meets."

The shield bearer was arguing with a Deltan

peltast much taller than himself, but a Warrior of
the Voice separated them before they could get into
the fight Moth was hoping for.

"I don't see what this has to do with astrology,"
Ri Tal protested.

"Just this. Our astrologers say they see the pat-
terns of destiny written in the stars—and what
could that destiny be but the unfolding of Sartor's
designs? A foreigner questioning our astrologers
here risks offending those charged with seeing
Sartor's will obeyed. So the man from Dastar with
whom you, Ri Tal, talk in Chal will never tell you
what he really thinks of our astrologers.

"But were you to talk to him in his native city, he
might tell you. And I, who have long been fascinated with prophecy in all its forms, have learned
what I could of the astrological lore of the Delta,
where the science of the stars is far older than ours,
and very, very different."

"Your point?"

"That not only do the two sciences contradict
each other, but both are shams. Oh, there are
honest astrologers, to be sure, but they are themselves deluded, and the rest are liars and cheats.
King Asp ignores his astrologer; you'd be wise to do
the same."

Ri Tal rubbed dust from his eyes. "If you set so
little store by prophecy, why were you so interested
in what your peltast friend had to say?"

"Of course I believe in prophecy!" Sklar Ton
declared, offended. "Do you take me for the kind of
fool who refuses to believe in anything until he can
hold it in his hands—and then doubts its memory
if someone takes it away? Not a day passes without

proving that divination with livers and entrails reveals great truths; what sane man could doubt this? But astrology? Best waste your time elsewhere."

"A man may fail to understand the meaning of a liver, or misconstrue that meaning, may he not?" Ri Tal asked.

"To be sure."

"And is not the reading of entrails still more difficult, and misinterpretation still more likely?"

"That, too, is self-evident."

"And might not a man, failing to interpret such omens correctly, believe that he had, in fact, been shown no true omen when in reality the failure was in himself?"

"Granted."

"Then," Ri Tal cried triumphantly, startling Moth, "in reading the meaning of the vast and living heavens, is it not still more likely that a man may err? Yet that does not prove that there is no truth there to be read!"

"Yet neither does it prove that there *is* any truth there. In fact, I think you argue now against yourself—for the heavens are so vast that any messages they reveal would be beyond mortal comprehension."

"But consider the grandeur of the heavens!" Ri Tal said. "Think what truths await us there, truths so vast, so magnificent, that were man to comprehend them he would become a god! Yet you turn your back on the heavens for the noisome guts of an animal soon to putrefy; you do this when every night the stars wheel above you. . . . I do not understand you, trader."

"Nor I you. Truths that no man can comprehend are not meant for me. I would rather study guts and learn whether or not my daughter will marry well. But this argument gets us nowhere. And besides, we're almost to the Fair."

"The Fair?" Moth asked. "I mean—you're sure?"

"Yes, though there won't be any Fair until we get there. You see that flat area up ahead?"

Tramu nodded, but no matter how much Moth craned his neck he couldn't see over the people in front of him. He suspected that neither could Tramu.

"That's it," Sklar Ton said. "Close enough to Kyborash so we have a chance to get back to the city if the Nomads try anything, far enough away so they can get away if *we* try anything."

"Careful around the Nomads," Ri Tal cautioned Moth. "Don't let one of them get your amulet off you or—"

"Or I might end up as a slave!" Moth finished. "I *know*, Father!"

"Your father's right to warn you," Sklar Ton said. "Nomads don't consider themselves bound by Fair law in the same way we do. The oath they take is to do nothing to disgrace their people. If they can get away with something—such as stealing the two of you—they won't feel they've disgraced their people. Just the opposite."

"And I'd hate to have to tell Tas Et and Pyota that you'd been stolen," Ri Tal told Tramu.

"Don't worry, uncle," Tramu said. "I'll be careful." Moth envied him his assurance, at the same time wishing his father would quit treating the two of them like children.

"It's not going to be all that dangerous," Sklar Ton said. "The Nomads have to pay the same penalties we do if they're caught breaking Fair law. And getting caught is so humiliating for them that they normally commit suicide—though the usual penalty for breaking Fair law is death anyway. So unless they're certain they can get away with something, they act as though they respect the law."

The caravan swung left to avoid a marshy hollow overgrown with red swampthorn and Moth was finally able to see the Fairground. The Nomads were lined up at the far end of a huge, gently sloping meadow; behind them the forest began, deep and dark and richly green. And—

"They're on top of their horses! They're sitting on them!" Moth said, amazed. Ri Tal and Sklar Ton burst into laughter.

After an instant during which he, too, stared, Tramu asked, "You mean you didn't know that they, uh, sat on top of their horses? I thought everybody knew that."

But Sklar Ton and Ri Tal laughed at him in turn, and when Moth joined in Tramu's face grew red. But his anger soon gave way to embarrassment, and in a moment he, too, was laughing.

"Why don't *our* warriors sit on top of their horses?" he asked.

"We don't have enough horses," Ri Tal said.

"Our warriors don't know how to get on a horse and stay on it anyway," Sklar Ton added. "They don't like to be reminded of that fact, either, which is why it's better not to mention anything about this back in the city."

"Why don't the Nomads ride on their horses
when they come into Kyborash?" Moth asked
Sklar Ton. "Mother said some of them came
once."

"They probably know it's more diplomatic not to
humiliate our warriors by doing something they
can't do," the trader said after a moment's thought.
"But I'm not really sure."

"Maybe they don't want us to learn how," Tramu
said excitedly.

"But they let us see them riding on top of their
horses here," Ri Tal pointed out. "So that can't be
it."

The city men's procession was spreading out
now, men and animals taking up places facing the
Nomads across the meadow. When they had posi-
tioned themselves in a straight line, a Warrior of
the Voice robed in white and yellow walked toward
the Nomad line.

A single Nomad rode forward to meet him.

"That's Casnut, son of Tlantut, one of their
Great Shamans," Sklar Ton whispered. "I was
hoping it would be him. He's Tlantlu, I think, and
the best judge they have. It's the Nomads' turn:
he'll be Judge of the Fair today. You'll have to give
him your oaths that you'll abide by the laws of the
Fair and submit to whatever punishment he de-
crees if you disobey the law."

"But he's a Nomad!" Tramu said.

"So much the better," Sklar Ton said firmly.
Moth looked at him in surprise. "Casnut's code of
honor is different from ours, but he's a totally
—and I mean *totally*—honorable man. If you met

him away from the Fair he would probably knife
you and steal everything you had, because he'd see
nothing wrong with that; but here he's Judge, and
he'll uphold the honor of the oaths sworn here with
his life, if need be. He'd sentence all his sons to
death by torture if his honor as the Judge required
it."

"I thought you said they didn't think there was
anything wrong with breaking the law," Tramu
said.

"Not with breaking the law, no, but violating
their oaths is a different matter."

While Sklar Ton talked Moth studied the shaman. Casnut was the strangest-looking human
being he had ever seen. He was exceedingly tall and
muscular, but lean to the point of gauntness. His
tremendous beard was divided into three braids,
the central braid hanging almost to his waist while
the other two were looped back over his shoulders
and interwoven with the hair from his head to form
a single thick braid that fell far below his waist
—and hair and beard were straw yellow shot with
silver, while his skin was a gray so dark it was
almost black.

"His skin . . ." Moth murmured. "He's—"

"Nomads get that way when they're old," Sklar
Ton said.

Over breeches and an open vest of red-brown
leather, the shaman wore a caftan of black goatskin
with the hair still on it. This was open at the neck
and had a great number of shiny ribbons attached
to it that had been made to look like snakes. Some
of the snakes had eyes and open jaws; others had
two or even three heads.

A confusion of metal objects hung from the caftan. There were two convex disks that looked a little like turtle shells, a small golden bow and seven tiny golden arrows, rows of gleaming copper mirrors, and the golden skeleton of a hawk almost a forearm in length and very cunningly contrived; and all these things jangled and clanged whenever the shaman moved or the wind stirred. The sound was somehow more than just dead metal striking dead metal: Moth could hear in it the hunting scream of a great hawk, the shrieking of a soul in torment, the sighing of a wind filling earth and sky—and yet it was still just the barely audible tinkling of a few metal trinkets.

From the shaman's cap hung seven more copper mirrors, and the cap itself was made from the skin of a brown owl with its feathers, head, outstretched wings, and tail all still intact. In his left hand Casnut held a small black drum, and on this he sometimes beat out quick, irregular rhythms in accompaniment to his words.

Casnut and the Warrior of the Voice finished their parley and gestured their retinues forward. Three Chaldan slaves hurried to the Warrior of the Voice carrying a bulky wooden throne inlaid with silver and copper, while a single Nomad, moving with measured dignity, brought the shaman a large, plain wicker stool, which he set beside the throne. Five Chaldan Warriors of the Hand armed with swords and carrying metal-plated shields ranged themselves in a semicircle behind the Warrior of the Voice's throne; five Nomad warriors, their clean-shaven faces disfigured by puckered ceremonial scars and faded tattoos, took up positions behind the stool. One of them laid a red blanket on it.

"It looks like they're equal, doesn't it?" Sklar Ton asked Ri Tal. "But don't let that fool you. The Warrior of the Voice is just here to lend Casnut his authority. Next year it'll be our turn, and Casnut will be lending a Warrior of the Voice *his* authority.

"Moth, Tramu, if he asks whether you are men or children, tell him you are men. Men are bound by their oaths where children are not, and no one not oath-bound is given the freedom of the Fair."

"We aren't children," Tramu said. "We've been initiated."

"Even so, remember," Sklar Ton said.

One by one the Nomads came before the shaman. Each led a single horse which he surrendered to the Judge, who held its reins while questioning the man.

"Don't they bow?" Moth asked.

"No," Ri Tal answered. "The horse is the important thing for them."

As each Nomad finished swearing his oath, the Judge returned his horse to him. Nomads who had taken their oaths were beginning to unroll blankets on which to display goods, set up tents, and bring forward horses and other animals to be traded.

"There aren't any Nomad firedancers this year," Sklar Ton said. "A pity; you boys would have enjoyed watching them. Women aren't allowed here on their own, but entertainers are sometimes admitted under the Judge's protection."

When all the Nomads had sworn, it was the city men's turn. Sometimes as individuals, but more often in groups, they performed twenty full prostrations apiece before the seated Nomad, smearing their faces in the dirt as they stretched out their hands to the Judge, imploring his mercy.

"That's not right," Moth said, outraged. "Why do we have to do that when the Nomads don't?"

"Do you have a horse to surrender?" Sklar Ton asked.

"No."

"Then keep quiet."

"Are you men?" Casnut demanded of the group before him.

"We are men," they replied.

"This is the law of the Fair: neither to do violence to any person who bears the amulet of the Fair and has sworn the Fair oath, nor to obtain goods or slaves from any person here who bears the amulet of the Fair and has sworn the Fair oath, unless that person consents to part with those goods or slaves for a mutually agreed-upon price. Do you swear this on your sacred honor, on the name of your family, upon that god whom you hold most sacred?"

"We do."

"The peace of the Fair be with you," the shaman and the Warrior of the Voice intoned together.

"He doesn't sound like a Nomad," Moth whispered to Tramu.

"What's a Nomad supposed to sound like?" Tramu whispered back. "Did you think they just grunted at each other, the way we did when we played at being Nomads?"

And Moth had to admit to himself that he'd expected just that, grunting savages—shrewd, perhaps, there wasn't anything in Moth's idea of

Nomads that said they couldn't be shrewd—but this man spoke like a Warrior of the Voice!

Moth paid little heed to the Chaldans and Deltans; all his attention was on the shaman, on the perfect economy and grace of his movements, so out of keeping with his costume and its barbaric confusion of ornaments; on the stern, merciless face with the laughing eyes; on the blue-green tattoos that marked his forehead and cheeks yet somehow did not disfigure him.

Like a mottle tree, Moth thought. The bark's all blotchy, but it's beautiful anyway.

"Are you men?"

"No."

The Royal Eunuchs! He had forgotten them. Their backs were to him; their voices sounded strange, soft, high, yet without definition.

"But neither are we children, or women. We beg leave to take the oath of the Fair."

There was a long silence. Then the shaman said, "Even if you are indeed neither children nor women, yet you are not men. Women have no honor, and neither do children, so why should you, you who are a third thing not a man?"

Moth was not sure which of the figures spoke. "Men possess honor because men—men such as yourself, Great Shaman; men such as your warriors, though your honor is greater than theirs; and men such as these merchants, though their honor is less than that of your warriors—all have the power and responsibility to choose for themselves to do that which is right. Women and children do not have that right; their choices are made for them by their fathers or brothers or husbands, and that is another part of a man's honor: a man accepts responsibility for others as well as for himself.

"Yet though we are not men, we are free to choose that which is right, with no obligation to parents or husbands. Though we are not men, we are responsible not only for ourselves but for countless others, for we are the rulers of our cities. And so we fulfill the second requirement of honor, since we accept responsibility for the well-being of our subjects. Thus we must be considered as capable of honor as any man."

The shaman nodded, ignoring his Co-Judge's frown. "It is fairly argued. Though I do not know whether you do, in fact, possess honor, I cannot state that you do not—and that is as much as I could say about many of the other city men who have sworn Fair oath to me today. But what of your family name? How can you swear upon that, you who will have no descendants?"

"Do not the Tlantlu have the custom of adoption?"

"They do."

"So it is with us. We are a family—a family in which every child is adopted."

"If I grant that, do you have a god or gods whom you hold most sacred, and in whose name you can swear the oath?"

"We do, though it is not a thing about which we are free to speak to those not of our kind."

The shaman beat out a long, complex rhythm on his drum. His movements disturbed the ornaments hanging from his costume.

He froze suddenly, as if listening to the jangling ornaments. Then he smiled, and his smile was like the laughter in his eyes, joyous and fierce.

"The spirits have tested you. You may swear the oath. But I warn you—should I find that even one of you is an oath-breaker, I will judge you all creatures without honor and sentence you to death."

"We will take oath under those terms, and gladly."

When Moth's turn to swear came he was terrified. What if the shaman took one look at him and said, "You look like a child to me. You'll have to prove you're a man"? And of course Moth would never be able to do so, because even though he wasn't really a child anymore, that was a secret that not even his mother knew, and there was no way to prove it without telling the shaman things he was forbidden to tell.

But when he stammered out the correct response, Casnut showed him the same fierce smile he had shown the eunuchs, and then it was over and Moth had been admitted to the Fair.

⚓️⚡ Chapter Seven ⚡⚓️

The Fair covered the meadow. Most of the Chaldans and Deltans had set up booths or tents, while the Nomads had spread out blankets on which to display their wares. The Nomads, warriors all, needed no one to protect them, but the merchants and traders from the cities were less self-assured, and small groups of Chaldan Warriors of the Hand and their Deltan counterparts circulated everywhere, eyeing the Nomads and each other with suspicious eyes, avoiding the Chosen as everyone not of their own retinues avoided them. Yet despite the universal mistrust, it was still a day for drinking and festivity, a day that might make your fortune if you were a merchant from the marsh city of Lustan, a day when a Nomad might trade a sickly mare that would never be a proper warrior's mount to some ignorant Chaldan who would give him in return a knife such as he could obtain in no other way, a day when a warrior of Chal might trade a pair of silver ear ornaments given him by his fifth daughter's husband for powdered beastflower worth twelve times as much.

"Do you see those two?" Sklar Ton asked, amused. He gestured toward the spot where the men dealing in drugs and medicines were setting up a market of their own in the traditional place, directly under the Judge's eyes. A Deltan whose black hair was as long as any Nomad's was arguing with a Nomad who had only a few long blond wisps on his otherwise bald head, though in every other way he looked like a young man.

"What about them?" Ri Tal asked.

"That Deltan is trying to sell him something to cure his baldness. He's claiming that it will give him back his hair in three days."

"So?" Ri Tal asked.

"The Fair ends at sunset, even if the Peace of the Fair extends till tomorrow morning. That means the Nomad will be two days north of here and the Deltan two days south before the Nomad has a chance to see if it really works."

"And if it doesn't?" Tramu asked.

"Then his only hope is that both he and the man who sold it to him will be at the next Fair, so he can bring a complaint before the Judge." Sklar Ton shrugged. "The man's a fool."

"Then why would anybody buy anything like that here?" Tramu asked. "If you can't tell if it's any good or not."

"The Judges can recognize the commoner medicinals and poisons. Snal, red ivorywort, powdered spiderwasp—or strangle-apples, for that matter. Things like that."

Tramu nodded, recognizing the names.

"But what's more important is that this is the only place any of us can obtain certain medicines, such as beastflower, which enables a man to share the soul of a beast for a time and—perhaps—gain some of its courage for himself. Or blueleaf, which produces a giddy intoxication that renders a man too weak to move his limbs, and grayleaf, which imparts the strength to overcome all obstacles for a day and a night. And then there is the opener of the way, which some men claim allows them to converse with spirits, ghosts, and gods; and the death-dream bud, which kills with delightful dreams. They all come from the same plant originally, somewhere in the far north, or so people say, though I don't know anyone who's actually seen the plant. In any case, we can only get them from the Nomads here at the Fair."

"Is that what you come here for?" Moth asked.

"I'm here to help your father. But that's what I'll be trading for until he needs me."

Ri Tal nodded. "I'll return for you as soon as I find what I need. Come on Moth, Tramu."

They followed Ri Tal from booth to booth across the littered ground, trying to stare at the Nomads without being too obvious about it or getting too close to any of them. They managed not to step on anything important, though they got yelled at twice for trampling the corner of someone's blanket.

Some of the Nomads were selling raw bone, sinew, hides of various kinds, antlers, and meat, as well as the things they fashioned from such materials: bone ornaments, fetishes, needles, beads, and knife handles; bone arrowheads with thin barbs that would break off in a wound; bowstrings of sinew; leather garments and footwear. Then there were the horses—Moth was afraid to get too close to them; they were big and didn't seem gentle and stupid like oxen—and the black and white animals that took the place of goats and sheep for the Nomads, big things like deer but almost as broad-shouldered as oxen, with strange antlers that weren't sharp and pointed like a deer's, but were more like ducks' feet that had been warped and twisted into odd shapes.

There were rare spices, oils, perfumes, and food-stuffs, a multitude of strange odors mingling in the air. There were strips of cloth, not particularly well woven, but spectacularly dyed—which was all that was important, since the Nomads were selling dyes, not cloth. The manufacturers of the brilliant pur-ple, crimson, and yellow dyes were closely guarded secrets, and the dyes fetched fantastic prices, espe-cially from the Deltans, though Ri Tal pointed out Dilea's father earnestly haggling with a Nomad displaying strips of vivid crimson cloth. And there were flint weapons and tools: arrowheads, knives, scrapers, axe-heads, even plowshares. The poorer people of the Empire were as unable to afford metal as the Nomads themselves, and a flint plowshare would outlast one of ordinary copper anyway.

The Nameless One watched the potter as he stepped up to a display of carved lapis and pre-tended to glance at it idly—yet another of his clumsy attempts to dissimulate the extent of his interest in just those jewels and precious substances that would interest the King's Coffinmaker.

The Taryaa had come to the Fair to discover how they could use the Nomads against King Asp. Not for a dozen generations had a conqueror so threat-

ened their hold on the cities they ruled, and when
Asp had executed the Taryaa who held power in
Lashll, he had done so in defiance of a secret
compact that had bound the Kings of Chal when
Asp's own ancestors were still starving goatherds.

It was not to be tolerated. The Taryaa would not
tolerate it.

But they had not survived the Sorcerers' War and
the millennia of sand and salt that had followed by
inviting confrontation. They dealt in indirection
and diversion, sowing plagues, pitting enemy rulers
against one another, encouraging assassinations
and fomenting rebellions, and they had endured
while those who had opposed them were dust.

It would be ideal if the Nomads declared war
against Chal independently, almost as good if they
could be persuaded to ally with certain Deltan
cities against the Empire. At the very least, the
Chosen knew that they could convince some of the
Nomads to serve the League as mercenaries. As
such they would be invaluable, for none of the
civilized peoples could match the speed and striking range of their horse-mounted warriors; Chaldan and Deltan chariots alike were good only to
speed warriors to the scene of battle.

But though the Taryaa laid plans that would not
bear fruit for millennia as a matter of course,
though their awareness encompassed not only the
great flood due now in three years but that far
greater flood due in thirteen generations, yet they
were ever alert to the possibilities of the spontane-
ous, to those chances that must be seized at once or
lost forever.

And if the potter was truly the King's

Coffinmaker and not just his agent, perhaps a way could be found to use him to disrupt the Seven-Year Festival and destroy King Asp's legitimacy, even kill him. . . .

The Seven-Year Festival. The Chaldan year was three hundred and sixty-four days long, made up of thirteen twenty-eight-day months. But when in spring the old year ended, it was followed, not by the first day of the new year, but by a day that was part of no month, no year, a day the Chaldans believed to be bounded on all sides by time while itself outside of time, a day when all things were as they had been on that first day, at the very moment of creation, when all was new and vital, when there was nothing but newness—or so, the Nameless One knew, the Warriors of the Voice declared to their people. And should the day seem no different from any other, why, the Warriors of the Voice explained, that was because those unable to perceive the difference had had their senses so befouled by immersion in the illusions of time that they were unable to perceive the ultimate reality of the Timeless Instant.

Since it was hardly to be expected that those of the lesser Sils would be able to free themselves of their illusions, the Warriors of the Voice proclaimed Festivals whose rites enabled the participants to comprehend some semblance of the revitalizing renewal. Six out of every seven years, the timeless days—which were all really the same day—that followed year-end were dedicated to the celebration of the renewal of the vegetal world (the once proud plant withering, then dry and dead; yet from the seed it has left behind—a seed as hard and dry and dead as what remains of the plant itself—a new plant will arise, a tiny green shoot struggling up through the close-packed earth, bursting free of the graveground's weight, reaching up toward the sun until the plant that had once withered and died stands swaying again in the breeze, green testimony to death's impermanence); but every seventh year the Festival was something more, for it was no mere plant that died and was resurrected, but the King of Chal himself. While the King lay dead in his coffin all Chal lay dead as well, and though a man might think himself alive, though he might cry, "I'm alive! I'm alive!" yet would he be deluded, for all life, said the Warriors of the Voice, was only the fire of Sartor's divine being burning within the flesh that the ignorant confused with their true selves.

Though that sacred flame was of Sartor alone, only through His anointed King might it enter the world, for all life radiated from the King like the rays of the sun. And yet that sun was not the King, but Sartor.

When the time has come for the King to die he takes the sword which has been crafted to this purpose alone, and with his hands he breaks it. The Nameless One had never seen a Seven-Year Festival, but a Taryaa had once witnessed a Festival, two hundred and sixty years before, and what it had seen was remembered by all of its kind:

The King takes the sword from the smith who has fashioned it for him, a sword finely made, intricately inlaid but no toy, a sword to serve a man well in battle and made of that magically tough copper known to the smiths of Chal alone. He bends the sword, flexes it, and then, straining, sweating, grunting, he breaks it—not easily but with supreme difficulty, bending it forward, placing his booted foot over its center and grasping it by hilt and tip, lifting, gasping, putting his whole life into breaking the blade—for that is what happens: he snaps the blade, but the effort is fatal; he has poured his whole life into it, and he is dead.

The King is placed in his coffin, the lid secured, and the coffin lowered into the ground. Seven shovelfuls of earth are heaped upon it while the women wail.

The King's eldest son gives the smith who had forged it the broken blade, begs the smith to tell him that the blade is not truly broken, that the King's death is illusion only. The King cannot be dead!

And while he pleads the women are wailing.

The blade is broken, the King is dead, the smith replies. The sword cannot be mended. And yet . . . He pauses, and a hush comes over the crowd. And yet, the sword can be returned to that primal state before it was a sword, when it was neither whole nor broken; and from that primal substance a new sword can be forged.

And when this has been done, new life will awaken in the King.

He dies and yet he returns, the Nameless One thought, gesturing for one of its warriors. The ultimate obscenity.

"I've found almost everything I need," Ri Tal said presently. "Let's find Sklar Ton."

"But there's so much left to see!" Tramu said.

"True, and I'm sorry. Perhaps we can look around some more this evening, after I finish. But now that we've seen everything—"

"Not everything!" Moth protested. "Not nearly everything!"

"Everything I was looking for," his father said, frowning. "Act like the men you're supposed to be. We have things of vital importance to do here."

"But you don't need *us* to do them!" Tramu said. "We can look at other things while you're busy." Glancing at Moth: "We'll stick close to the Warriors of the Hand and Voice all the time, and we won't do anything dangerous, I promise!"

"So do I," Moth said.

"No. I promised to keep you safe, and I intend to do so."

"We're no longer children, Father," Moth said with as much dignity as he could muster. "We'll be very careful, I promise. Please?"

"No."

But Tramu persisted long after Moth had given up, and Ri Tal finally amazed Moth by granting them his permission, though he made them listen to all his warnings all over again.

When he was gone, Moth looked at Tramu.

"You just have to last longer than they can," his cousin said smugly.

"Does it work with your father?"

"Sometimes, but he's good at it himself. Come on, let's go look at the *real* Nomad stuff. I can see all the pretty jewels I want at home."

A daysixth later found them at the ivory-carvers' booth. It was larger than most, all of red silk, and filled with figurines and jewelry carved from a glossy white substance like bone, but far lovelier. Some of the carvings depicted animals unlike any Moth had ever seen; others portrayed strange man-beast combinations that he supposed were either gods or demons; still others were just lovely. Moth was watching a gaunt, fastidious-looking, stooped young man, his head wrapped in cream-yellow silk, who was painstakingly carving the figure of a young girl from a block of ivory, when someone behind them called, "Hey, you two!"

Moth looked up. A Deltan was watching them. He was only three or four years older than they were, the strip of brightly patterned cloth wrapped around his head proclaiming him an artisan like the ivory-carvers, though his bearing and voice were as insolent as Syrr Avyyrno's shield bearer's.

"What do you want?" Tramu demanded, matching the Deltan's tone.

"I don't want anything. It's your father who wants you."

Moth was instantly suspicious. "Why?"

"How should I know?"

"I mean, why did he send you?"

"He's busy. Looking at a piece of sky metal he's trying to talk my father into selling him."

"Sky metal?" Tramu asked skeptically, though Moth could see that the Deltan had caught his interest. "Where would somebody like you get sky metal?"

The Deltan sneered. "It fell out of the sky. Where did you think sky metal comes from, anyway?"

"Where is he?" Tramu asked.

"We have our tent set up over there"—he

pointed—"at the edge of the meadow, behind that
stand of trees."

"How do we know you're telling the truth?"
Moth said.

"About what?"

"About my father being there."

The Deltan shrugged, disgusted. "All they asked
me to do was tell you where he is. If you don't want
to believe me, that's up to you." He started to turn
away.

"Where'd you say it was?" Tramu asked.

The Deltan pointed again. "There. Just beyond
those trees."

He turned and walked away.

"I don't know," Moth said. "It's so far away from
everything else—"

"Come on!" Tramu said. "It's not like he was a
Nomad, or anything. He wasn't even a warrior."

"Even so—"

"Anyway, he isn't much older than we are." He
paused, stared challengingly at Moth. "You're not
afraid, are you?"

Moth remembered his father groveling before
Syrr Avyyrno that morning, the contempt he had
surprised on Tramu's face. And they were under the
protection of the Peace of the Fair.

"No. I guess not."

"Then let's go."

Just past the trees, someone struck Moth on the
head from behind, knocking him to his knees. He
looked up, dazed, to see the Deltan who'd given
them the message standing over him, grinning. He
had a short, heavy wooden club in his hand, and
the long blond braid—the Nomad braid—that the

cloth wrapped around his head had concealed was now flopping free. Two other Nomads were standing over Tramu's fallen body. Moth tried to get to his feet, but the false Deltan hit him with the club again, and he fell.

He lay there, unable to move or open his eyes, vaguely aware that someone was tying his hands behind his back, thrusting a wad of dry leaves into his mouth and gagging him.

He passed out, only to be brought half-awake again by the sound of someone shouting. He managed to force his eyes open again in time to see a spear skewer the false Deltan's chest, and then his captor collapsed onto him and he lost consciousness for good.

❧ Chapter Eight ❧

Warm. He was warm, drifting.

A woman was singing a strange lilting song in a language he had never heard before. Within her voice he floated safe, protected from the pain, from—

Memory grabbed, cold metal twisting in his gut: the Nomad. He'd been kidnapped—and then somebody had killed the Nomad. Rescued him.

He opened his eyes to blinding whiteness. The light was like a knife twisting in his head, behind his eyes. He tried to sit up, fell back, too sick and weak to do anything but lie there with his eyes squeezed tightly shut.

"You're awake, I see." He froze. It was the voice of the woman who'd been singing. She was somewhere behind him. "Don't be afraid. You'll be home again soon enough."

Home? He forced his eyes open again, squinted, tried to make them focus. The brightness was just sunlight shining through white silk. He was in a large, airy tent, lying on a heap of silken cushions.

Beside him, Tramu lay sleeping with his mouth open.

He managed to sit up, twisted around so he could see the woman.

"How do you feel? Better?" The voice was that of a woman, but the white robes, the mouth mask of scarlet silk, the smooth brown skin and unnaturally large, bulging pink eyes all told him that he faced a Royal Eunuch.

An enemy.

"How do you feel?" the eunuch repeated in its woman's voice. It was kneeling by a small fire, heating water in an unglazed clay pot.

"I feel—all right, Your Highness," Moth said. He was very afraid. "Just a little weak."

"No dizziness? No bad taste in your mouth?" The voice, strangely, reminded him of his mother's.

He started to shake his head, felt the world spin, saliva pool at the back of his throat. "A little . . . Your Highness. And the light hurts my eyes."

"Ah." The eunuch took the pot from the fire, poured the water from it into two cups. "Then drink some of this. It will make you feel better."

Moth accepted the cup, looked at it doubtfully. A thick reddish twig was slowly staining the water brown.

"There is no need to fear *me,* child. You are here, in my tent, because I rescued you from the Nomads who kidnapped you, but I am no Nomad. You are still at the Fair, and you will be free to return to your family soon."

"Then—why am I here?" He took a cautious sip, felt better immediately, and took another sip.

"What do you want from me?"

"I need your help. You see, it is very important that I learn how the two of you came to be kidnapped by Nomads disguised as my people."

"I don't understand."

"To rescue you we had to kill the three Nomads who had captured you. And we will have to justify killing them to the Judge of the Fair, or he will have all of my kind here put to death for violating Fair law. Now do you understand why I must find out more about what happened?"

Moth nodded, terrified again. It wants to find out what I'm going to tell the Judge before it lets me see him, he realized, remembering how the shaman had said that if one of the eunuchs should prove itself to be without honor, they would all be killed. If it thinks I'm going to say the wrong thing, it will have me killed before I can tell the Judge anything.

"You owe me a certain debt of gratitude for saving you from lives of slavery," the eunuch continued. "We will see the Judge of the Fair after you and your brother have answered my questions, and then you will be free to go."

"I'll tell you whatever you need to know, sir."

The eunuch's face above the mask crinkled in what was evidently a smile. "You need not fear me. If you would prefer, I can send for your father and have him here by your side while I question you, though I would rather question you and your brother alone."

"My cousin, sir," Moth said.

"You and your cousin alone, then. Because, you see, I need to know everything that happened, and if either of you did anything that was . . . not really wrong, perhaps, but still a bit foolish or against your father's wishes—"

"There wasn't anything like that, sir," Moth said quickly. He hesitated a moment, then added, "Maybe we were a bit foolish, though."

"Of course. And out of that debt of gratitude you owe me, perhaps you will tell me about these things you did that were a little more foolish than they ought to have been. There is no need for your father to know of them; you can send for him when we have finished."

"Thank you, Your Highness, but—well, can you send for him if it gets too late?"

"Certainly. But you need not call me 'Your Highness'—that is a title for a king or a queen, and I am neither. Speak to me as you would to an aunt; if I had a name you could call me by it, but since I have none"—soft, trilling laughter—"then call me nothing at all. But you, child, you must have a name?"

"Moth, son of Ri Tal the potter, sir."

"No titles, Moth, son of Ri Tal. And would you call your aunt 'sir'?" The voice was clear and quick like running water, soft and smooth. Almost a woman's, but more assured than any woman's voice Moth had ever heard. And yet it still somehow reminded him of his mother's voice.

"May I . . . ask you another question?" he ventured. The infusion seemed to have cleared his head; he was beginning to feel a little better.

"Of course. Ask me whatever you like."

"Will Tramu"—he gestured toward his sleeping cousin—"be all right soon?"

"Yes. He must have swallowed more of the

blueleaf they gagged him with than you did, so it will take him longer to rid himself of it."

"That was what they put in our mouths?"

"Yes, mixed with ordinary leaves. To keep you from waking up before they got you safely away from here. But it will not harm him in any way."

"I think I remember now, sir, but—may I ask you another question? You said you rescued us?"

The eunuch's laughter was another brief snatch of birdsong.

"My people rescued you. One of our artisans saw a man he didn't know, but who was dressed as a Deltan, telling you to go to one of our tents where he knew that we didn't have any tents."

"The ivory-carver?" Moth asked.

"Yes."

"I didn't think he even noticed us." He paused, took another sip of the infusion, glanced up at the eunuch and was caught by its mild pink gaze.

Like a rabbit, he realized. It has eyes like a rabbit.

Somehow that only made it all the more frightening.

"What do you want me to tell you?" If he told the eunuch what it wanted the Judge to hear, it would let him go. Only he had no way of knowing what it wanted him to say.

"Tell me everything that happened. But relax, Moth, son of Ri Tal. Relax. Whatever was planned here was no fault of yours. You bear no blame for what happened."

"Well, we were looking at the ivory-carvers' booth and—"

He broke off as the eunuch held up a hand.

"No, Moth, I want you to tell me *everything,*

starting with when you first reached the Fair. They must have decided to capture you some time earlier."

Moth nodded, and haltingly told the eunuch everything that had happened since he had first sighted the meadow, leaving out only the reasons that had brought Ri Tal to the Fair.

"And that's all, sir," he said finally.

"Tell me more about what the Nomad said to you. He told you that your father was looking at a piece of sky metal?"

Moth watched himself weighing and testing the question to see if it was safe to answer. "Yes. That's why Tramu was so excited. His father is a smith."

"Of course," the eunuch said, as if that explained everything, and Moth finally relaxed.

"That's all I know," Moth said. "But—can I ask you another question?"

"Yes, Moth."

"Then—why did they want *us?*"

"Because the two of you are young. Perhaps they thought they could trick you more easily."

They did, Moth thought. "But why—what good would we be to them? Why would they all risk their lives just for the two of us?"

"All three of them were young—none of them had earned any ceremonial scars or tattoos yet. Capturing the two of you here, in defiance of Fair law, would have been a way of proving their bravery and earning their manhood scars."

"You mean, like a sort of initiation?"

"Exactly. And the fact that you and your cousin have no special value as slaves would prove that they had done it not out of greed, but for the exploit alone."

The eunuch laughed, another snatch of birdsong, sweet but strange. Moth found himself focusing on the inhumanity of that laughter. The eunuch was *different*, incomprehensible, not to be trusted.

"Can we send for my father now, sir?" he asked.

"Soon, Moth. As soon as your cousin awakens and I've heard his story. Is he sensible, your cousin?"

"Tramu?" Moth asked. The eunuch would be able to check everything Moth told it against what Tramu said when he woke up. I was right not to try lying to it, he realized, and was surprised at the relief he felt.

"Is your cousin sensible?" the eunuch repeated.

"Very sensible. Just a little too brave sometimes."

"That is not necessarily bad," the eunuch said. "You said his father is a smith?"

"Yes. That's why his hair's so red."

"All smiths are passionate. But your hair is red as well as black. Was your mother a smith's daughter?"

"Yes." He began to feel more comfortable: family was a safe topic.

"Among us, you know, smiths have black or brown hair like everyone else. But they are as rash as your redheaded smiths."

"Tramu is sometimes a little rash," Moth admitted.

"Like all smiths."

"Maybe I should try to wake him. It must be getting late."

"He'll feel much better if we allow him to sleep a bit longer. And it's not really that late. But how shall we—Ah!" the smooth brown skin around the soft pink eyes crinkled with what Moth suddenly recognized as amusement. "Have you ever seen the Delta?" the eunuch asked.

"No. I was born in Chal, but all I can remember is Kyborash."

"Would you like me to tell you stories about the Delta while we wait for your cousin to awaken?"

"Please, sir!" Moth said. "I'd love that!" There was no danger in listening to stories—and besides, he was being treated like a prince or some great warrior's son, not like the son of a mere potter. "Please!" he repeated.

"Certainly." The Royal Eunuch seated itself on a cushion near Moth. Its eyes are softer-looking than real people's, Moth decided.

"I will tell you something of Bierecia, where I was born. Though it is not strange to me, it will be to you, for there is nothing like it in all Chal.

"Bierecia is a rich city, for its people alone know the secrets of capturing the great marsh clam we call the Olein-Te, with its tusks of the purest, smoothest white. There is no finer material, none worth a sixtieth as much for the carving of beautiful things. You will see none of it here, for it is too precious to leave the Delta.

"Long ago Bierecia consisted of fourteen separate islands, and my people traveled between them in boats. But as the centuries passed they first linked the islands with bridges, then extended the islands themselves with stone taken from the mainland, until, some nine thousand years ago, thirteen of them had become one great city.

"Only the fourteenth island, Gwar-chi, remains
separate. Its shores are cliffs of black rock, unassail-
able except by means of a great stairway of white
marble, and on its summit, looking out over all
Bierecia and down on the Sea of Marshes and out
to the great Ocean glinting blue-green and silver in
the sun, stands the Royal Palace.

"I was born there, the son of King Astorang-
aroakanival and his Queen, the Lady Lamprias-
tifal. I was very young when I was selected to
become what I am, but though the Taryaa (for that
is what we call ourselves) took me from my family
and . . . made me what I am, I was required to
return to my father's palace for two weeks of every
year. Yet though there is glamour enough in the life
of a King Who Reigns But Does Not Rule, it is all
empty pretense to one who has lived the life of a
Taryaa. And beneath the glamour there was always
the stink of rotting fish, my younger sister, Flastuf-
isa, chattering nonsense, and my father pouting and
sickly, flying into petty rages that only my mother
and the servitors listened to. . . ."

For some time Moth had been staring openmouthed at the eunuch, totally amazed that he, a
potter's son, was being told such things. He shut his
mouth, moistened dry lips: it was not safe to know
the secrets of the great unless you yourself were
great.

Again the trilling laugh, but the amusement
Moth was learning to read in the exposed parts of
the strange face robbed the moment of its menace.

"Have no fear, Moth, son to Ri Tal the Potter: I
will tell you nothing to make you fear that I need to

silence you. The Taryaa do not rule through awe or fear; our power is inherent in what we are. I know what must remain silent, and that I will never reveal; as for the rest, I am free to share it with whomever I wish, and they may think of it what they will."

Moth shook his head, uncomprehending.

"But I have already told you of myself, of my kind. Tell me more about yourself."

"About myself?"

"The life of a potter of Kyborash is as strange to me as the life of a King of Bierecia is to you. Tell me. of yourself, Moth."

"But— I've only just been initiated. And I couldn't tell you about what we do in the potting compound anyway. I'm sorry, I don't know what to tell you."

"Tell me what brought you to the Fair, then."

The King's coffin. The one thing he'd kept from the eunuch. But he was sworn on his true name not to mention it.

"Tramu and I wanted to see it. We'd never seen one before, and Tas Et—"

"And who is Tas Et?" the eunuch asked, and Moth couldn't keep himself from giving a little sigh of relief.

"Tramu's father."

"A smith, then. Is he a good smith?"

"He's a very good smith. Tas No Sil says he'll be the Sil Smith someday, and—" Moth caught himself, furiously reviewed his words.

The eunuch saw his sudden tension, drew tentative conclusions even as Moth relaxed again.

"I came to the Fair to buy horses," the eunuch

told Moth. "But things did not go as I had hoped, and I will return to my city with only a few, and those not of the finest quality."

"I'm sorry," Moth said.

"It is of little importance. But you, what brought your father here? The Fair is a strange place for a potter. Unless your father is the Sil Potter, of course."

Pride struggled with discretion. And even if the eunuch was lying to him, trying to trick him, he still might be safer if it realized how important his father was. "He's not the Ri Sil, not yet anyway, but he's here on Sil business," Moth said, congratulating himself on having conveyed his father's importance without revealing any secrets. "He used to direct all the Sil's affairs in Chal," he added. "That's why I was born there."

"I can see that your father is no ordinary potter."

"No," Moth agreed, flattered.

"May I venture a guess? Is your father going to be making something for the Seven-Year Festival?" The eunuch held up a quick hand. "No, don't say anything. Anyone realizing that there was a Master Potter of Kyborash here this year would have guessed the same thing, but let my final guess remain my secret. Tell me nothing."

Moth felt relief surge over him: the eunuch had known Ri Tal's secret all along. It must have known what he was doing every time he avoided saying anything about why his father was here, and it had been telling him the truth when it said that all it wanted was to find out what had really happened with the Nomads. And none of that had been anything it would have to silence Moth for. He'd been right not to try lying to it.

He was safe.

"Thank you," he said, meaning it.

"For what? For respecting a secret? But that is little more than common courtesy."

From the way the dark skin crinkled above the scarlet mouth mask, Moth could tell that the other was smiling at him again. He tried to imagine what the eunuch's mouth looked like. Was it really toothless? What if he—Moth felt greatly daring for even thinking of the question—what if he asked about it?

But Sklar Ton's words came back to him, sobering him. Even in Kyborash men who tried to penetrate the Women's Mystery died, and why should this ruler of strange cities guard its secrets any less jealously than Moth's own mother did hers?

It probably looks just like an old woman, but without the wrinkles, Moth told himself firmly.

"Would you like to hear more about my people?" the eunuch asked.

Moth smiled and nodded, then listened entranced as the eunuch began telling him of the campaign the men of Lustan had undertaken against the pirate city of pu-Assan.

⚙ Chapter Nine ⚙

The eunuch was concluding the tale when Moth finally heard Tramu moan.

"Keep still," the eunuch warned him. "I must sing him into a good awakening."

Tramu was shaking, snarling wordlessly with teeth clenched, sweat beading his agonized face. His body had gone rigid, every muscle straining against every other.

He looks like he's dying, Moth thought.

The eunuch crossed its hands on its breast and began again the soft swirling song that had eased Moth into wakefulness. The liquid voice soothed Moth anew, and within moments Tramu's forehead began to smooth, his hands to unclench.

The scarlet silk fluttered as the eunuch sang. Moth felt free and light, like a leaf on the wind; with every liquid cadence his companion's voice grew clearer, more beautiful, more meaningful. . . .

And Tramu was relaxing, almost smiling. His eyelids fluttered; he groaned, levered himself up on one elbow, and squinted at Moth and the eunuch.

"Hello, Tramu," the eunuch said, holding out a

cup of the brown infusion. "Drink this. It will make you feel much better."

Tramu just stared at the cup in the eunuch's outstretched hand.

"Don't worry, Tramu," Moth said. "It really will make you feel much better. We're safe. They rescued us from the Nomads!"

"What Nomads?" Tramu took the cup and scowled at it, but did not drink.

"You remember," Moth said. "The Nomads who kidnapped us."

"No."

"Some Nomads tried to kidnap you, but my people rescued you," the eunuch explained. "I'll have you back to your uncle soon."

"Why not now?" Tramu's voice was shrill.

"There's nothing to be afraid of here, cousin," Moth said as soothingly as he could, remembering how afraid he'd felt when he'd first awakened. "And you should have seen what you looked like just now before the Royal Eunuch sang you back to health. You looked like you were dying. You should be grateful."

"Grateful?" A muscle in Tramu's cheek began to twitch.

"You have my word as a Taryaa that as soon as you tell me what happened to you, you may rejoin Ri Tal," the eunuch said.

"What is he talking about?" Tramu asked Moth.

"Calm down, cousin. He just needs us to tell him everything that happened so he can tell the Judge about it," Moth said. "About the Nomad who told us about the sky metal, and how they tried to kidnap us."

"He wasn't a Nomad," Tramu said belligerently, slurring his words slightly. "He was a Deltan."

What was wrong with Tramu? Didn't he realize how dangerous it was to say that?

"No, he wasn't a Deltan, that's just what he was dressed like. But I saw him later, when he hit me, and—"

The eunuch held up its hand and Moth fell silent. "Let him remember for himself, Moth. That way he may recall something that you yourself missed."

Tramu ignored the eunuch. "He really was a Nomad? You're sure?"

Moth glanced at the eunuch, who nodded, before answering. "Yes. I'm sure, Tramu. He had long yellow hair under that cloth he had wrapped around his head. In a braid, the way Nomads wear their hair. He couldn't have been from the Delta."

Tramu shook his head, looking confused and lost. "I don't remember. My head hurts."

"You'll feel better if you drink your tea, cousin."

"They gave you blueleaf after they hit you," the eunuch explained patiently. "That's why you're feeling so confused. The infusion will make you feel better."

"I don't know what you're talking about!"

The eunuch looked at Moth. "Perhaps you had better tell him everything from the beginning, after all, and see if it helps his memory."

So Moth repeated what had happened from the time the false Deltan had told them Ri Tal was waiting for them to seeing the man die.

"Very good, Moth," the eunuch said as Tramu glared at his cousin. "I am known to be an excellent judge of a man's truthfulness: you have given me the truth as you know it."

The eunuch was watching Tramu's eyes, saw the fear there. *There is something he's afraid of betraying to me,* it realized.

"Don't you remember anything?" Moth demanded.

Tramu started to say something, then shook his head. "Just what you said, about him telling us to go see your father."

"You may recall more when the blueleaf wears off completely," the eunuch told him. "And remember, smith's son, you owe me no little debt of gratitude. When you've told me everything you can, we'll get your uncle and take our story to the Judge. But you have nothing to fear. I promise you that."

"All right, but you better make your promise good—"

Tramu's still drugged! That's crazy; you can't threaten someone like a eunuch! Moth thought, even as the eunuch said patiently, "Remember, the Judge has sworn to have us killed if we violate Fair law. My life and that of my fellows depends on seeing that you are returned safely."

Tramu nodded, satisfied. "Good. Because my father's very important, and King Asp will help him get me back."

"Your cousin told me how important your father is now," the Nameless One said, emphasizing the word *now* and watching Tramu very carefully.

Tramu balled his fists and stared at Moth. "What *exactly* did you tell him, cousin?" he demanded.

"Nothing secret. Just who we were, and that your

father's Tas Et and our grandfather's Tas No Sil.
That's all."

"Your cousin is right to be suspicious," the
eunuch said, while deciding what use to make of
the information it had just gained. "Too much
misguided trust has already gotten the two of you
kidnapped once today, and my people and yours
are not always the best of friends."

He's not angry at Tramu, Moth realized, relieved.

Tramu was drinking his fourth cup of the brown
infusion, Moth his seventh, when one of the Nameless One's Deltan warriors finally entered with Ri
Tal and Sklar Ton.

Moth and Tramu told them what had happened.
Ri Tal listened impassively until they had finished,
then suddenly hit Moth so hard he knocked him
down. He started yelling at both of them for their
stupidity, then abruptly remembered where he was
and fell silent.

Moth picked himself up, afraid of what his father
was going to do next—but after a moment Ri Tal
just grinned at him, relieved.

"Were I rich, or powerful, I would gladly do
whatever was in my power to thank you," Ri Tal
said when the eunuch had told him of its part in the
events. "But I am only a potter—"

"A Master Potter of Kyborash, are you not?" the
eunuch asked.

"Yes," Ri Tal admitted, pleased but a little wary.

"Then there is indeed something you can do for
me. I have a great need for the services of a Master
Potter of Kyborash. But first, Tramu, your nephew

—his father is Tas Et, the smith?"

"Yes," Ri Tal said. "My wife is second daughter to Tas No Sil; his eldest daughter, Pyota, married Tas Et.

"And is Tas Et a good smith?"

"An extraordinary smith, as Tas No Sil himself admits."

"Excellent. I have some business to attend to in Kyborash. I will call upon you at your home in three days. If you could see that Tas Et is also present, I would be most grateful, and the two of you might well learn something to your advantage."

"Never will my home have been so honored," Ri Tal assured him, and Moth felt so proud that he couldn't keep himself from grinning idiotically.

Walking back to Kyborash the next morning, Moth thought about how strange it had all been, how utterly unlike anything he had ever imagined could happen to him. He had seen the Fair and the Nomads atop their horses, seen the shaman Casnut and even talked with him; he had been kidnapped by a Nomad warrior and rescued by a Deltan eunuch, and yet here he was walking back to Kyborash and everything was just as it had been before.

Except, he realized, except that I've met one of the rulers of the Delta and he treated me like a friend.

❧ Chapter Ten ❦

The Royal Eunuch had come to speak to Ri Tal and Tas Et. The eunuch's burly driver sat on his cart in front of the house chewing a reed; two other Deltan warriors, tall men in undecorated copper armor with swords slung across their backs, stood outside the doorslit conversing in low tones and eyeing everyone who passed the house. And they, in turn, were being covertly watched by all of Moth's neighbors.

But Moth too was outside the house, banished to the garden. It was not fair, not fair at all; if it hadn't been for him Ri Tal would never have met the eunuch, but Moth had still been sent outside when all he wanted to do was stand in the dim interior of the anteroom and listen to the conversation he knew was going on in the sunlit central courtyard. He wouldn't interfere, wouldn't make any noise or be any trouble to anyone.

He thought of excuse after excuse to return to the house, questions he urgently needed to ask Kuan, things he was sure she would be grateful to know. But though he made up his mind to try to go inside again and again, his resolve always failed when it came time to pass the guards, although he told himself that they'd seen their master greet him as a friend, although he was sure they knew he was a lawful member of Ri Tal's household and entitled to enter his own house whenever he wanted to. Time and again he returned to the garden without having attempted to get in.

It was not just that he was afraid of what his father might do to him, or even that he was afraid of the guards. What he really feared was the shame of having the watching neighbors see him denied entry to his own house, after he'd told them all about how well the Royal Eunuch had treated him, and how the Pink-Eyed had been fascinated by every detail of Moth's daily life, even curious about the kinds of houses he and his cousin lived in and what sort of food they ate.

It was late afternoon and Moth was standing not far from the house, trying to work up the courage to get closer still, when he heard his uncle yell something inside. The warriors tensed, and the one in the cart picked up his sword while one of the guards yelled a quick question in through the doorslit, but they relaxed as soon as they heard their master's reply.

A moment later Tas Et emerged, brushed past the guards, and stalked past Moth, pausing only long enough to tell him, "I love your father like a brother, nephew, but he's a fool!"

Moth turned to watch him as he made his way with quick, angry strides down the street toward the inner city. The two guards also watched him go; one said something to the other, and they both laughed. Moth felt confused and angry and ashamed.

Some time later the Royal Eunuch emerged from the house. It paused a moment to say good-bye to Moth, then climbed onto its cart with its warriors and departed. Moth watched the cart until it was out of sight, then darted into the house. But his father had retired to the potting compound with orders that he was not to be disturbed, and when Moth tried to ask his mother if she'd overheard anything, he was sent back to the garden.

"Do you know why the Royal Eunuch came here to see Tas Et and myself?" Moth's father finally asked at dinner.

"No. Mother wouldn't tell me."

"That's as it should be. But what he wanted was to persuade Tas Et and myself to undertake a certain kind of manufacture for him for which he would have paid us exceedingly well. It seems that the gods of his city—"

"Swilth, Lord of Fishes, and Pith-Mia-Sim of the Winds and Agoen, Lord of the Sky, and—"

"And all their other gods. Don't interrupt. The gods of his city have conceived a desire for offerings made from neither clay nor metal alone, but rather from the two together. And since the gods of Bierecia desire these objects to be crafted as exquisitely as possible, he came here to ask us to make them for him."

"Are you going to make them?"

"No, though I would like to. But I am sealed to the clay alone, as Tas Et is sealed to the forge and the forge alone; neither of us may undertake such a project."

"I heard uncle yelling," Moth said. "And he told me that he loved you but that you were a fool."

Ri Tal sighed. "He has a smith's temper, but you must not hold it against him. He was angry because the eunuch suggested that you and Tramu, both being young enough to be sealed to your Sils without yet having been sealed to them to the exclusion of all else, could become pottersmiths, RiTases, and learn to make such things."

"I would like that," Moth said.

"So would I, but the idea made Tas Et furious. He said that he was a maker of swords, of strong, shining weapons, not of clay pots that shatter when you blow too hard upon them, and that neither he nor Tramu would ever have anything to do with the Pink-Eyed's offer.

"He had reason, I suppose, for though the Ri Sil is the elder, the Tas Sil is the more highly honored. Yet— But no matter. Tas Et refused. Still, if a way could be found to do this thing, to make of you a RiTas, would you consent to be sealed to Sartor's Forge Aspect as well as to the clay?"

"Yes," Moth said immediately, not needing to consider.

"It could bring you great wealth, son, and perhaps in time honor beyond anything I can hope to achieve. Perhaps you could become, not the Sil Potter, but the first Sil RiTas."

"Yes," Moth said. "I would like that very much, Father."

"But the way would be difficult, son. You would have to bear within you two of Sartor's Aspects, and if you proved too weak to hold them in balance within you they might well tear you apart. They might kill you. You might end up in the cage."

"I am strong, Father. I know I am strong enough."

"This is a different kind of strength. If you take this road, your way will be far, far harder than mine ever was. Yet who is to say what heights you might reach—and if not you yourself, then your sons or your sons' sons?"

"I will try it, Father," Moth said. "I will do it."

"You go too fast and not fast enough all at once, son. You cannot simply try it, like a fruit you can bite into and then toss away if it has worms in it. Once sealed to a Mystery you are sealed to it for life, for better or for worse."

"Would I have to work in the garden and barley field like a potter?"

"No. Probably not. But you would have to work very, very hard in the forge and the potting compound."

"I would enter into it, Father."

"You are sure?"

"Yes."

"Good. Yet it may well never come to pass. You will need the permission of both Ri Cer Sil and Tas No Sil—and of the Warriors of the Voice as well. I'll ask Ri Cer Sil tomorrow."

"I'm sure he'll agree," Kuan said. "He has always been a friend to you."

"A friend, yes, but this is a matter of Sil law. Still, I hope he will grant us his permission."

The next day Moth was working in the barley field by the river when Tramu stopped to talk to him.

"Father said that the un-man from the Delta

tried to talk him into making me a potter," Tramu said.

"There is nothing wrong with working with the clay," Moth said.

"To be sure, to be sure—nothing wrong for you, but for me, for a smith! I was born to be a smith; I have been raised for the forge—and then to suggest I put it all aside and begin playing with mud—"

"There is nothing wrong with the clay!"

"Nothing, I meant no offense, cousin. After all, we too delve the earth in search of the Earth Mother's children, but, well—look at you now! You and your father both work in the fields all year. No smith has to do that. Our craft is so valuable, so demanding, that the Warriors of the Voice supply us with everything we need."

"Father said that if I become a RiTas I won't ever have to work in the fields again."

"But still, cousin, you would have to spend some of each day working with the clay—and during that time you would not be doing the work of the forge. Smithcraft is not something that can be done a little at a time, like weaving—it demands your whole heart and soul. That's why somebody like Tas Gly will never be a good smith despite his nimble hands. And it is better to be a smith than a potter."

"No," Moth said.

"For me it is better. And, cousin, would you not truly rather be a smith?"

"No!"

"Truly, cousin?"

"Truly."

"Then why do you want to be a RiTas?"

* * *

"Ri Cer Sil has given his permission," Ri Tal said that evening. "And Tas No Sil has said that it may be possible. But Moth has so little chance— Tas No Sil said that Moth may undergo the initiations for silver and gold, but only if the smith initiating him will bequeath him his own tools. Tas No Sil said that no one whose father was not a smith, not even his own grandson, could learn the secrets of the forge without being helped by the spirits of another smith's tools. But what smith would give his tools to a boy with one black eyebrow?"

"Father will leave his tools to Tas Et," Kuan said.

"Obviously."

"Perhaps we could arrange a marriage."

"No." Ri Tal bit his lip. "In Kyborash today there are only thirteen marriageable smiths' daughters, but there are seventeen smiths with sons. Moth will never marry a smith's daughter."

"Perhaps a smith with neither sons nor daughters—"

"There is none."

"Then one from another city?"

"Moth cannot leave Kyborash if he is to learn from me to be a potter as well as a smith, and he cannot stay here if he is to learn smithcraft from a smith in another city."

"If he could be a smith, any kind of smith, even a jeweler—!"

"If. I know how much it would mean to you, Kuan. But I see no hope for it. None at all."

"Then I can't be a smith, Father?"

"I'm sorry, son. I had hoped— No. You'll be a potter like me—but a far, far greater potter than I am. Your dolthe is that of a great man. I thought I had learned its secret when the Pink-Eyed made its offer, but— No matter."

Moth bit back tears. Only children cried, and he was no longer a child.

The next day Moth was working in the vegetable patch, weeding the herbs and spices and killing the insects that fed on them, when he saw Tramu talking to a tall, redheaded boy wearing a smith's soul on the double chain around his neck. They were coming toward him. Moth looked away, hoping that neither of them had seen the envy twisting his face.

He yanked savagely at a weed. The weed resisted. He pulled harder. Suddenly it slipped free of the earth and he fell over backward.

Picking himself up off the ground, he tensed himself to ignore the laughter he expected to hear. But Tramu and his friend had been looking in another direction. They hadn't even noticed he was there.

He went back to his weeding.

❧ Chapter Eleven ❦

While he waited for Sklar Ton to emerge from the Siltemple, Moth watched the slaves and artisans preparing the Great Square for the Festival. He'd been watching the Temple gate for at least a day-sixth, but he had no objection to waiting. The longer it took to get his father's message to Sklar Ton, the longer until his mother got the chance to put him to work.

Tramu doesn't have to work in the fields, he thought. It's not fair.

For long weeks men had been laboring on the brick platform upon which the Festival drama would be enacted. The platform stood two body-lengths high and was thirty-six bodylengths long and twenty-four wide; from the center of the square where Moth was standing it blocked the view of the Palace of Warriors and hid the part of the Warriors' Wall containing his Sil's shrine.

Behind him he heard the whining yet melodious voice of Lapp Wur, the exorcist: he was standing too close to the cage. He moved a dozen steps closer to the platform. Any farther, and he would have been unable to get a good look at the people coming out of the Siltemple.

On the right end of the platform, a Warrior of the Voice and an astrologer in a black siltunic decorated with dirty white moons were supervising the women of the Queen's retinue in the construction of the Palace of Reeds. The women wore dresses of yellow linen; the Palace was being woven of the butter-yellow reeds that grew nowhere but in the Palace Lake at Chal. Each corner of the square building was oriented to one of the Four Quarters of the world: when King Asp took up residence in it, it would become the Ommaret, the still mid-point at the center of the world around which all else revolves.

Rising from the left end of the platform was the red and yellow enameled step-pyramid with the blue godhouse at its top. Between the miniature ziggurat and the Palace of Reeds, slaves and free artisans were erecting screens, dark-grained Deltan wood inlaid with copper for the swordsmith to stand behind, painted and lacquered wood to hide the other dignitaries.

A slave bent almost double beneath a load of bricks jostled Moth, knocking him sprawling in the dust. He picked himself up angrily, turned back to see the slave already climbing the platform with his load and Tramu rounding the cage, coming in Moth's direction. With him was a girl with thick, curly red hair and a silver bracelet on her left wrist that proclaimed she'd begun her Temple training for the women's mysteries.

"Moth!" Tramu shouted.

"Hello, Tramu." Moth recognized the girl.

"Hello, Rafti. Sartor guide you."

"And you, Moth." She smiled, baring perfect teeth. She was much prettier than he'd remembered. "Moth, there was something I wanted to talk to Tramu about right now, and—"

"What?" Tramu demanded.

"I'd rather not talk about it with Moth here."

"Why not? He's my cousin."

"Yes, but you know there are things we can't talk about except with other smiths."

"Hah. You're not a smith, Rafti, you're a smith's daughter. And I can't think of anything you'd need to tell me right now that I wouldn't want my cousin to hear."

"Mother says the smith-bred should stay faithful to their own."

"To your father, she means? Tas Gly's a terrible goldsmith, Rafti. Maybe even the worst ever. I prefer Moth."

"Better my father than a potter, even if he isn't the best goldsmith in Kyborash!" Moth realized she was close to tears.

"I can talk to Tramu later," he said, but they both ignored him.

"You mean, better than Ri Tal my uncle, or Moth my cousin?" Tramu asked.

"Yes! Look at your cousin, all covered with dirt like a field slave!"

"Somebody pushed me!" Moth said, beginning to get angry.

"The Tas Sil's *different*, Tramu. You *know* that!"

"Different, yes, but not like you're making it sound. Clay comes from the Earth Mother just like metal, Rafti. The Ri and Tas are brother Sils. Even your father should have taught you that."

"He taught me to know my own kind, which is more than your family did for you! Your hair's red, Tramu, but your cousin's is speckled like a dryfrog, and you don't seem to be able to see the difference."

"At least my father's a *good* potter," Moth said.

"I see the difference, all right, but I don't pretend it means something it doesn't," Tramu said. "Grandfather picked Ri Tal for his daughter's husband. He could have had your father if he wanted him. He didn't want him, and I don't think he made a mistake."

"You're still awfully young, Tramu—"

"Three months older than you."

"Then don't you think it's about time you started to grow up?" Rafti spun on her heel and strode away. Moth followed her progress through the confusion of the market for a while, then turned back to his cousin.

"Thank you, Tramu." He tried to make the words sound formal and dignified, in keeping with the gratitude he felt.

"Beautiful, isn't she?" Tramu asked. "And clever. I like her—or I used to, anyway. It's a pity about her mother, though."

"What are you talking about?"

"Marriage."

"Huh?" Thinking: It's not fair, just because his father's a smith he gets to—

It wasn't fair.

"Don't look so shocked, cousin. Her mother's put her up to marrying me, and that's why she's acting so strange."

"You're sure?"

"Of course. She never really said so, of course, just hints about it all the time, but I've been hearing about it for a while. Father gets angry every time her mother tries to sneak the idea into a conversation, but Mother thinks it's funny."

"You're not getting married, then?"

"Not to Rafti. Maybe to somebody else."

"Who?"

"I don't know yet."

"Aren't you still a bit young?"

"Older than you, cousin. I visited the hierodules yesterday."

Moth knew better than to believe him. He just looked skeptical.

"You're too young."

"Father took me. Smith custom's different, Moth. That's why Rafti's mother is so interested all of a sudden."

"Still—"

"Of course I'm too young to get married, but I'll be eleven next month, don't forget. And when Father . . . you know . . ."

Moth nodded.

"Well, then Mother'll be able to get me any bride she wants. So Rafti's mother's trying to get me first."

"She knows about it?"

"Of course not. She just knows I'm the best husband she could find for Rafti. Not that Mother would let me marry the daughter of such a paw-handed goldsmith even if I wanted to. Even Father'd rather have me marry a good potter's daughter, and you know he takes the idea that we're a people apart very seriously. And he's right, you know, cousin, not like Rafti made it sound, but—"

"But different. I know."

"Anyway, her mother's stupid. Her father, too. I'm surprised they ever let him become a goldsmith, even after eighteen years as a silversmith. Stupid, the both of them."

"Not Rafti, though."

"No. You like her, cousin?"

"Not anymore. But she's still, I don't know . . ."

"Sure. It's because she's a smith's daughter."

"I wouldn't want Tas Gly for a father."

"That's not what I meant. It doesn't have anything to do with Tas Gly himself. But you'll never see a smith's wife creeping around hiding behind her husband like most men's wives."

"Mother's not like that," Moth agreed.

"No, she isn't. But it's good that you don't like Rafti. She'll probably end up like her mother."

"Ugh. Hey, tell me if you see Sklar Ton coming out of the Siltemple, will you? I've got a message for him from Father."

"Sure."

They watched the men and women on the platform for a while; then Moth glanced around, making sure no one was within hearing distance, and asked in a low voice, "How's it coming?"

"It's almost finished. Father let me spell one of his blowpipers on part of the scabbard. It's beautiful."

"The scabbard?"

"Yes."

"Have you seen"—looking around again, his voice falling to a whisper—"the blade yet?"

"Not yet. I was going to sneak into the forge and look at it—"

"What about the guards?" Moth interrupted.

"There aren't any. They'd be too hard to keep secret. That's why we're getting a two-story house inside the walls when this is all over."

"Luck."

"Yes. Anyway, right now Father and his blow-pipers all sleep in the forge, but I could sneak past them. And I was going to, but Father told me if he caught me trying it he'd cut off two of my toes himself, and if I got away with it without getting caught, I might kill King Asp. So I decided not to do it after all. How's the coffin coming?"

"Not so loud!"

"Sorry."

"It's four days finished."

"You've seen it?"

"I helped make it. Parts of it, anyway."

"But you've seen the whole thing?"

"Yes. It's wonderful!"

"What's it look like?"

"Sort of like a boat long enough for two men to stretch out in. And it's got a lid that Father sculpted to look just like King Asp."

"You're sure about that?"

"Yes. All those jewels and those amber eyes—"

"You've seen the King many times, no doubt."

"To be sure—just not yet, unfortunately. But if King Asp doesn't look like Father made him look, then he doesn't look like a King should. I mean, of course he looks like a King should, but—"

"Yes?"

"But if he doesn't look like Father made him

look, then he doesn't look the best way for a King to look."

"Maybe you'll change your mind when you see him."

"Maybe you'll change yours when you see the coffin. If you can get close enough to the platform to see it at all."

"I'll get close enough. Hey, isn't that Sklar Ton?"

"Yes. See you later."

"Sartor's luck, cousin. You better hurry."

The trader was almost out of the square before Moth caught up with him and gave him Ri Tal's message.

"Tell him not to worry," Sklar Ton said, and continued on his way.

Moth made his way through the market and out the gate, then set off down the Street of the Thieving Warrior toward home. Rounding a corner onto the Street of the Slave of Drea'Est, he saw Yeshun and Shuner, Ri Cer Sil's twin sons. They were too much older than Moth to be close friends, but he liked them both.

"Yeshun!" he called, hurrying. "Shuner! Wait for me!"

"I've got a riddle for you, Moth," Shuner said when Moth caught up with them. "What has—"

"Don't be a fool, Shuner," Yeshun interrupted. To Moth he said, "I just asked him that riddle, and now he's trying to get you to answer it for him."

"I was going to ask him a different riddle," Shuner protested.

"No, you weren't. Look, you've got to keep exercising your wits if you ever want to earn your

Ri. You can't keep on pretending it doesn't matter."

"I'm better on the wheel than you are."

"Much better. But you're going to be a potter, not a field slave, it just isn't good enough to be clever with your hands. You're going to be a priest, Shuner, like Father—making pots that look good isn't enough. If you don't understand the Mysteries, your pots will be dead. Sure, you can position the clay right on the wheel, but can you position it right in your soul, where Sartor shapes it?"

"Maybe I'd better leave the two of you alone," Moth said.

"Don't worry," Yeshun said. "We won't talk about any Mysteries you aren't ready for yet. But, Shuner, you've got to practice your riddles: you've got to develop your wits if you want to master the Higher Mysteries. Even King Asp does riddles. Doesn't he, Moth?"

"So everybody says."

"Here, Moth," Shuner said, taking a half-eaten piece of flatbread out of his belt pouch. "You want some? We've both had all we can eat."

"No, thanks. I'm fasting."

"It's about time for your first clayquest, isn't it?" Yeshun asked.

"I'm leaving tomorrow. I've been fasting for three days."

"Still hungry?"

"Starving," Moth admitted.

"You'll be all right by tonight. Not that you stop wanting to eat."

"You don't have very long for your quest, do you?" Shuner asked. "Because of the Festival."

"Six days."

"That should be long enough," Yeshun said. "I always get weak after five days of fasting."

"I don't," Shuner said.

"You're better at it than I am. You're better at almost everything than I am, damn it, but you just let your head sleep."

"Maybe I'm not very clever."

"You are when you want to be."

"That's my street," Moth said. "I'll see you later. Luck."

"Luck. Sartor grant you good clay," Yeshun said.

"Sartor's luck," Shuner added.

Moth passed through the house and out into the potting compound without speaking to his mother. When night fell he took the necklace of clay beads from around his neck and buried it, thanking the Earth Mother for the years he had been allowed to wear it. Henceforth he would wear a necklace made from clay he himself had found, or none at all.

He daubed his body with the seven clays and prostrated himself once to each of the Four Quarters, then took the birdstone his father had given him, an intricately carved piece of basalt about the size of his thumb attached to a slender linen cord, and twirled it until it sang.

Above him the stars shone clear and cold, Sartor's Nighteyes, watching him as he began the Ritual of Prayer and Propitiation.

❧ Chapter Twelve ❧

Moth set out at first light, the dawn only a pale glow in the east, the moon still bright overhead. Naked except for a rope belt from which hung the pouch containing the birdstone and his saucer and trowel and cloth bag, his skin freshly daubed with the seven clays (the still-wet clays cold against his skin, the early-morning wind chill and biting), he paused in the street outside his house only long enough to thank the house-guardian for having sheltered him, then made his way out of the city and upriver.

Every sixty paces he prostrated himself to the Four Quarters, listened to the birdstone's song, and implored Sartor's aid. Every three hundred and sixty paces he repeated the full Ritual of Prayer and Propitiation, muttering the words under his breath to keep them secret from anyone who might chance across him.

When he encountered other human beings, he averted his eyes. He spoke to no one and no one spoke to him.

Early in the afternoon he reached the guardhouse

blocking the path above the Nacre's narrow gorge. His appearance proclaimed his identity and mission; he made the four prostrations and passed by unchallenged.

Below him the Nacre foamed, roaring with a thousand drunken voices, drowning out the birdstone's song. The narrow path hugged the wall of the gorge. Sometimes the going was so difficult that he was forced to make his prostrations hunched up like a leafworm; once he almost fell. Small streams and falls blocked his way: he forded them, leaping the smallest despite the danger of slipping on the wet rock and falling to the river below.

He was far beyond the path he had taken the first time he'd accompanied his father in search of clay before he began to hear the birdstone's song through the river-roar.

When darkness came, he curled up and slept naked and unprotected on the chill stone. Awakening, he could only remember that his dreams had been joyous.

Dawn was breaking. He stood up, stretched, and did the full Ritual of Prayer and Propitiation before continuing on.

The rock was chill, black, devoid of vegetation: the Earth Mother's naked bones.

The sun rose, reached its zenith, and had begun to descend before Moth passed beyond the limit of his previous explorations. Now, whenever he came across a stream or fall, he stopped and swung the birdstone, listening and looking in the calm silence that followed for a sign that this was the stream that would lead him to the clay he sought.

But something—the voice of a fall, a rock the

shape of a human skull, something wrong with the way the sunlight played upon the water—warned him away from every stream he found, and the fear began to grow in him that he would find no stream he could follow and would be forced to return clayless to Kyborash, there to live without beads or honor until a year had passed and he could again attempt clayquest.

Night fell. He curled up, slept.

Early in the morning of the fourth day—the last day before he had to turn and make his way back to Kyborash—the path led him down out of the gorge into a broad valley where the Nacre's roar was only a gentle mutter. The sight of trees and bushes, the warm smell of grass, cheered him; his hunger was long gone, and his light-headedness he attributed to the excitement knotting his stomach muscles. It was hard to keep himself from running and leaping.

The path had led him away from the Nacre and up into the hills when he found the stream. He swung the birdstone, listened to its song, then turned his attention to the stream, found welcome in every ripple.

The tight knot in his belly dissolved. He felt joyous, giddy, yet still very aware of the fact that if he had to follow this stream any great distance there would be no time to try another.

But he thrust his doubts aside and did a full Ritual, then prostrated himself sixty times to the stream and asked its spirit, its Unslith, for permission to follow it.

The sense of welcome emanating from the waters continued unchanged, and he knew the Unslith had granted him its permission.

He turned his back on the path and began following the stream up toward the snow-peaked mountains. The stream had changed its course too recently for tanglethorn to have choked the old streambed, and the foothills were not yet too steep for rapid progress, so the going was easy.

Later, when the foothills had become mountains and the sun was falling toward the western horizon, the air growing cool, Moth scrambled up a particularly steep grade to find himself on a wide, flat ledge.

He turned back, looked down at the ledges and grades below him. Like a ziggurat, he thought. Sartor's Ziggurat.

He followed the stream inward until he came to a deep, turbulent pool fed by two separate waterfalls cascading from the lip of what looked like the same ledge, about five bodylengths over his head.

Above him he pictured ledge after ledge, the mountain stretching ever higher, the ledges growing narrower, until finally, at the top, Sartor sat in state in the blue godhouse of the sky.

Maybe I won't find any clay, he thought. I'll just keep climbing higher and higher, all the way up through the snow to Him—

The falls were about ten bodylengths apart. Moth spun the birdstone, examined the falls in the silence following the song. They were too different in ways he could feel but not name to be twin forks of a single stream, or overflows from a single pool: he was certain that each fall was fed by a different stream.

He could follow only one. He prostrated himself to each fall and asked its Unslith for guidance, but received no enlightenment. Neither fall welcomed him; neither rejected him.

He spun the stone again, watched and listened, spun it again. And again.

He had to decide soon: the day was almost gone. He spun the stone again. Again and again.

A flight of red-winged birds overhead, veering off to the right. An omen?

He had no choice but to take it as an omen. He put the birdstone back in his belt pouch, began to climb the rock face. It was damp but rough, providing plenty of finger- and toeholds. He had a bad moment when a chunk of rock came away in his hand, but his fingers found another projection before he could fall, and within instants he was up over the top.

He had been right: the falls were fed by different streams. And the other stream emerged from a hole in the rock only six or seven bodylengths from the edge of the ledge upon which he was standing.

He looked back, down, seeing the Nacre far below. A sudden certainty stole over him. The certainty made it easier to continue, helped him fight his growing exhaustion and consciousness of the possibility of failure, helped him ignore the slight dizziness that he only now realized had been growing within him since he'd begun his ascent.

The late afternoon sun painted the rocks with deep, rich colors. He continued on, up.

A little later, climbing a shallow grade where the stream meandered through numerous quick bends, he found a bed of yellow clay exposed.

Yellow—the False Emperor. A doubtful omen. But not one that he could reject.

He knelt and crossed his arms on his breast. He could feel the silence all around him as he said, "Sartor All-Highest, Merciful Patron, I, Sartor-ban-i-Tresh, Your faithful worshiper, obeyer of Your King of Chal, Asp Son of Vitrus, initiated priest of Your Ri Sil, do beg of You Your aid in this, my first clayquest. Lend me Your Strength, O Greatest of Gods. Lend me Your Wisdom, O Creator of All Things. Smile upon me and intercede for me with these, the Spirits of Stream and Earth."

He repeated the prayer seven times, then prostrated himself to the stream and said, "Hear me, Unslith, Stream-spirit. I, Sartor-ban-i-Tresh, twice-born child of the Earth Mother, thank you in the name of Sartor All-Highest for revealing this clay to me. Accept of me my life's water, that I offer you as sign of my gratitude, and intercede for me with the Spirit of the Clay if I meet with your favor."

Extending his left hand in the Gesture of Submission, he pursed his lips, leaned forward, and spat into the stream.

As his spittle struck the water, panic seized him. The sky was crushing him beneath its infinite weight; the earth gaped open beneath his feet; the stream was slithering from its bed to suffocate him in its shining coils.

He leapt to his feet, spun around, and ran.

Sixty strides, and the sky returned to the heavens. The sun glistened innocently off the clear waters of the stream. The earth was solid beneath his feet. His fear was gone, fading from his memory.

The stream-spirit was willing, he thought, but the clay was not. Or—perhaps the Unslith wanted me to know that it did not reject me, but that it wishes me to find finer clays.

Prostrating himself to the Four Quarters, he prayed, "Sartor All-Highest, grant me Your guidance. Earth Mother, intercede with Your Children for me." And once again his certainty bubbled within him.

The way grew ever steeper, the mesas and ledges smaller and separated by longer and longer stretches of sheer cliff, yet he felt little fatigue as he scrambled for finger- and toeholds on the vertical cliff-faces. Time seemed to have stopped: the sun should have set daysixths ago, yet still it hung, red and unmoving, above the western horizon.

It was still hanging there when he climbed through the spray of a miniature waterfall and realized that he had come upon a mesa at least as large as the one his father had shown him on that first trip, years ago. The stream was gentler here, clear over smooth pebbles; on either side of it grew long gray-green grasses.

He soon found a bed of clay. The clay was reddish, mixed with sand; the stream-spirit accepted his life's water and did not drive him away, but when he moistened the clay and allowed it to dry, a chalky white scum formed. Though the clay had shown itself unsuitable, he thanked the spirit of the clay before continuing on.

Within moments he had come across another bed of clay, and this clay was neither red nor yellow, nor tan nor brown nor gray nor brownblack: it was no proper river clay at all, but the white clay found only in rare hollows high in the hills, and

Moth knew that its presence there by the stream-bed was a miracle.

He thanked Sartor, then dug some of the white clay from the ground with his blackwood trowel. Certain as he was that its presence was proof of miraculous intervention, he was almost tempted to fill his sack without testing the clay; but in the end reason prevailed: the tests existed not only to see if the clay was suitable for his use, but to determine if the spirit of the clay found him acceptable, and he would certainly offend the spirit by neglecting the ritual.

He moistened the clay and allowed it to dry on his saucer. No scum seemed to form, but when it was thoroughly dry he examined it very carefully to make sure the clay's whiteness had not camou-flaged any scum. It had not: the clay was clean.

He kneaded some of the clay mass into a rope, then bent the rope into a ring. He felt a certain tension as he worked, for the white clays required delicate handling and rarely forgave a potter his errors, and he had little experience with them. But the ring did not crack.

He had found the clay from which he would make his darsath, his soul-shadow. And it was a finer clay than he had ever imagined could be his.

The sun was setting at last, and he felt all the exhaustion that he had somehow been spared earlier come flooding over him. He slept.

Before dawn the next morning he filled his cloth bag with nine trowelfuls of the creamy clay, one for each year he had borne a name, and, taking the utmost care not to drop it, returned it to his belt pouch. Its weight felt good at his side, a constant reminder of the miraculous gift he had been granted.

He found himself running, leaping down the gentler slopes, jumping a bodylength or even two at a time through the predawn darkness, clambering blind down cliff-faces with the reckless speed of a suction-footed lizard.

He had not yet paused to sleep again when, on the morning of the sixth day, he was stopped by three Warriors of the Voice. They questioned him but let him pass.

The closer he got to the city, the more warriors he encountered, but no one else stopped him for questioning. Twice he passed oxcarts loaded with purple-leaved ang branches. The branches would be used to feed the fires in the trench separating Kyborash from the profane world during the Festival.

He arrived home late in the afternoon. The Festival was to start at dusk, but, like the women and the other men not yet fully initiated, he would take no part in it until morning.

"You have returned with very fine clay indeed," Ri Tal said after inspecting Moth's sack. "Prepare and bury it, then prostrate yourself three hundred and sixty times to each of the Four Quarters, thanking Sartor with a prayer of your own invention each time. When you have finished you may eat—but remember, take no more than nine mouthfuls of barley mush and drink no water. For every extra mouthful you will spend a year hungry; for every sip of water you will endure a year of drought. Do you understand?"

Moth nodded.

"Good. Sleep tonight with your head resting over your buried clay. Sartor will send you a dream, and that dream will reveal to you the shaping of your soul-shadow."

"What if I don't dream, Father?"

"Sartor will send you a dream. You may not remember it immediately when you awaken, but in time it will return to you."

"But what if I dream more than one dream?"

"Then you must choose the true dream. And you must be careful not to let a pleasant but false dream sway you from one fearful but true. Do not let the vision of a simple form, easy to grasp and within your power to shape, tempt you from your true darsath, though of it you see only a tiny part, and that beyond your power to shape.

"From the clay you have found you will shape only the shadow of the shadow of your true soul, and it need be no more like your true soul than an infant is like the man he will become. Yet as that infant has within him the sleeping reality of his future self, so must this darsath reflect your true soul.

"Hurry now. You must tread the sand and ashes into your clay and bury it quickly, for your weakness will soon be upon you, and you must eat before dusk."

After Moth's mother had spooned the nine bites of mush into his mouth, she anointed him with scented sesame oil and kissed him. He kissed her back, then left her for the potting compound. With every mouthful he had swallowed, more strength had drained from him, and it was almost more than he could do to push aside the hanging veiling the doorslit and stagger out to where he'd buried his clay.

Not even the knowledge that the Seven-Year Festival had begun was enough to keep him awake.

⤨⤨ Chapter Thirteen ⤨⤨

"Slowly, Sartor-ban-i-Tresh." His father's voice. "Awaken slowly, gently, awaken and hold onto your dream. Say nothing, Sartor-ban-i-Tresh: awaken and remember and say nothing."

Moth yawned and opened his eyes. It was still dark. All he wanted to do was go back to sleep.

"Hold onto your dream, Sartor-ban-i-Tresh!"

What? Oh. Something about . . .

. . . Baalkunti, the primeval island, rising from the waters of creation, an island of clay. . . . But Baalkunti continued to extend itself upward out of the waters until Moth could see that it was really a head, a head of clay on a long neck . . . rising higher and higher, the neck growing longer and longer . . . grass sprouting from the top of the head, but not green grass, no, red and black grass—

That's me, Moth realized. That's *my* head.

—but blades of yellow grass were sprouting among the blades of red and black, and all the grass was lengthening, growing longer and longer until it hid the head completely, until it fell to the Ocean itself.

Suddenly there were birds. Birds beyond counting, the infinite sky black with their numbers, but far away, all the birds flying so high that they were just clouds of tiny, darting specks, like swarming midges. . . .

One speck growing larger, black, taking on form, a bird diving down *straight into his eyes*—

And the clay head opened like a shy-lily unfolding to greet the dawn, became the world. He saw Kyborash—

And attacking it, a horde of Nomads on horseback, their leader a man of clay. In his left hand he held the reins of his horse, and where his right hand should have been there grew a blade of gleaming metal.

The man of clay was Moth.

He was older, a man, not a boy, and his face resembled that of Ri Tal, yet harder somehow, and crueler. He was dressed as the shaman Moth had seen at the Fair had been, in a caftan of black goat hide and breeches of red leather. From the caftan hung mirrors of copper and the golden skeletons of many hawks; his long hair was braided into separate strands of black and red and tied back from his face with a live serpent the color of amber. The snake hissed and coiled and dripped yellow venom from its fangs, and the shaman's eyes, *his* eyes, his sun-yellow eyes, burned with hatred—

Yet all this was at the same time a small cylinder of red-, black-, and yellow-glazed clay with wings of red copper.

"Is it clear, Sartor-ban-i-Tresh? Don't try to understand it now. Just hold it clear in your mind.

Study it so you will never forget it. . . . Do you have it?"

"It has me," Moth whispered.

"Good. You must never forget it. But the Festival is beginning. Go inside and dress yourself."

When Moth made no move to comply, he asked, "Is your dream clear in your mind? Do you need more time?"

"No." Moth shook his head.

"Then hurry!"

Moth stumbled to his feet, groped his way through the doorslit. The room was lit by only a tiny oil lamp that gave off more smoke than light. Moth struggled into his gray linen undertunic and belted the siltunic of scarlet wool over it, slipped his feet into his worn sandals. Ri Tal thrust a staff into his hand. In the dim light Moth was unable to see it clearly, but he knew that a design appropriate to his new station in life had been carved into it.

"Hurry!" Ri Tal said. "It's almost dawn."

Kuan was waiting in the courtyard. She combed Moth's hair back, then together the three left the house and made their way to the walled inner city. They were stopped several times by warriors guarding the sacred precincts, but once they crossed the planks laid down over the smoldering wood in the Firetrench they were free of harassment, for within the circle of fire Kyborash had returned to the time before time began, before there were warriors and laws, before the creation of the universe. Before the first King reigned in Chal.

And yet, Moth thought, nothing's different. Everything looks just the same, and I still feel like I always have.

"Tell me what happened last night, Father," he said.

"When night fell, King Asp paid homage to Sartor in the square's eighty-one shrines," Ri Tal said as they walked. "Then he worshiped at the shrine inside the Palace of Warriors, and at the shrine in his own Palace.

"After Sartor had accepted his homage in each of the lesser shrines, King Asp ascended the ziggurat in the Siltemple to light a torch from the sacred flame. From the Square, we could all see him climbing the steps, though no lamp was lit and there was only a sliver of moon. It was as if he himself were aflame, though he shed no light. I do not know how to explain it.

"As he climbed the steps he became harder and harder to see, until, just before he passed within the godhouse, Sartor's Nighteyes shone clearly through him. When he emerged again he held in his hand a torch burning with the Flame of Creation. He held it high for all to see, then ran down the steps and out through the Temple and into the square.

"There were too many men separating us for me to see his face, but people said it was alight with a joy greater than other men could bear, and I myself heard him laughing as he ran. Men would throw themselves into his path, to be burned by the sacred flame, and he laughed and made his way to the gate.

"There he gave the torch to Prince LasTvil. The Prince took the torch and ran from the inner city the length of the Avenue of King Delanipal the Conqueror, out through the West Gate, and on until he reached the Firetrench, and into the trench he threw his torch."

Kuan took up the story. "The flames leapt up and the Festival began. I was outside the Firetrench with the other women, and I saw the flames come swimming like quick-darting fish through the wood. The ang branches flared yellow and we sang songs of praise to the King. Could you hear us, Moth?"

"I was asleep, Mother."

They cut through an alley and entered the Street of the False-hearted Hierophant. A little farther and they left the narrow, twisting streets laid out when the city was still Drea'Est for the broad, straight Avenue of King Delanipal the Conqueror. Dawn was breaking. Moth could make out other families on their way toward the city's heart. There were hushed conversations all around them, the sound of sandaled feet slapping the paving stones. They were close enough to the inner city now to hear the crowd in the Great Square murmuring to itself with the voice of a thousand tiny waterfalls.

Ri Tal quickened his step. Moth began to fall behind.

"Slow down, Father," he pleaded. "Please. I can't walk that fast."

"If you can't walk, you'll have to run."

Kuan caught her husband's arm. "Please go slower, Tal. We'll be there soon enough, and he's tired from all his fasting. I can't keep up with you either."

"We'll be late," Ri Tal predicted gloomily as he slowed his pace. "All the potterpariahs and leadsmiths and slaves will get there first. They'll get to see everything while we stand by the Wall of Merchants and crane our necks."

Ri Tal was right: they had no hope of getting anywhere near the platform. The square swarmed with people of all stations—Warriors of the Hand in blue, smiths in red and gold, potters in scarlet, scribes in gray, astrologers in moon-crescented black, sellers of songs in brown edged with pink, entrail readers in gray splashed with red, slaves, confectioners, boatmen, brewers, basket makers, sculptors, and chisel workers, men of every Sil, each dressed in the colors of his station and accompanied by wife and children whose dress reflected his, yet all crowded together without regard for rank, field slaves in ragged gray linen kilts pressed up against weavers in gaudy wool. The smell of oil and sweat hung heavy in the air.

It's all my fault, Moth thought. If I'd walked faster, we'd have been in time.

"I'm sorry, Father," he said.

"Don't worry, son," Ri Tal said, smiling and putting his arm around Moth. "We didn't have a chance anyway. I had to let you sleep late after your clayquest or you'd never have made it here at all."

More people kept arriving. Moth was surrounded by strange accents and unfamiliar dialects. As the unending stream of latecomers flowed in through the gate, Moth and his parents were pressed back and to the right, until they found themselves in front of the gate to the King's Palace.

But the King had spent the night in the square hut of yellow reeds on the platform, and Moth's family was about as far from the platform as it was possible to be and still remain in the Great Square.

"The Palace of Reeds is not the cradle woven for King Asp by his mother's servants, but it is no different from that cradle," a hook-nosed man in scribe's gray was explaining to a boy whose nose declared him his son. "When King Asp comes forth into the light of day he will have become a man and— Look!"

The first ray of the morning sun had struck the platform.

"The King!" a Warrior of the Voice cried. The crowd began to shout, "KING ASP! KING ASP! KING ASP!"

And the King emerged from the Palace of Reeds.

He was tall, very tall, yet not so tall as Moth had expected him to be, and though his shoulders were strong he was no smith: the coffin Ri Tal had fashioned for him was overlarge. He wore a long yellow tunic embroidered in purple and blue over an undergarment of cloth of gold, and in his left hand he carried a scepter of gleaming red copper. His long brown hair was parted in the middle and fell in luxuriant oiled curls past his shoulders. His skin was a deep brown, darker even than his hair, and his eyes were huge and yellow like the eyes of a great hunting cat. On this day he wore no crown, but green pearls gleamed in his long beard and he wore disks of red copper in his ears. He was barefoot.

He gazed out at the crowd and cried, "I am a King!" in a voice louder and deeper than any herald's. "I am a lord, I am great, I am mighty! I have arisen from the dead, I am a warrior, I am a prince, and I am glorious, for I am Asp son of Vitrus son of Hanrab! Suppliant of Sartor of the Many Aspects am I, a servant unyielding, subduing the lands of His foes. I am a King mighty in battle, a destroyer of cities and forests, victorious over enemies, King of the Four Quarters, Prince of a multitude of lands and of all Kings! I am Asp, King of Chal and of all other cities, Asp to whom enemies prostrate themselves, Asp the ruler of all men, Asp the proclaimer of Sartor!"

He has the voice of a King! Moth thought.

The King stepped forward. A slave dressed as a Lashllite warrior emerged from behind the screen and put sandals of copper upon his feet.

"I am Asp, King of Kings, conqueror of the Lashllites! Their warriors I slew and heaped their bodies before the gate of their city! Their King I slew and all his priests; their temple I razed, taking great wealth of gold and silver; their gods I overthrew, destroying their images; and upon the site of their temple I raised a tower to Sartor ten times the height of a man, of brick plated with gold! And at the base of that tower I placed an image of Sartor all of gold and copper and twice the height of a man!"

The King took a second step forward. Queen Sishal and her son, Prince LasTvil, stepped from behind a screen of golden feathers. The Queen prostrated herself to her husband and kissed his feet; the Prince knelt and presented his father with a copper-bladed sword.

"I am Asp, King of all Chal, King of all lands! The peoples of Latunsal and Gwetand rose against me in rebellion; I prepared an expedition against them and with vigorous assault I besieged and took their cities; three thousand of their warriors I destroyed; I filled the streets of their cities with corpses; their houses I burned; many warriors I took alive for slaves and their spoils in abundance I carried off; their cities I overthrew, razed, and burned!"

The King began to walk slowly forward ("One step for every year of his life," Moth heard the scribe whisper), and with every step he took he recounted more victories. When he halted again, the Master of Warriors, a tall man dressed all in blue, emerged from behind a screen. He prostrated himself before the King, then rose and stood proudly behind him.

"I am King Asp, King of Kings, Sil Warrior of the Hand and Voice, the greatest warrior of all times by the sufferance of Sartor! To my Master of Warriors I give this sword, for he has served me well in battle, as my sword has served me well!" the King cried, and the Master of Warriors stepped forward to receive his sword.

The King took another step, and the Sil Masters of all but one of the eighty-two lesser Sils stepped from behind their screens to prostrate themselves before their King. One by one they crawled forward to kiss his feet and pledge him their fealty. Moth could see their lips moving, but their voices were inaudible.

To each Sil Master King Asp gave a green pearl from his beard.

"I am Asp, the Sil of Sils!" he cried. His voice was as mighty as before, but he paused now and again as if to catch his breath. "I am the most glorious of rulers, the most favored of Sartor, and I am the most generous of men! To these, the Sil Masters of the Lesser Priesthoods, I show my generosity with gifts of pearls as precious as cities!"

The Sil Masters prostrated themselves, and the King took a final step forward. From behind a screen of bleached werewood emerged the Voice of Sartor, his head concealed in a white hood, while from behind a screen of precious metals stepped Tas Et. Tas Et was dressed all in metal, in cunningly wrought mail that flashed red and silver and gold in the sun, and no part of his body or face could be seen. In his right hand the smith held a great sword sheathed in a scabbard of gold inlaid with copper. Moving slowly, the smith knelt before the King and held out the sword to him, but even as the King reached for it the Voice of Sartor stepped forward and snatched it from the smith's grasp.

"Sartor grants King Asp his life!" the Voice cried, and his tones were almost as mighty as the King's. The King took the sword from the Voice's hands.

"I am Asp!" he cried. "I have arisen from the dead, I am a warrior, I am a prince, and I am great and glorious, for I am Asp, King of Kings! I am Asp, and this sword"—he drew the copper blade from its scabbard—"is none other than myself. I name it Asp son of Vitrus son of Hanrab, the proclaimer of Sartor, the worshiper of Sartor, the exalter of Sartor, a servant unyielding, King of all Chal!"

And the Sil Masters crept forward on their knees and kissed the blade.

Then the Voice of Sartor cried, "Listen, for I speak the words of Sartor All-Highest. Know you, King of Chal, that you have sinned against your master! For seven years have you been the mightiest of men, but though you are the greatest warrior the world has ever known, though the noblest of men have been as dirt beneath your feet, yet as they are to you, so are you to Sartor! Seven years have you been the husbandman of the All-Highest, nothing more; and though you have served Him as no other man could have served Him, though you be still the greatest and most glorious of men, though you tread the empires of Ashlu beneath your feet, yet are you but a man and your service is not sufficient. You have failed your god!"

"I have conquered many lands for Sartor!" the King cried. "I have built many temples, raised many towers, caused to be made many images. I have spread the fear of the All-Highest throughout the Four Quarters!"

"All this you have done, and more. Yet you have failed Sartor, you have sinned against Him, and for this you must die!"

"What sin have I committed?"

"You have been a man only, and not a god."

"Sil Tas," the King pleaded, turning to Tas Et, "will you not die for me, that I may live and Sartor may be appeased?"

"I will die for my King!" Tas Et cried, and his voice was not at all the voice of the uncle Moth knew. "Let Sartor take my life instead, for King Asp is a great King, the Sil of Sils, and the best of men!"

But the King shook his head and cried, "No! You have given me this blade that is my life, O Master Smith, and I cannot return a death for a life, for I am a just King and the most generous of men! Yet I fear death, for I am only a man, and all men fear dying! Is there no one else here who will die for me?"

"I will die for you, Father!" Prince LasTvil cried in a voice thin and high, though he was already a man.

"Alas, my son," the King said, "to give you life and then take it back—what kind of man would I be then? And how, were I not the best of men, could I be the most glorious of Kings?"

"Yet I beg you, Father, let Sartor take my life instead of yours!"

"And should I die in battle, who then would rule all Chal? No, LasTvil son of Asp son of Vitrus, the time has not yet come for you to give your life to Sartor!"

The King turned to the Lesser Sil Masters. "And you, my Sil Masters, is there one among you who will die in my stead?"

And they cried out that they would die for him.

"Yet I cannot take all of your lives, for I am a just and a generous King, and how should I choose among you? No, there is no one among you I can permit to die for me. I must die, and no man may make my passing any easier."

The King laid down his scepter. He threw off his embroidered tunic. He kicked off his copper sandals, and with his left hand he tore his undergarment of cloth of gold from his body, so that he stood naked in front of his people.

He brandished the gleaming sword. "I am Asp son of Vitrus son of Hanrab, and I must die to appease the just anger of Sartor All-Highest!" he cried in a ragged voice, and many of the people crowding the square cried out and rent their garments.

"No!" a man with the clear voice of a seller of

songs cried from the crowd. "King Asp is a good King, a just King! He cannot die!"

The hooded Voice of Sartor stepped forward and held up his hand. The crowd fell silent.

"Die he must!" the hooded warrior cried. "So it has been ordained, and so it must be. Yet"—the Voice turned to the King—"you die not alone, O King, for Sartor is with you! Die you must, die you shall: your death approaches you on fiery wings and you may not deny it! Yet it is the will of Sartor that before death claims you, you may ask a single gift of any of your subjects, and the power of Sartor shall come to you through that gift! Choose, O King, and choose quickly, for your time draws near!"

"A dead man needs little that the living may grant him!" the King cried. "Yet I would ask my Master of Warriors to give me something of his, that I might die"—his voice failed him; he paused, gasping for breath, then finished—"that I might die as a warrior!"

The Master of Warriors sheathed the sword the King had given him. He stripped the gloves from his hands. Stepping forward, he fitted a glove over the King's left hand. The King held his hand aloft and the amber beading the dark leather glowed in the bright morning sun. Then the King grasped the sword named Asp in his gloved hand and allowed the Master of Warriors to fit the other glove to his right hand.

Gripping the pommel in both hands, Asp held the red blade overhead. The sun caught it as he cried, "To You, Sartor, Master, to You and You alone I surrender my life!"

And taking the sword in his gloved hands, his naked brown body gleaming with sweat, his white teeth flashing as he grimaced in the agony of his exertion, the King bent the sword named Asp over his knee, forcing it slowly out of shape, bending it back until it was straight again, then farther back, until it was again bowed as far out of shape as he could bend it. Again and again he bent the blade, his powerful muscles like slow-swimming metal fish beneath his sweat-shiny brown skin as he strained without ceasing.

Until, suddenly, it was over, and the King held the two fragments of his life aloft, and died.

The Voice of Sartor stepped forward, knelt by the King's body. "King Asp is dead!" he cried, rising to his feet. "The life Sartor gave His husbandman, He has demanded from him."

The Sil Masters surged forward to confront the white-robed figure.

"I speak for the Lesser Sils!" the Sil Astrologer cried in a musical voice. He turned to the massed people in the square. "King Asp was more than a man! He was not as you or I; he cannot be dead!"

"He was a man," the Voice replied. "A great man, a mighty man, the most glorious of men—but he was only a man, and all men die! Examine his body for yourselves if you do not believe me!"

One by one the Sil Masters stepped forward to kneel by their fallen King and examine him. The Sil Astrologer was the last. He rose slowly to his feet and turned to face the crowd.

"King Asp is dead!" he cried. "He is dead and his limbs grow stiff, his body grows cold! This I have seen with my own eyes, felt with my own hands.

The King is dead and Chal is dead and we—we are no more what we were! We are nothing, no one, creatures without names, without—" And the Sil Astrologer broke down and wept, and the people in the square did likewise.

"Wait!" the Master of Warriors cried, and the weeping ceased. "The Smith has not yet spoken!"

Tas Et moved slowly across the platform to the fallen King. He bent with agonizing slowness to examine, not the naked body, but the broken sword. He rose, holding the two pieces of the sword he had forged.

"The blade named Asp son of Vitrus son of Hanrab is truly broken. The King is dead," he said, and though his voice did not seem loud, Moth could hear him clearly.

"He is dead!" the smith cried. "Let him be placed in his coffin!" And fourteen princes from fourteen cities King Asp had conquered came forward bearing the King's coffin.

The princes lifted the King's body and with due reverence placed it within the boat-shaped coffin. They sealed the lid in place.

"He is dead and in his coffin. Let him be buried," Tas Et said, and a hole was made in the brick platform and the boat bearing the King's coffin was laid within it. Seven times seven shovelfuls of earth were heaped upon its carven lid.

"He is dead," Tas Et repeated. "He is dead, and yet—" The crowd was silent, waiting. "And yet—" He paused again, then cried, "And yet he may live again, if it be the will of Sartor All-Highest!"

The smith held the broken sword above his head. "This is the sword named Asp son of Vitrus son of

Hanrab. Should it be the will of Sartor, it may be
returned to the time before it was a sword, to that
state in which it is neither whole nor broken, and if
it then be forged anew the King shall live again!"

Moth wept and cried out with joy.

"I am no longer the Voice of Sartor," the Voice of
Sartor cried, "for the King is dead and there is no
Chal. Yet still do I know somewhat of the will of
Sartor, and if those who were Chal be willing, then
it is the will of Sartor also that King Asp be restored
to life. Is this your will, you who were his people?"

"Yes!" Moth screamed, and his voice was lost in
the roar of the crowd's assent.

"So shall it be!" the hooded warrior cried, and
Tas Et took the broken blade and made his way to
the back of the platform, where he was lost to view.

The silence grew and grew, and there was something strange to it, something that frightened Moth.
It went on and on. Moth was afraid it would never
end. It was heavy, sullen, fierce; it bore him down
beneath its weight, and he knew that it would crush
him if he did not cry out loud, and yet he could not.

And then suddenly it was gone, and there were
voices all around him.

"What happens now?" he asked. "What happens
next?"

"Anything!" a field slave standing behind Ri Tal
said before the potter could answer. "Anything at
all!" And the slave let out a great whoop of joy and
ran up to a slavemaster in a black and white siltunic
and knocked him to the ground.

"Anything," Ri Tal said slowly. His voice was
strange, far away. "There is no law in Chal now, no
Chal, nothing! The void has taken us back, and we

no longer know who we were or what we were. I may be your father, I remember I was, once; or I may be your grandson or your mother's mother or nobody at all—"

"Father!"

"No," Ri Tal said reflectively. "No, I'm not your father." His voice quickened. "I'm a purple ming bird, and all the women in blue are my wives!"

He let out a shrill, trilling cry. "You're a moth, aren't you? Be careful, moth. Ming birds eat moths. But I'm not hungry, not quite yet, little moth. . . ."

He turned and disappeared suddenly into the crowd.

"Mother?" But Kuan too was gone.

All around him people were singing and dancing and speaking in strange tongues. Men were crouching low to the ground, their hands covering their eyes. Fights were breaking out all over the Great Square, and men and women were coupling without regard for rank or station.

Chapter Fourteen

The people in the Great Square had gone mad. They gibbered, drooled, fought, and coupled like animals; old men laughed and played silly children's games. A Warrior of the Voice gave his costume of yellow and white wool to a woman, who began giving orders to a weaver, who ran over to a field slave and traded his many-colored siltunic for the slave's gray kilt, then returned and knelt before the woman and tried to dig through the hard clay brick of the square.

But it was more than madness—or more than other people's madness, Moth realized as he pushed his way through the crowd toward one of the lesser gates. For over there he saw a man sitting calmly on empty air, there another with great blue bubbles where his eyes should have been, there another who winked in and out of existence, over there a man with three shadows, one red, one blue, and one purple, and *there*—

Madness. He had to get away or he'd end up in the cage. If he could make his way out over the Firetrench to his uncle's house where they were reforging the Blade That Had Been Broken—

A hand caught his arm—Sklar Ton, looking cheerful, unmussed, and, above all, normal. Moth's panic vanished as suddenly as it had begun, and a great calm came over him.

"Ah, young man, I see you're confused. You see madness about you, and more than madness, impossible things, so that you fear that you yourself may have gone mad. Is this not so?"

"Yes," Moth admitted.

"You must understand—and I say this with all the goodwill in the world—that you *are* mad. And, of course, so am I, and so are all these other good people around us. We are mad because we fail to apprehend the reality of our situation."

"Go on," Moth said, fascinated. It was as if each word Sklar Ton spoke revealed a new truth, something never before imagined, only to have that truth superseded before he could grasp it by the next word Sklar Ton spoke.

"The death of King Asp has returned us to a state of primordial chaos, and in this primordial state, nothing has yet been given a name. And thus, being unnamed, everything you see and hear and feel around you is without existence."

Moth nodded.

"So, since we and our surroundings are as yet all unreal—why, it is possible that we may become or experience anything whatsoever, since there is no limit to the unreal."

"And so you think us mad?"

"By no means. Our madness is that, instead of accepting the unreality of everything we see and are, we cling to names that we have not yet been given and that have no existence. You, I suppose, think yourself a young man named Moth, the son of Ri Tal the potter?"

"Yes."

"Therein lies your error, for by assigning names and hence granting existence to things that are not real, you prove yourself mad! As are we all, in this time and place, if you grant me the use of such terms."

He paused, looking suddenly confused. Moth felt an urge to help him, and with the urge to help came the necessary words, an upwelling of meaning and understanding.

"I believe you have missed a vital point," he said.

"Yes?"

"Since nothing has a name, it is impossible for us to divide the world into those things that are named and so exist, and those things that are not named and so do not exist. Thus, since nothing may be said either to exist or not to exist, any name may be appropriate to anything, and it is not madness to grant any name we desire to ourselves or to anything upon which our fancy lights."

"You convince me."

"Thank you," Moth said.

"You would then consider it permissible for me to call myself Sklar Ton and to call you Moth?"

"Quite permissible. But not—necessary."

"An excellent point! Yet I choose to remain Sklar Ton. But not Sklar Ton the trader. Rather, Sklar Ton the prophet!"

"A splendid choice. If you would care to exercise your gift. . . ."

"Nothing could please me more."

Sklar Ton closed his eyes. His green siltunic flickered blue, then faded to black. He held his hands together in front of him, palms up.

Flames began to dance in his cupped hands. His eyelids lifted to reveal pools of light-devouring night. The color drained from his skin, as though sucked into the void that stared out at Moth from behind the prophet's face.

"Your birth was an abomination. Your every breath is blasphemy. Every instant that you remain alive brings us all closer to annihilation. But though you glory in desolation, though your only food be hatred and the powers of death come at your command, yet you too shall be overthrown and destroyed, and all your triumphs shall come to naught, even as the evil now growing within you shall be destroyed—"

The prophet clapped his burning hands to his eyes. When he took his hands away the flames were in his eyes, mad flames, and his powerful hands were clenching and unclenching convulsively. Then the hands came up again, still twisting convulsively, as they leapt for Moth's throat.

Moth broke free, tried to push him away. Sklar Ton's hands were ripping at his siltunic.

Tas Et's house. I have to get to—

But he was already there, on the street outside his uncle's house.

Inside the house, someone was screaming.

◆❧ Chapter Fifteen ❧◆

There was something he had to do. He could feel the need, the urgency, yet it was somehow sundered from him, abstract and meaningless.

His body was running with sweat. Was that it? The breeze brought the rich odor of mud to his nostrils, tempting him to rip off his clothes and throw himself into the green water of the canal whose reflection he could see between two houses. He could breathe through a hollow reed, never have to come up for air, never have to face the sun again.

Was that what he needed to do? He considered it, decided that it would perhaps be better just to sit down calmly in the shade of the wall behind him while he thought things through.

He took off his sandals and wriggled his toes in the dust, ignoring the voices from the house. The dust was cool between his toes; each toe was like a little swimming fish.

I am Moth, he realized suddenly. "Moth!" he cried aloud, delighted with the sound of his name. Not the furry creature with a cylindrical body, fan-shaped antennae, and great scarlet wings that

146

lost their brilliance if you so much as brushed against them with your finger, but Moth, the son of Ri Tal. Of course.

And yet, for a few instants, hadn't he been . . . someone else?

No. Not someone else. Not exactly. His thoughts felt like things seen underwater, murky and blurred, yet vibrant. But even though he had remained Moth, the son of Ri Tal, Master Potter of Kyborash, he had been, somehow, a *different* Moth . . .

Screams, shouts, a cry of pain; the sounds of a struggle threatened to disrupt his concentration. He listened for an instant, but no one called his name. He returned to his thoughts.

. . . a Moth who had been neither altogether himself nor altogether someone else, since both Moths had continued to bear the name of Moth, the son of Ri Tal, Master Potter of Kyborash. . . .

A Nomad stuck his head out of the doorslit of the house across the street. He was tall, gaunt, his graying face scarred and tattooed, his hair a blond so pale it was almost white. In his right hand he held a sword, and his leather breeches and vest were smeared with fresh blood.

. . . yet all the same, this other Moth—no, because he was not an *other*, he was . . .

The Nomad stared at Moth for a long instant, then glanced up and down the street. There was no one else to be seen. He stepped out of the doorway, yelled something back over his shoulder. Two more Nomads burst from the house, swords in their hands. The taller was wounded and held his blood-stained left arm close to his side. The other was carrying a leather sack.

He threw the sack to the man with the pale hair, who caught it and slung it over his shoulder. The wounded man gestured at Moth and asked the pale-haired man something. Moth listened attentively, but no one spoke his name.

The man who had been carrying the sack said something to the tall man, and all three Nomads looked away from Moth. The pale-haired man shouted something in a deep, ragged voice.

Tas Et's house! The house from which the Nomads had just emerged was Tas Et's house, and this was important. Since his uncle's house was outside of Kyborash's walls, he must have left the zone delimited by the Firetrench; he was back in the world of time and names. He existed, and his name was Moth. Moth? But that was only his usename. Didn't he also have another name, a truename? His heart raced with excitement as his truename suddenly came to him, complete and whole: Sartorban-i-Tresh. How could he have forgotten it?

A fourth Nomad, riding a great dappled gray horse and leading three other horses by their reins, appeared around the corner of Tas Et's house.

Even as the man with the pale hair tossed the sack to the fourth Nomad, the full signification of Moth's truename finally burst on him and he was himself again. But it was too late—the other three Nomads had mounted, were galloping away.

"Nomads!" he cried. The dust the horses had raised was already beginning to settle. "Nomads! Help!"

From Tas Et's house he heard an answering shout.

He scrambled up and ran across the street and into the darkness inside the house, tripped over a body. He fell sprawling, lay for a frozen instant with his cheek wet with half-congealed blood, staring into the dead eyes of a blond Nomad.

A fly was walking slowly across the Nomad's left eyeball. The eye was blue.

"Untie me, infant!" someone yelled from behind him. "If you value your life, untie me!"

Moth pushed himself away from the corpse and turned, rubbed at the blood on his cheek, staring.

"Hurry!" The man's pale blue tunic was stained red from his many wounds; his lips were wet with blood foam. Moth recognized him immediately: the Master of Warriors.

"Come here!" the Master screamed at him.

There were dead men all around, some of them Nomads, the others Chaldan warriors. The Master of Warriors was propped up against the bodies of two of his slain comrades. His legs were tied, and the rope with which his hands had been lashed together had been looped around his neck in such a way that he had no choice but to stare at his hands.

Blood was still welling sluggishly from where his thumbs had been.

Moth pushed himself up off the corpse, stumbled over to the Master of Warriors. His fingers fumbled at the knots.

"Master." His voice seemed to be coming from somewhere far away. "I can't—"

"My dagger. At my side."

"It's not there."

"One of theirs, then—" Gesturing with his head. "Over there!" His voice was raw and ragged.

"My uncle—"

"A knife! Get a knife!"

The second Nomad had a knife half-hidden under his body. It was slippery with blood. Moth pulled it free and wiped it on the dead man's clothes, then sawed at the ropes around the Master of Warriors' wrists.

"Faster!" The Master's voice was a fading whisper. Moth sawed harder. "Did you see them? The Nomads?"

"Yes." He had one wrist free. "They rode away on their horses."

"Were any of my warriors there?"

"No, Master." Moth freed the other hand. The warrior extended one of the fingers of his right hand and forced himself to touch the stump where his left thumb had been without flinching. Moth could see the scream trying to force its way past his clenched jaw.

"Why did they cut off your thumbs, Master?" Moth asked.

"Why? You ask me why?" His eyes never left his mutilated hands. "They left me here to tell children how they defeated me and stole my King's life from me. How they left me less than a man," he whispered, and closed his eyes.

"What do you want me to do, Master?" The Master of Warriors said nothing. "What do you want me to do?" Moth yelled at him.

His right eye opened, closed again. "Too late. Get . . ." He was unconscious.

"I'll find somebody!" Moth said. "I'll—"

A wordless, bubbling scream suddenly came from behind the red and gold hanging hiding the entrance to the forge. Then another, shriller shriek of agony that seemed as though it could never have been torn from a human throat.

"Uncle?" Moth shouted. "Tramu?" But there was only the agonized shrieking and wailing.

The Master stirred without regaining consciousness.

"Uncle, is that you?" Moth cried. There was no answer. "I can't go in there!" Moth shouted. "I'm just a potter's son! Uncle? I'll get a smith. Just wait, I'll find someone! I promise!"

The shrieking followed him out into the street.

"Help me!" he cried as he ran. "Somebody help me!"

No one answered him.

He darted into a house, looking for somebody, anybody. It was deserted.

In the next house he found three dead Chaldan warriors.

He ran blindly then, afraid to enter any other houses. His lungs were on fire; he no longer knew what he was shouting. He ran.

A hand caught him by the arm. "What's wrong, little Ri?"

A warrior in Chaldan blue, the sun gleaming off his breastplate and helmet.

"You're alive," Moth croaked, overcome by the wonder of it.

"And why shouldn't I be?"

"Tas Et's house!" Moth gasped. "All dead. My uncle—he was forging the blade, and the Nomads —Nomads on horses—

"You can't get into the forge!" he yelled after the running warrior. "You need a smith!"

He leaned against the wall and tried to catch his breath. His mouth was thick with saliva. He spat, wiped his lips with his left hand, started back to Tas Et's house.

By the time he got there, dead warriors and Nomads were being dragged from the surrounding houses. Three Warriors of the Voice were standing with drawn swords in front of the doorslit. They refused to let him enter.

"But he's my uncle!"

"It doesn't make any difference," the warrior on the left said. "Nobody gets in but King Tvil."

King Tvil. Prince LasTvil had become King Tvil. The natural order was restored.

It did not seem very important.

"Then can I talk to my cousin, Reverence? My cousin Tramu? Is he in there?"

"You can't talk to anybody," the warrior in the middle said. He looked younger than the others and still carried himself like a Warrior of the Hand. "The Nomads cut their tongues out. So go away." Then he added, more kindly, "Go home and tell the rest of your family, boy. They should know."

"Maybe he knows something, though," the oldest warrior said. "What's your name?"

"Moth, son of Ri Tal the Master Potter, Reverence," Moth said.

"Go home, Moth. We'll find you again if we have any questions."

He was almost home before the tears came. He tried to wipe them away, but could not make them stop, so he continued walking.

The house was still sealed. He would have to look for his parents within the city walls.

The fire still smoldered in some stretches of the Firetrench but most of the flames were out. Moth jumped the trench and entered the inner city.

Some of the people he saw on the street were still in various states of confusion and undress, but most were again garbed as befitted their stations. Warriors in groups of three were everywhere.

Moth's tears and red face branded him as one of those still manifesting the Festival confusion; people avoided him, pretended not to see him.

Once he saw Sklar Ton, but the trader glowered at him with such hatred that Moth turned and ran the other way.

He finally found Ri Tal and Kuan in the Street of the Thieving Warrior. His mother's dress was ripped and Ri Tal had lost his staff; the two shuffled arthritically forward, their eyes downcast.

"Mother!" Moth cried. "Father!" He ran to them.

They threw their arms around him and kissed him.

"We were afraid you'd been killed," Kuan said, almost sobbing. "We heard that Nomads stole the sword and killed Tas Et—"

"They almost killed me too," Moth said. "I saw them stealing it, and the warriors said they cut out Tas Et's tongue and Tramu's too—"

"They aren't dead?" Ri Tal asked.

"No, but the warriors guarding their house wouldn't let me in."

"Tell me what happened."

Ri Tal hesitated for a moment after Moth finished telling him what he'd seen, then said, "The Palace Guard took King Asp's body away to be buried in Chal. They took the coffin I made for him out of the ground, and six of them carried it to an oxcart and they took it away."

"They're not going to bury you with him, are they, Father?" Moth asked.

Ri Tal smiled grimly. "There's no place in the Royal Realm for potters, son. Just warriors and their families."

"What's going to happen to them, Father? To Tramu and Pyota and Tas Et?"

Ri Tal started to speak, closed his mouth again.

"Aren't you pleased to know that your father's coffin will rest forever in the Great Necropolis at Chal?" Kuan asked hurriedly.

"Mother—" Moth began. His father cuffed him. "But what about *Tramu*?" he wailed.

"I don't know," Ri Tal said harshly. "Don't ask me any questions about them. Not now, not ever."

When they arrived home Ri Tal forbade him to leave the house.

At sunset the following day, Moth later learned, Tas Et was impaled on a stake in the Great Square, and next to him was the thumbless Master of Warriors. Pyota, Tramu, and Tas Et's four blow-pipers watched the two men's agonies from the cage in the center of the square.

One of the blowpipers died from his wounds, and another went mad. He was taken from the cage and stoned to death.

After six days without food or water, Pyota, Tramu, and the surviving blowpipers were sold at a public auction. The Tas Sil of Nanlasur, a Chaldan city where lead was mined, bought them for mine slaves.

Ri Tal forbade Moth ever to speak of them to him again, and before allowing him to leave the house made him swear an oath never to go to Nanlasur.

Ri Tal had told his son nothing of Tas Et's agonies on the stake, but the other young potters and smiths soon filled in the gaps in his knowledge. The King, they said, had watched the victims' agonies all night by torchlight while his musicians played for him. The smith was strong, and the Painmaster, Tepes Ban Sil, a clever man—or so the King was reported to have remarked. He was also said to have added that it was a pity his servant's cleverness did not extend to furnishing a tongueless man with a more articulate voice.

Tas Et had been impaled at sunset. He lived till shortly after dawn.

"The Nomads did this to our family," Ri Tal told Moth the day he finally allowed him to leave the house. "They tried to steal you; they murdered your uncle. Hate them with all your soul."

And Moth hated the Nomads. But no Nomad had impaled his uncle, no Nomad had sold his aunt and cousin into slavery, and he hated King Tvil far more than he hated the Nomads.

He was not stupid; he told no one that he dreamed of someday seeing King Tvil's son forced to watch his father writhing on a sharpened stake, as Tvil had forced Tramu to watch Tas Et.

Such dreams were madness for a potter's son. But though he shared his secret thoughts with no one, neither did he try to forget them.

And when Tas No, his grandfather (Tas No Sil no longer; that name had been lost to him when he was stripped of his position as High Smith), asked Ri Tal if Moth might be allowed to learn smithcraft, so that he who now had no one to whom he might leave his tools when he died could ensure that they lived after him, Moth did not object.

Ri Tal wanted Moth to make pretty pots and ceramic statuettes with metal decorations to be traded to the men of the Delta.

Moth wanted to make weapons.

Chapter Sixteen

When the setting sun touched the mountains on the western horizon, Moth would be twelve. And before it set again he would be either a man of two souls and two names, sealed to both potting compound and forge, betrothed to Rafti—or he would be dead. Not everyone survived the manhood rituals, and he had to undergo initiation in two Sils before the day was over.

Sartor, be merciful! he prayed. He remembered the day he had found the white clay: a miracle. Surely Sartor would not have wasted a miracle on someone doomed to die in ordeal.

In the two years since King Asp's death, King Tvil had made peace with the Delta, the better to pursue his war with the Nomads. Taxes had been raised again and again, and Ri Tal had been forced to sell his own wares in the market to meet them.

But though the war had ended when a lone Nomad had come riding into Kyborash to throw the broken pieces of Asp's dead life in the dust before the entrance to the Palace of the King, the taxes continued unabated. And Ri Tal told his son that their only hope of meeting Snae Tka's demands was the profit he hoped to derive from the new manufactures Moth was to make for the Royal Eunuch.

So Moth's life had been devoted almost entirely to the pursuit of his two crafts. He had no time for amusement, little time to devote to those friends who had not turned from him after the events of the Festival. And whatever vision had come to Sklar Ton while he had been Sklar Ton the prophet, he still hated Moth for it.

When his grandfather had taken him into the forge to learn the smithsecrets, the old man had forged for him a silver soul, a thick oval pendant with a tiny golden sun-flame in its center. Moth wore it on a silver chain around his neck, where it dangled beside the clay talisman he wore on a leather thong. And with the new talisman had come a new name, Sartor-ban-ea-Sar, Sartor in the Fire Burning Low, a name that Tas No said had come to Moth because of the manner in which he had been singled out to become a smith.

It seemed to Moth that his two souls bore a kinship to each other, for all that one had a name of beginning and the other a name of ending. But of this he said nothing to his grandfather, and he revealed his new name to no one else.

Moth's father had taught Sartor-ban-i-Tresh to make useware, first shaping a base, then piling the coils upon it until he had a vase or bowl; he had taught him to make a kiln, and the ways of burning wood to obtain the right charcoals. Sartor-ban-i-Tresh learned to fire that which he shaped, and when he _ finally fired the coil-built and hand-molded soul talisman he had made for himself (struggling each morning to make the clay reproduce dream forms from the previous night, Ri Tal looking at his attempts and shaking his head or, more rarely, smiling, but in any case ordering Moth to destroy them, until, at last, the day came when the form was acceptable), the talisman did not crack.

That day Ri Tal took the dolthe he had made for his son so many years previously in Chal, and he journeyed far from Kyborash to bury it in a place where no man would ever find it.

"Your true soul lies buried far from here, sealed within a stout glazed jar," Ri Tal told his son the day after Sartor-ban-i-Tresh had removed the fired talisman from the kiln he had made. "But though you will never see your true soul with the eyes of your body, yet it is not different from the darsath that you now wear around your neck. The hidden soul will change every time you make for yourself a new darsath to wear; yet it is shaper as well as shaped, and it will guide you as your hands give form to the visible talisman. But never forget that the visible soul you wear around your neck is shaper as well as shaped, and beware of damaging your true soul, for should your darsath crack three successive times in the firing, your true soul, your precious dolthe, will be wounded beyond hope of healing."

But Moth had two souls. Though he spent his mornings in the potting compound, his afternoons were spent learning the ways of the smiths from Tas No. Sartor-ban-ea-Sar learned to make a blowpipe from a reed with a clay tuyere at the end to direct the stream of air; he learned the rituals for working the clay from which the smiths made their tuyeres and molds.

Yet their rituals were not those of the potters, and Moth was Ri as well as Tas: when he worked clay in the smithy he had to perform the rituals of both Sils. Tas No gave him a small part of the forge to be his alone, and there he performed the potter's rituals in the proper secrecy.

First he was taught to tend the forgefire. He was careful, knowing that his life was forfeit if he let the fire die before its time. Then he learned to make the small sacrifices needed to ready the forge for the workings that he was being taught: the proper method of crushing the barley and millet, the words to be said and the gestures to be made as he threw the insects (one of them always the great scarlet moth that was his namesake) into the flames.

He begged Tas No to teach him the animal sacrifices necessary for the forging of weapons, but though his grandfather had grown hesitant and timid, almost doddering—his age fallen upon him all at once, like a collapsing wall—yet he was firm in his refusal. Sartor-ban-ea-Sar would learn only that which he needed to know in order to make things of beauty.

"But your hammer and his family," Moth pleaded. "Surely your tools will be unhappy if they never again have a chance to undertake the great workings—"

"No." Moth opened his mouth to protest but Tas No cut him off with a sharp, angry gesture. And when he was at last sure that Moth was going to remain silent, he finally began teaching him the secret rites for making and extinguishing the forge-fire.

Only a few weeks ago Tas No had forged a new soul for him, taking the metal of the old soul and melting it in a fire that Sartor-ban-ea-Sar alone had made and tended. With the forging of his new soul, Moth felt anew the antagonism that was building between Sartor-ban-i-Tresh and Sartor-ban-ea-Sar.

Sartor-ban-i-Tresh had become simple, patient, loving; he enjoyed looking out over the barley fields, enjoyed feeling the cool canal water on his skin as he waded in the irrigation canals, enjoyed the sight of the setting sun. He was happy and content: he knew who he was and what he was, and he had no longing for anything else.

Sartor-ban-ea-Sar was different. He loved and pitied old Tas No, he felt a certain affection mingled with contempt for his parents, and he never ceased to think of Tramu, but for the rest of the world he had only suspicion and hatred.

Sartor-ban-i-Tresh wanted to delight. Sartor-ban-ea-Sar wanted to destroy. There had been a time when the two souls had been one, and Moth still could not always tell them apart, yet they were distinct now, and grew more different with each passing day.

Sometimes Moth felt that neither soul was his, that he was a third being, nameless and alone, and that the two souls fought for dominion of what should have been, not theirs, but *his*.

While Moth's two souls had been separating and growing apart from each other, Rafti had reached the age of twelve and completed the initiation into the Women's Mystery she had begun two years before, when, with the other girls her age, she had begun her training in the Siltemple. For six months she had been a veiled hierodule in the Siltemple, her companionship at the disposal of anyone who could pay the Temple's price. When she was returned to her family her mother, Kytra, had attempted to raise the money for a good brideprice by selling her services, for Tas Gly, her father, was a poor smith and the family was without money. Yet though Rafti was a handsome girl blossoming into beauty, none of those who had known her at the Temple seemed to remember her with longing, and she brought her family little money. So Tas Gly decided that she must be married quickly, lest her beauty fade before it could find her a husband.

But though there were more smiths' sons in Kyborash than there were smiths' daughters for them to marry, the sons one and all refused Tas Gly's daughter, preferring to find their brides in other cities. At last she was left with no one, for without a dowry she could not hope to find a husband outside Kyborash. So though Moth was no true smith—or so, Tas Ayri, who had been Moth's friend while Tramu still lived the life of a young smith, jeered—yet for all his dappled hair and black eyebrow he was somewhat of a smith, and Rafti had no choice but to marry a smith.

So the marriage had been arranged, though Rafti was a year older than Moth, though Tas Gly hated Tas No for the insult he fancied the old man had done his family by spurning Rafti as Tramu's bride, though Rafti and Moth bore each other no love and

Moth knew that Rafti would be as happy to learn of his death in the manhood rites as she would be to learn that he had survived them to marry her.

It was spring; the potting compound was cool. Nine days yet remained before the beginning of the Spring Inundation, when Moth would join the other men for the three days' labor in the Temple barley fields that all men owed Sartor. Those three days every year of plowing and sowing, of dragging the wooden harrow with its stone teeth over the land and breaking up clods of earth with stone hammers, would be the only field work Moth would ever do again. No smith worked his land; that was left for his wife and children, and for his slaves, if he was rich enough to own any.

Three days a year: the only field work he would ever do again—if he survived to do it this first time.

The Ri came for him promptly at dusk. In the fading light he could see that all save his father had hidden their faces behind half-masks of fired clay; they wore scarlet robes thickly daubed with mud, and they were singing the Ri Chant, that others might know them for what they were and avert their eyes.

They took Moth and tied his hands and feet. They rolled up small aromatic leaves and shoved them into his nostrils, that he might not know by smell where they were taking him. They put damp soil in his ears, that he might not hear their words; they put a lump of fire-hardened clay in his mouth and tied his jaw shut. Ri Tal placed a half-mask of fired clay without eyeholes over the upper part of Moth's face, blinding him.

They lifted him to their shoulders and carried him from the compound.

The leaves in his nostrils felt cold; their fumes chilled him. He was dizzy, confused, terrified. He could do nothing. Though his ears had been plugged he could hear the Ri singing.

At last they lowered him to the ground. Rough fingers dug the earth from his ears: he could hear again.

"Many years ago the mother's child within you died and you became a child of the clay. *Is this not true? Answer!*"

But the clay in his mouth made speech impossible.

"He does not answer," the speaker stated, and Moth recognized his voice: Ri Cer Sil. "Is this because he is no true child of the clay?"

"He is a true child of the clay. He has a name." His father's voice.

"You swear this to be true?"

"I swear it by my name, and with Sartor as my witness."

"Then he is a true child of the clay. Why, then, does he not answer?"

"Perhaps he is disobedient," another voice suggested, and Moth tensed, recognizing Ri Shar, the potter who had argued most adamantly against allowing him to become a man of two Sils.

"Perhaps," Ri Cer Sil said. "If that be true, then he must die."

I can't answer with this thing in my mouth! Moth wanted to shout.

"Yet perhaps he is unwilling to speak for good

reasons of his own," suggested a voice that Moth recognized as Yeshun's.

"Perhaps. Yet if that be so, still must he die, for what are his reasons to us?"

The clay in his mouth sucked the lifewater from his mouth and throat, choking him. He struggled against the ropes that bound him, tried to force his jaws apart and spit the clay from his mouth. The lump was expanding, choking him.

"Perhaps the Earth Mother prevents him from speaking." Ri Tal's voice.

"Perhaps. If that be true, then may he live."

"Yet how shall we learn why he does not answer us?" Yeshun asked.

"We must ask the Earth Mother." They sang a long chant without words, suddenly fell silent.

"She does not answer." Moth did not recognize the voice.

"If She rejects him, he must die." Ri Shar's voice. "If he be not Her son, if he be son to a human mother, then he must die."

"Yet She does not answer."

"We must test him." Ri Cer Sil's voice.

"Yes."

"Yes." A new voice. "Let the Earth Mother take him."

"She must eat him; he must enter Her womb."

"Yes."

"If he be true son to Her, he will be born anew."

"Yet first She must eat him." Moth could no longer recognize any of the voices.

"But what of Her jaws? Her terrible, grinding jaws?" cried a voice that might have been his father's.

"If She tears him to pieces with Her jaws, he will not live."

"No. Yet She must eat him if he is to be born again."

"He must be eaten."

Silence. Moth struggled against his bonds.

"See him struggle."

"He cannot escape Her."

"Call Her, that She may eat him."

"She comes."

Moth heard the noise then, a low whistling, growing louder and deeper, beginning to roar. . . .

The clay muffled his scream. Around him he could hear the men bursting into song.

"She is here!"

"She opens Her mouth!"

"Do you see Her teeth, Her teeth of black stone, fierce and sharp?"

"She will eat him!"

"No! Do not let Her not eat him!"

"She must eat him. Lower him into Her mouth."

"See Her teeth. How they grind, how they grind! She will eat him!"

Moth was lifted by many hands. He dangled face down.

"Her teeth! Her teeth!" They were lowering him. He could smell the damp earth coming closer, feel Her teeth going round and round his body. The earth smell was all around him. Blood trickled down his body onto his face. And still they lowered him.

He tried to cry out, tried to swear to Her that he was Her son, Her husband, that he had no other mother or wife but Her, but no sound escaped his lips.

"She eats him!" came the cry, and he was falling.

He was wedged into the damp earth, and a voice was speaking to him.

"Listen to me, Sartor-ban-i-Tresh," the voice said. "Listen to me, for I am your mother, the Earth Mother, the bride of Sartor. Listen to me, for though I have eaten you, yet may you live.

"With my sharp teeth I have severed the ropes that bound you. You are in my throat; you must make your way downward into my womb. Listen to me, and know that if you heed me you need never die. Do not try to speak—I know that you cannot speak, for was it not I who arranged it so?—but make your way down through my throat, down through my body and into my womb."

The damp hard earth was all around him. He could not move his shoulders. He began wriggling his head, kicking with his legs, trying to force himself down Her throat.

"Quickly, Sartor-ban-i-Tresh, or I will squeeze you with the great muscles of my throat and you will be eaten."

Was the clay around him moister? It was colder, he was sure it was colder, and it was getting slipperier. . . . He wriggled like a fish trying to swim down through the river ooze, and his shoulders broke free. He fell, landed on damp clay. He reached out, felt smooth stone walls tight all around him.

"You are in my womb, Sartor-ban-i-Tresh," the voice whispered to him. "Listen, and I will reveal to you the meaning of all things. I will tell you how the world was created.

"At first there was nothing but the waters, vast, formless, without beginning or end. But on the first day the sun arose from the waters, and the sun was Sartor. Sartor looked out upon the waters and found them beautiful.

"But soon Sartor decided that the waters were too empty. So He created me, and I was Baalkunti, the first land. Baalkunti, the primal hill.

"Sartor admired Baalkunti for a time, but soon He decided I was too bare, so He created grasses and flowering plants and naro palms with which to clothe me.

"Sartor admired the beauty of His creation for a time, but then He decided that the world would be more pleasing to Him still if it contained yet more kinds of life, so He took from me moist clay, and from this clay He fashioned the first fish to swim in the waters around the world. But then it seemed to Him that the land had too little life, so one by one He created the land animals, delighting in forming each and every one from my clay. And when He had filled the land and waters with life, He realized that the sky too was void of pleasing creatures, so He created the birds.

"But Sartor grew bored with knowing all that was to happen, so He fashioned lesser gods to create new things for Him, that He might be surprised and delighted by their creations. And for a time all was as He wished.

"But the gods came to Him, and said, 'You have made the birds to share the sky with us, and this is not right. So Sartor gave the birds legs upon which to stand and commanded them to alight each and every one for part of the day or night, and the gods were satisfied for a while.

"But soon the gods came to Sartor and said, 'We have no temples.' So Sartor created great temples for them, and they were happy for a while. But after a time the gods came to Sartor and said, 'We have no worshipers. Our temples are empty and no one brings us offerings.' So Sartor created mankind to worship the gods.

"And the gods came again to Sartor, but He held up His hand that they might not speak. 'I will create nothing more for you,' He told them, 'for I tire of creation. Should you desire anything, you must make it for yourselves or command mankind to make it for you, for I have created men to be creators of small things, as you are the creators of greater things and I am the creator of All.' And Sartor became hot and fiery and withdrew to a place where none of the gods dared approach Him. And He would speak no more to them, but only to me, Baalkunti, First-Born of His creations. And for this the gods hate Sartor.

"The gods are lazy and when they must labor they grow angry and punish mankind, but they delight in beauty. This is why the potters of other lands shape clay to create pottery, that they may delight their gods, so that the gods may be astonished and withhold their wrath.

"But know, Sartor-ban-i-Tresh, that I, Baalkunti, the Earth Mother, First-Born of Sartor, Older Than the Gods, took pity on the potters of Chal, for they knew not Sartor but only the gods. To them and to them alone I revealed the true secret of Sartor's nature, that they might become the Ri Sil.

"It is right and just that your pots be sold to those who know not Sartor, to be given to their gods, for the gods are real and Sartor created men to delight and astonish them. But know you also that you exist to delight and astonish Sartor All-Highest, and that those pots which you create from me, from Baalkunti, the Earth Mother, whose secret name only the Ri potters of Chal know—those pots that you create for Sartor will hold within them your life, and should He accept them of you, then for as long as it pleases Him for your pots to endure, for that long shall your soul survive. And if your pots please Sartor for all eternity, then life immortal shall be yours. And this I, Baalkunti, First-Born of Sartor, promise you.

"But now the time has come for you to be reborn of me as a man. Reach up with your hands, find the passage from the darkness of my womb up into the outer world. Follow the passage up and out of the earth, and you shall be reborn."

Moth struggled up and out, until his head was free of the earth his mother, and strong hands seized him and pulled him free. He felt a great contentment, like a warm, sweet pool within him.

"He is born!" the Ri Sil cried. "Let us take his mask from his eyes, let him take the clay from his mouth, let him be clothed as a man should be clothed, and let him be given his staff, for on this day he has become a man and a Ri!"

As the sun rose, the Sil Potter explained to Moth the true meaning of the potter's wheel, of the circle that has no beginning and is without end, the circle that is immortality and the union of male and female, that which is perfect and without a second.

The sun broke free of the eastern horizon, and Sartor-ban-i-Tresh, Sartor of the Setting Sun, was a man. The potters crowded around him, kissing him on the cheeks and congratulating him. Yeshun, himself Ri Yeshun for more than a year now, kept slapping him on the back, and even Ri Shar apologized to him and said that he accepted the Earth Mother's judgment.

But with the sunrise came the men of the Tas Sil for Moth, that Sartor-ban-ea-Sar might prove himself or die in the attempt.

And Moth knew that if Sartor-ban-ea-Sar died before Sartor All-Highest accepted of Sartor-ban-i-Tresh a pot, then Sartor-ban-i-Tresh died also.

❦ Chapter Seventeen ❧

They were all around him, faces hidden by masks of silver, gold, copper. He could feel the furnace heat on his naked back; they had taken his soul silver from around his neck, placed it in a crucible above the flames.

He could feel the metal sweating. Soon it would be soft as flesh, soon weak as water. . . .

"Listen," the masked smiths whispered. "Listen and learn how all things began. Soon you will be in the flames: listen and survive."

"Before the world was made, there were only Kiwan and Neetir, alone in the abyss of night," a smith masked in copper said, and Moth recognized Tas No's voice. "There was neither birth nor death, nor hunger nor satisfaction, and there was nothing to do, so Kiwan and Neetir fought. Each time They fought They made new laws to govern how They were to fight, and each abided by the laws.

"Once when They were fighting, Neetir decided that Kiwan had broken the law. This had never happened before, and Neetir did not know what to do, but finally She decided, 'If Kiwan can break our

172

laws, then so can I,' and She gave birth to Sartor, to help Her battle against Kiwan. This is how birth came into the universe.

"Sartor and Neetir fought against Kiwan, and Kiwan was destroyed. This is how death first came into being. Sartor tore out Kiwan's heart and ate it. This filled Him with a great strength and a great fury, and He ate the rest of Her body. Then He turned on Neetir, His mother, and killed Her as He had killed Kiwan. But though Neetir was dead, Her tears continued to flow. We know them as rain, and when they fall to earth they become the Nacre's waters.

"After Sartor killed Neetir, He looked around Him for someone else He could fight and kill, but the universe was empty of all but Neetir's dead body. And looking at Her body, His fury left Him as He realized how beautiful Neetir and Kiwan had been, and how even in death Neetir was still beautiful. Sartor determined to fill the emptiness of the abyss around Him with Her beauty.

"From Neetir's bones and flesh, Sartor created the heavens and hells, and filled them with gods and demons. He made them beautiful, in memory of that beauty which had been Neetir's and Kiwan's, and He made them terrible, for such was His nature. What Sartor loved more than all else was killing and bloodshed, so He made the gods and demons to fight among themselves and to fight against Him, for they were stupid and did not know that Sartor had created them and was stronger than them all.

"From Neetir's face He plucked one of Her great yellow eyes, and blew upon it so that it grew fiery and hot and became the sun, to light the abyss for Him.

"For ages uncountable Sartor labored to create new heavens and hells, new gods and new demons, from Neetir's body. When He grew thirsty from His labors, He would create bowls in which to catch Neetir's falling tears, so that He could drink them and quench His thirst."

Tas No fell silent, and a burly smith masked in gold took up the narrative. "In the whole universe there is nothing so precious as Neetir's tears, and Sartor wished none of them to escape Him." The smith's voice was high, quavering, the voice of an old man trying to entertain an infant, though he was still in the full flower of his manhood.

"One day Sartor noticed that there was a place in the universe where it often rained, and that this rain just fell and fell forever, and was drunk by nobody.

"'This is not right,' Sartor said to Himself, and He determined to make a great bowl in which to catch the rain as it fell, so that He might drink it Himself.

"Now, this was not a new idea for Sartor. The universe is full of the bowls He has made. We call them stars, and they are so far away from us that they seem tiny, and all we can see of them is the light glistening off the waters they contain.

"Sartor took the winds where He wished to create His great bowl, and plaited them together. From them He made a basket, and in this basket He constructed His bowl.

"Then Sartor reached out with His seven long, long arms, and with each arm He grasped a star.

Each star He grasped was a great bowl filled with the water of Neetir's tears. He began to dance, and as He danced He spun the bowls around Him in a circle. When He let go of the bowls they continued to circle around Him, for such was His will.

"Now, moving water always deposits clay. You do not need to be told this, I am sure: you have seen how the Spring Inundation leaves fresh soil behind on the fields. Not all soil is good clay, but the clay deposited in the seven bowls was the very best clay in all the universe."

A smith masked in silver took up the narrative.

"When the clay was ready, Sartor fashioned it into a perfect bowl, wide and round with a flat bottom and high sides. Then He took the sun from the pouch in which He kept it and used it to fire the bowl.

"When the bowl was fired, Sartor spat upon it inside and out, that it might be glazed and better hold water. But though it was a perfectly formed bowl, Sartor was not yet satisfied with it. He took the earth from beneath His fingernails—and He has seven fingernails on every finger, and seven fingers on every hand, and He has seven hands. These earths were of all different colors, red and white and green and blue and brown and gray and silver and gold and many other colors besides, and from them He made beautiful paints. Then, using His tongue as a paintbrush, He painted the inside of the bowl with magical birds and animals and plants and fishes and men.

"Sartor ordered the sun to circle the bowl, to melt the glaze and fix the designs He had made to the bowl. But His work had made Him thirsty—in

all the universe there is no one with a thirst like
Sartor's—and He knew that it would not rain
where He was for another five months. The stars He
had set spinning were still too muddy to drink
from, so He went off to another part of the universe
where rain was falling, and He could quench His
thirst.

"The sun circled the bowl, and for a time it was
content. But soon it realized that the designs Sartor
had painted on the bowl were the most beautiful
things it had ever seen. The sun stared and stared at
the bowl. It was so fascinated that it forgot Sartor's
orders and came closer and closer to the bowl,
for the figures Sartor had painted were so small
that the sun could not see them well from far
away.

"The sun came so close that its heat melted the
bowl's clay sides and cracked the bottom. All the
glaze melted and ran out through the cracks. The
men and animals and fishes and birds and plants
that Sartor had painted on the bowl also melted.

"When the sun realized what it had done, it
retreated high into the sky. The bowl cooled again,
and all of the molten figures grew hard."

A smith in a mask of copper continued.

"One of the figures was a giant man with an anvil
for one fist and a hammer for the other. He was all
of copper, and his body was covered with stubby
branches and small knobs, while his eyes were
green malachite. This was Raburr. He felt cold, and
that was how he knew he was alive.

" 'I am Raburr and I am alive,' he said. He stood
up and looked around him. The great bowl was
cracked everywhere, and there were great gaping

holes in it through which he could see the distant stars.

"'This will not do,' Raburr thought to himself, and the great anvil that was his fist grew fiery red with his anger. 'Sartor wants this bowl to catch the rain, but it has holes in it and all the water will escape. I am Raburr; I will patch the holes so the bowl will hold water for Sartor.'

"He called out to all the birds and plants and men and animals and fishes, 'We must mend the world! Come and listen to me. I am Raburr; I know what we must do.'

"When the birds and plants and men and animals and fishes heard Raburr's voice they all said to themselves, 'We can hear, so we must be alive. We will listen to Raburr.' And they gathered around him.

"'We must all help to save the world for Sartor,' Raburr said. 'I know what we must do. The plants can help by growing roots and holding the soil together.'

"'This we will do, and gladly,' all the plants said.

"'The birds can help by weaving the winds together so that they become gentle and do not carry off the soil,' Raburr said.

"'We will do this, and gladly,' all the birds said.

"Then Raburr said, 'I will take the fish and animals and men and hammer them into plugs with which to fill the holes and cracks in the world.'

"'We will not do this,' the fish said. 'We are beautiful as we are, and we will not change.' But the men and animals said, 'We will do this, and gladly, for the love of Sartor.'

"So Raburr began hammering. But the first men

and animals he tried to hammer into shape cracked and broke. That is why there are no three-headed men and animals.

"When Raburr saw what he had done, he grew angry and the mighty anvil of his fist grew hot. Now, it happened that there were at this time the broken pieces of the body of the last three-headed animal upon the anvil, and as Raburr's anger waxed hot the broken pieces grew soft. And Raburr, seeing this, wondered at it. 'Perhaps,' he thought, 'I can hammer the pieces of this body into shape now that it is soft.' And he tried it, and made of the body of the last three-headed animal a perfect plug with which to mend one of the holes in the world.

"So Raburr began hammering all the two-headed men and animals into the right shapes to plug the holes in the great bowl. Whenever his anger cooled, he had only to think of the waters escaping from Sartor's bowl to grow angry again.

"Now, when the sun had retreated into the sky it had turned its face away from the world, for it did not want to look upon the destruction it had caused. But the sun heard Raburr hammering and turned its face again to the world.

"'Stop, Raburr!' the sun cried. 'Sartor created all of you alike to be beautiful, and to delight His eyes; yet you, who are only one of His creations, are destroying the rest. You do great evil, Raburr!'

"Raburr knew that the sun spoke truth. 'But what must I do?' he asked. 'I must patch the earth so that it will hold the rains.'

"The sun replied, 'From each man and animal take the heart. The rest of the body you may use to fill the holes in the world, but the heart you must hammer into the shape of the creature you took it from. I will send down my fires to the animals and men that you shape, so they will be alive, and not altogether hard and rigid, but like in part to molten metal. That way you will not be destroying Sartor's creations.'

"Raburr thought on this, and he knew it was good. He did as the sun had commanded him. This is why men and animals are warm, and fish are not.

"But when Raburr had hammered all the men and animals into shape there was still one great hole left. So he called the birds one by one from the sky, and with each of them he did as he had done with the men and animals. From their hearts he made little birds, and into these little birds the sun breathed the fires that made them warm and alive.

"But when Raburr had hammered all the birds into shape and placed them all in the ground, there was still a small gap left to be filled.

"'If I do not fill this hole, all the water will drain out and be lost,' he said to himself. 'I am big enough to fill this hole, but who is there to hammer me into shape?'

"'Fish,' he cried, 'will you hammer me into shape, that I may patch this bowl for Sartor?'

"'We will not,' the fish replied.

"Raburr called on the little men, and on the little birds, and on the little animals, but they were too busy with their own affairs and did not heed him.

"'Plants,' he cried, 'can you hammer me into shape, that I may patch this bowl for Sartor?'

"'We would, and gladly,' the plants replied, 'but

we are rooted and cannot move to come to your aid.'

"'Sun,' Raburr cried, 'can you hammer me into shape, that I may patch this bowl for Sartor?'

"'I cannot hammer you into shape,' said the sun, 'for I have no arms. Only Sartor can help you. I will call Him. Hammer your ears shut and put clay on them while I call for Him.'"

Another smith took up the story.

"The sun roared out Sartor's name. The sun's roar was so mighty that the birds and animals and men were too small to hear it, but the fish were still great and the sun's roar deafened them for all time. This is why fish have no ears.

"Sartor heard the sun's roar and came striding across the heavens.

"'What have you done to my beautiful bowl, O faithless Sun?' Sartor demanded.

"'Forgive me,' the sun begged. 'It was fascination with the beauty of your creations that made me forget myself and approach the bowl so that I might better observe them.'

"'I will forgive you, O Sun,' Sartor said, 'for my creation was indeed too beautiful for one such as you to resist.'

"'O Sartor,' Raburr cried, 'for love of You I have attempted to patch Your great bowl, but there is no one save You who may hammer me into shape so that I may plug the last hole and finish my work.'

"Then Sartor looked again at the world, and He saw that its sides had melted down and that it would never again hold water. But He looked also at the work Raburr had done for love of Him, and He was pleased.

"'I will grant you your wish,' He told Raburr, and He took from him his heart. Sartor hammered the rest of Raburr's copper body into shape, and with it He filled the last gap in the world. From Raburr's heart Sartor made a tiny Raburr, and into the tiny Raburr He breathed life and heat.

"'You shall be a smith, and so shall all your descendants,' Sartor told the tiny Raburr. 'For the labors you have done from love of Me you shall be honored evermore, but because you destroyed all the two-headed and three-headed men and animals, all smiths shall forever be a people apart, both more and less than other men. What say you to this?'

"And Raburr said it was just.

"Sartor called the fish to him and addressed them thus: 'O Fish, I love you for your beauty, and yet I am angry with you. You wished to retain the forms I gave you, and for that you bear no blame. But neither is it just that you be greater than the men and birds and animals who sacrificed their forms for love of Me. Henceforth you shall be no larger than any other creatures. Since you refused to use your arms to help Raburr, you shall be without arms. Nor shall you have legs, for a creature with legs but without arms would be an abomination. What say you to this, O Fish?'

"And the fish said it was just, though in truth they were angry with Sartor's judgment, for they had not the courage to defy Him. Sartor took from the fish their hearts and from these hearts He fashioned tiny armless, legless fish. But though He breathed life into the tiny fish, He gave them no warmth.

"Then Sartor took the bodies of the fish and from them He hammered out a silver water bowl, and this He called the moon. He placed the moon in the sky to catch the rain, so that He might drink when He was thirsty.

"Yet He feared that the sun would become fascinated and destroy His new water bowl as it had destroyed the first bowl. So He took the sun in one hand and the moon in another, and He set them to spinning around the earth, so that when the moon was in the sky the sun was below the earth. But the sun begged to be allowed to look upon the moon's beauty, and Sartor took pity on it and told it that sometimes He would allow the moon to share the day sky with the sun. And the sun was glad, and thanked Sartor.

"When Sartor drinks from His silver bowl, His great black lips hide it from us; this is why we cannot always see the whole moon at night. Sometimes when His thirst is great His lips cover the whole moon, and we cannot see it at all.

"Because Sartor's silver bowl is so much smaller than the world, it is not large enough to catch all the rain that falls; so some of this rain reaches the earth, where it flows into the River Nacre and brings life and nourishment to the plants and fishes and birds and animals and men."

The story was over. The smiths stood frozen, silent, reverent, but Moth wanted to scream at them, "Is that all? Is that all you have to tell me?" Sartor-ban-ea-Sar hungered for tales of weapons forged for killing, but this—this was another pretty story, sufficient, perhaps, to satisfy the curiosity of a simple potter like Sartor-ban-i-Tresh, but with nothing to offer Sartor-ban-ea-Sar.

They're hiding the true smithsecrets from me, he realized. I'll never learn to forge weapons; all they're going to teach me is how to make pots out of metal instead of clay.

"The little Ri looks angry!" a smith masked in gold said, and Moth heard laughter ripple through the Sil.

"Good!" said a smith masked in red copper. "Good, Sartor-ban-ea-Sar! Feel angry, be angry, for the anger you feel is Raburr's life flame burning within you. Feeling that anger, you touch your smithsoul, and as the sun breathed life into Raburr, so you must learn to breathe your smithsoul into the flames of the furnace, that they may live and that their life may be that of Raburr."

And, still laughing, they taught him to use his anger as a road to the fires that burned hot and still within him.

I was wrong, Moth realized. This is it; they're teaching me the real smithsecrets. All that other was just to make me ready.

"You are not yet a man," they warned him when the instruction was over. "You have learned to breathe Raburr's flaming soul into the furnace flames, but you must also have the strength of soul to protect the Raburr flame from the spirits of the fish. The fish still hate Raburr for the punishment Sartor visited upon them, and they will fight you for possession of your forgefire. And though the fishflames glow as though they held the sun's true fires, yet they are cold, and all that comes from a furnace in which the fishflames burn is accursed."

"Listen, Sartor-ban-ea-Sar," a smith said. "Your

soul silver lies melting in a clay crucible in that furnace, and until now we have kept it from harm. But the time has come for you to show your smith's strength. From the melted silver a new soul must be fashioned. The fashioning is beyond you, and we will do it for you—but first you yourself must take the silver from the furnace without tongs or forceps. If Raburr is strong in you, you will defeat the fishflames, and take your soul silver from the furnace without being burned. If you are too weak to protect the furnace from them, you will be burned and we will kill you—but if the soul you breathe into the flames be truly Raburr's, you need have no fear."

This is real, he thought. I can die here.

"Will you do this?" they demanded together.

"I will."

"Begin." A conical copper vessel full of some dark, noisome liquid was thrust into his hands.

"Drink this. Now."

"What is it?"

"Fire."

It burned his mouth and throat with the fires of spices and the fire of flames; it had a greasy texture and the taste of putrescent flesh.

"Drink it all."

He wanted to gag. Tears were streaming from his eyes, but he conquered his body's aversion, finished the liquid.

"Sit cross-legged there, in front of the furnace. No, closer. Still closer—good. There, where you cannot tell the heat from the furnace from the heat rising within your body. . . ."

Moth stared at the three blowpipers, the slender

reeds entering their silver masks giving them the look of grotesque birds.

"Close your eyes." He closed his eyes. "Now, look within yourself, find the artery of fire, the hassa. . . ."

It was there, a thread-thin canal filled with ascending flame. It wove back and forth within him like a swaying serpent, and with every breath he took the flames leapt high. . . . And now it began to grow, the flames thrusting ever more fiercely . . . the flame canal swelling . . . as thick now as his little finger . . . now swollen to the size of an arm . . . the flames growing fiercer . . .

The artery of flame fills his body.

Within the envelope of his skin he is a torch, all dazzling flame and currents of blast air.

He has no body. He can hear the other flames all around him, making noises like children cracking beans between their teeth. . . . He is inside the furnace, a single grass blade of flame in an orange-red meadow, feeling the three streams of cold air fanning his being into paradoxical brilliance. . . . Above him he can see the clay crucible in which his soul silver lies melting . . . he can feel the restless agitation of the melting metal, the firm support of the clay.

His soul silver is almost molten. Soon he will remove it from the furnace. He feels only confidence—

And suddenly the fishflames are pressing inward, trying to root themselves in the charcoal floor above which he dances. He pushes them back with the strength of his will, keeps their false fires from touching his soul silver, but he knows that if he returns to his body and sets his will to protecting it from the furnace flames, the fish spirits will stamp his soul silver with their chill death before he can pluck it from the furnace.

Raburr! he cries in a voice all hisses and crackles and sighs. Raburr, noble ancestor!

He directs his anger inward, through the channel of his anger to the blaze within his soul, through the white heat at the core of his self, out and back again, questing—

Raburr, First Smith, aid me in my time of trouble!

And he feels it, a sense of presence approaching from far away, suddenly taking root within him, making of the fires of his soul a habitation for itself.

I command you by your secret name. Raburr, ancestor, I compel you to reveal yourself to me!

There is no answer.

Raburr, by your name I command you to answer me!

Then he feels the presence within him reaching out, merging with the flames of the furnace.

I am not Raburr.

He feels no fear, only rage that he should be thus invaded.

Who are you? Answer me! I compel you in the name of Sartor, in the name of—

Those names are useless against me. They mean nothing to me. But I will give you a name by which you may compel me, Sartor-ban-ea-Sar. I will give you this name if you will forge an oath upon your anvil that you will perform for me one service.

And if I refuse?

Then you will die. Yet I mean you no harm.

And why, spirit, should I trust you?

Because only through me can you reach Raburr, Sartor-ban-ea-Sar. Because I know your truename: your soul is mine, to do with as I choose, and yet I have let you live. Is that not reason enough to trust me?

What service do you ask of me?

I would forge of you a weapon against one who is your enemy as well as mine.

And that is all you want of me?

Is it not enough?

Moth has no choice: I swear to do you this one service, spirit—but only if you swear first that all you have told me is true and that you mean me no harm, and swear this upon your truename.

Agreed. I swear to you, Sartor-ban-ea-Sar, that I mean you no harm, and this I swear upon my anvil that is broken, this I swear upon my truename, which is Sartor-ban-u-Quarr, whom you knew as Tas Et.

Tas Et is dead.

Yet I am he, though even now Tepes Ban thrusts the stake through me, though Tvil watches laughing as my life's blood gushes from me, and I call down upon him my smith's death curse.

Tas Et dies, the flames whisper, and yet I am he. Do you not know my voice, nephew? Am I not Tas Et, your uncle?

You have his voice.

You do not yet believe? Then look upon me now in my death agony and *see* me!

The naked man twists weakly on the stake that protrudes from his shoulder. His ears and nose are gone, hacked off; pink foam drips from his mouth.

His eyes are open, staring from the flames at Moth.

The blood-foamed lips move: Do you want to join me on the stake, nephew? Feel my agony for your own? Is that what it will take to make you believe?

Enough, uncle! I believe!

Then swear, nephew. Swear that I may make of you the weapon of my revenge.

I, Sartor-ban-ea-Sar, swear upon my anvil that Sartor-ban-u-Quarr may make of me a weapon for his revenge. May the stone crack, may my hammer shatter if I am not true to my oath.

The vision fades.

I have sworn to obey you, uncle. But you have chosen a poor instrument for your vengeance.

The flames hiss orange, yellow, crimson. And outside, the pale fishflames, cold as winter stars, pressing inward. He does not have the strength to fight them any longer.

Help me, uncle. I compel you by your name, and by the oath you swore. Help me survive the fishflames.

The secret is hatred, nephew. Draw upon the fires of my hatred, use them to destroy the fishflames, for they are not true flames and they can be destroyed by fire. Through me you draw upon the fires of Raburr's anger. Take of me the burning—

And Moth looks at the pale fishflames through the eyes of his uncle's hatred, and wherever his gaze falls the fishflames burn with a great roar and are consumed.

When there are no more fishflames to menace the furnace he lets himself return to his body—

To find himself being held down by two silver-masked smiths while his body spasmed and convulsed against the ground and against their restraining arms. His sweat, rank and strange-smelling like that of an animal, had turned the dust and dirt in which he'd been rolling into greasy mud, coating him, like a slip of liquid clay on a pot. His mouth was sour with the taste of blood.

He spasmed one last time and was still, lying aching and exhausted on the yellow earth. The two silver-masked smiths cautiously loosed their holds on him. Just as cautiously he sat up, spat black blood, and got to his feet.

Tas Et? he asked within him, and saw again the bloodstained mask of his uncle's face. He shuddered.

He did not want the weight of his uncle's vengeance.

"The fire," a copper mask said. "Take your soul silver from the fire." And Moth made of his anger a glove of flame hotter than the furnace fires and took the silver from the crucible without harm.

But when he handed it to the waiting smith it was already hard, already formed: a curving tooth of a blade sharp enough to sever the wings of a fly in flight. It had a hole in the blunt end through which his amulet chains could go.

Behind their masks the smiths made small anxious, excited noises. Feet shuffled; someone coughed. Yet none of them spoke until the soul dangled from the double chain around his neck.

Then they taught him to use the handleless stone hammer and the other tools of the hammer's family —the forceps, tongs, and stone anvil, the files made from the special copper taken from a secret mine.

And in all his tools Moth could sense Tas Et's spirit, and to each of them he pledged anew his hatred.

"He will be a great weaponsmith." Tas Et's voice, booming in the silence; but though all the smiths heard it, none of them recognized it. They sighed, and Tas No said, "If it be right, I will teach him to forge weapons."

Moth took his soul silver from the flames early in the afternoon. By nightfall, Moth, named Sartor-ban-i-Tresh of the Ri Sil and Sartor-ban-ea-Sar of the Tas Sil, was betrothed to Rafti, her family his family, though after the customs of the smiths the marriage would not be consummated for another two years.

And when they had exchanged marriage tokens and the time had come for Rafti to give him the chaste, ceremonial kiss with which their pledge was to be sealed, she whispered, "I'm pleased that you survived, husband."

That night, lying on his pallet in the darkness of his parents' house, Sartor-ban-i-Tresh wondered about his coming life with Rafti; but within Sartor-ban-ea-Sar there was only the fearsome weight of his oath, the terrifying prospect of life as his uncle's avenger.

ᚙᚖᚙ Chapter Eighteen ᚙᚖᚙ

"Look!" Moth's gaze followed his mother's pointing finger. Someone in copper armor was coming out of the King's Gate.

"Is that—?" Kuan asked.

"Not this time," Tas Gly said, his voice overindulgent, condescending. Moth detested him as he, in turn, despised Moth.

"It's nobody important," the goldsmith added. "Just another warrior." Tas Gly was small for a smith, shorter than Ri Tal; his face was narrow, ferret-sleek, and overly clever; his every gesture conveyed a sense of abnormal tensions only precariously held in check.

My futurefather, Moth thought, as the goldsmith moistened his lips with little darting movements of his tongue.

"And whoever he was," Tas Gly told Kuan, "he's gone back inside."

"You're right," Kuan said. "Sorry. I guess I'm a little overexcited."

"Well, what's wrong with that, Mother?" Moth demanded in what he hoped was a light tone, his gaze fixed on Tas Gly's face. The goldsmith wouldn't meet his eyes, which pleased him. "It isn't every day you get to see the King and Prince SarVas."

"Of course not," Tas Gly said. He grimaced, sucked at his lips, wiped them dry with the back of his right hand. "It's just that, well, Moth, it sometimes makes me nervous the way your mother always leaps ahead of things—"

"My wife has very quick wits," Ri Tal said.

"She's a fine woman," Tas Gly affirmed. "You should be proud of her."

"I am," Ri Tal said. "Very proud."

"But I do get a little overexcited sometimes," Kuan said.

There was a momentary lull in the conversation. Voices crowded in on Moth from all sides, fruit sellers, sweetmeat vendors, people like himself standing idly in the Great Square while they waited for King Tvil's eldest son to begin his circuit of the shrines—

No, he thought. Not people like me. There isn't anyone else like me.

"You're not looking well, Moth," Kytra said. She was a large, bulky woman with a predatory nose and teeth too large for her mouth. "Do you feel all right?"

"I'm fine." His father looked sharply at him. Moth nodded slightly, and Ri Tal gestured covertly to Tas No. The two men moved closer to Moth.

"Are you sure? You look a little ill to me. One of my uncles was an exorcist; I know about these things. You've got to start taking care of yourself now, if only for our sakes. We're your family too, now."

"I guess I'm just a little overexcited myself, futuremother." He tried to force a smile, felt the tremors begin.

Not now! he pleaded. Please, uncle, not now!

He felt it coming over him, struggled against it. Tas No and Ri Tal moved in to hold him tightly, supporting him and keeping him from falling, while Kuan moved smoothly forward to conceal what was happening from Rafti's parents.

"Try to keep it from showing in your face," Tas No whispered.

"You must tell me how you achieve that phenomenal calm, Kytra," Moth's mother said. "I've always admired that in you, your calm."

"It's nothing you can learn," Tas Gly replied for his wife. "Kytra's just got it and we don't, that's all. She's always been calm. Haven't you, dear?"

"When I wanted to be," Kytra said. "But I was wild when I felt like it. Wilder than Rafti."

"There's nothing wrong with Rafti," Tas Gly said.

"And there's nothing wrong with being a little wild," Kytra said. "That's all she is, a little wild, just as I was, and I settled down quickly enough when I got married." She reached out and squeezed her husband's narrow hand. To Kuan she said, "Rafti will settle down soon enough. Your son won't have any problems with her."

"I'm not worried," Kuan said.

They were all so far away . . . receding, diminishing. . . .

"I wish you wouldn't say things like that about Rafti," Tas Gly said.

"I'm sure she meant no harm," Kuan said. "I like Rafti. It's a pity she can't be here with us now."

They were all so far away now, but not far enough away that he couldn't hear his mother forcing herself into a sickening parody of friendliness. It disgusted him.

I'm sorry, Mother, he thought.

"A pity for her, maybe, but a good thing for your son," the goldsmith said. "He'll be thankful enough for all the time she's spent as a hierodule when the time comes to consummate their marriage."

"I'm sure you're right," Kuan said. "Isn't that—?"

"The King!" Kytra said, standing straighter. "And the Prince is right behind him!"

Their strong hands held him. He could feel some of the rigidity leave his body.

Tas Et? he asked.

Yes.

Months had passed since the first time Kuan had asked him about his fits.

"I've been having them since I was initiated as a smith," he told her. His father looked grim but compassionate. For a moment Moth was overwhelmed by the need to tell them everything. I've got a ghost in me, he wanted to shout, Tas Et's ghost, and whenever he haunts me I go into a fit.

He was no longer a child; he bit down on his tongue, said nothing.

"Why?" Kuan asked. "Is Sartor punishing you for something?"

"No. I'm all right, Mother. I just can't talk about this."

"Smithsecrets?" Ri Tal asked.

"Yes." He was grateful for the excuse.

"You can't tell us anything about your fits without betraying something you swore to keep secret?" Kuan demanded.

"No."

"And the times you run away from us and hide in the trees or in the barley field, the times you cry and laugh for daysixths at a time—you can't tell us about those, either?"

"Kuan, he can't tell you anything. Or Sartor *would* punish him. But—I think I know what the trouble is. And I wouldn't be breaking any oaths by telling you. Son, may I?"

Moth nodded.

"It's because he suddenly has two souls where before he had only one. Remember how we used to fight the first few years we were married? It was hard for me to get used to having a smith's daughter as a wife, even harder for you to learn to live with a potter for a husband. Well, Moth has both a potter and a smith inside him now, and it will probably take a long time for the two of them to learn to live in peace with each other, just as it took us a long time."

"But what if his souls never stop fighting? I don't want to see him in the cage, like—" She broke off. "I just don't want to see him in the cage."

Ri Tal took a long time to answer. "They'll have to learn to live together," he said finally. "But until they do, we have to keep people from learning about his fits. I don't want him in the cage any more than you do."

"Of course not," Kuan said. "Moth, is it— You know, when women are first initiated the spirits of foreign women sometimes visit them and demand a party, with singing and dancing and fine clothes. And they keep coming back again and again until the women join the Women's Mystery."

"What are you trying to suggest?" Ri Tal asked. "There is no mystery for the two-souled."

"What can we do, then? Just wait, and hope it passes? What if his fits never cease?"

"They will."

"But if they don't?"

"Would you feel better if I asked your father's advice?"

"Much better."

"I'll take Moth to see him now. I'd meant to talk to him soon anyway."

Tas No greeted them at the doorslit, ushered them inside. Carya brought beer.

"You know about Moth's fits?" Ri Tal asked when Carya left.

"Yes."

"Kuan and I are both scared somebody will see him and report him."

"You're right to be frightened," Tas No admitted. "So am I. But I don't know what to do."

"I told Kuan I thought his fits would go away if we could keep them secret for a while—"

"Perhaps. But what if someone learns of them first?"

"I can stay out of sight until the fits stop," Moth offered. "Not go out of the house, stay in the forge or the potting compound."

"You can't spend all your time hiding," Tas No said. "What about Tas Gly and Kytra? What about *Rafti?*"

"Rafti wouldn't betray me," Moth said.

"Kuan trusts Rafti too," Ri Tal said. "And even if Tas Gly and his wife dislike us, they—"

"No."

"No?"

"They don't *dislike* me, Ri Tal. They hate me. First of all, because when I was the Tas Sil I made it clear that I would never let Tas Gly so much as attempt to become a coppersmith, much less a weaponsmith. And then, because Tas Gly is sure I was the one who told Tas Et that Rafti wasn't good enough for Tramu. I didn't have to tell Tas Et anything—he was smart enough to realize for himself that no daughter of Tas Gly could ever have been right for Tramu—but Tas Gly would love to revenge himself on me for all the ways he thinks I humiliated him. He'd be perfectly willing to sacrifice you and Kuan and Moth in the attempt."

"So? Even if you're right, I still don't think it makes any difference. Moth's the only husband he's ever going to find for Rafti, and he knows it. He's poor, and he's too greedy to risk having to support an unmarried daughter for the rest of his life just for some petty vengeance."

"You underestimate him."

"I don't want to see my son in the cage any more than you do— Less: I remember Sul. But I'm sure we can trust Tas Gly's greed where we could never trust his honor."

"I hope you're right," Tas No said. "But I wish

we could have found Moth another bride."

"I like Rafti," Moth said.

"Are you sure we can't?" Ri Tal asked Tas No, ignoring Moth. "Perhaps we could still find someone else. If not here, then in some other city. Maybe someone with mixed blood like Moth—"

"Impossible," Tas No said. "Moth *has* to marry a full-blooded smith's daughter, or the Tas Sil would refuse to let him learn the smithsecrets. I wouldn't let him myself, in their place—it's not a question of likes and dislikes, it's a question of right and wrong. And I tried other cities. She was the only smith's daughter I found whose family would consent to a marriage with your son."

"I still wish we could have found somebody else," Ri Tal said. "Or at least somebody with different parents. Moth and Kuan both seem to like Rafti."

"I'm not scared of Tas Gly," Moth said. "He's happy to have me around so he can gloat about Tramu and Tas Et. But there are a lot of other people who do worry me. Sklar Ton, for one. He's always spying on me, ever since the Festival."

"Spying on all of us," Tas No said. "He still blames us for what happened then, and he's not alone. I haven't had very many friends since the Festival. Until your two souls reconcile themselves to each other, your father and I will have to protect you."

"Thank you, Grandfather," Moth said. There was no way he could tell them that it was Tas Et's ghost struggling with his souls that caused his fits. That Tas Et wouldn't leave him until King Tvil and his house were destroyed.

Or until Moth had destroyed himself in the attempt. —

What do you want from me? Moth asked the ghost. The fit was over; Tas Et had again taken up residence in his body. You can't do anything to him here; he's surrounded by warriors.

I just want to watch him. I just want to watch him through your eyes and hate him while I die.

"Futurefather," Moth said loudly, letting Tas No and Ri Tal know that he was once again in control of himself, "futurefather, have you heard about the vase Father has been commissioned to make for King Tvil's new necropolis?"

"No," Tas Gly said. "Tell me about it."

Moth's father let go of his son's arm, moved forward. "The King was so pleased with the coffin I made for his father that he's asked me to make him a vase for his water-of-life."

Moth watched the King in his heavy copper armor leading his son from shrine to shrine. The boy couldn't have been more than six years old; he moved with straining stiffness, as though barely able to sustain the weight of his golden armor.

"Such a pretty prince," Kytra said. "But he looks so little— How is a boy like that going to kill a lion?"

The whole thing's a fraud, Moth thought. Somebody will kill the lion for him, then he'll pretend to have killed it himself.

The King and his son worshiped briefly at each of the shrines along the King's Wall, then made their way down the Warriors' Wall.

Moth lost sight of them just before the King led his son through the Warriors' Gate to worship at the shrine in the Warriors' Palace. The cage blocked his view.

❦ Chapter Nineteen ❧

The vase swelled upward from its flat base, flaring into roundness, then tapering to rise into a long slender neck. Moth had thrown it before daybreak, squatting over the hole in the ground containing his wheel, one hand darting out to keep the wheel spinning, then back to the clay as his fingers pulled and stretched the revolving mass into shape.

He'd trimmed the excess clay from the neck, smoothed the lip with a piece of soft leather. Placing the vase where the first rays of the sun would warm it, he'd kept careful watch over it throughout the morning, turning it again and again to keep the sun from drying any one part of it too quickly.

It was a small vase, deceptively simple, yet Sartor-ban-i-Tresh had been well pleased with it. It needed only to be fired and glazed—a single color, he'd decided, perhaps a deep red—to be perfect.

But his father had ordered him to ring the slender neck with incised grooves so that when the vase had been fired and glazed, Moth could wind it with the colorful threads his mother spun from the

fibers of the stinging nettle, the ends of the threads
to be fixed in place with small wooden pins. This in
mimicry of the smith's true inlay work, of his silver
and gold wires hammered into union with the
metal surfaces they adorned.

Sartor-ban-i-Tresh was a potter. He loved the
seven clays, loved the forms they assumed when he
shaped them; often he felt himself no more than a
midwife helping the Earth Mother's children from
Her dark womb into the world of light and air. And
no matter how pretty brightly colored threads
might seem, he knew they could only hinder his
efforts to make manifest the true spirit of the clay,
the sacred beauty which only a potter's hands and
fires could reveal to mankind.

Sartor-ban-i-Tresh was shamed and angered by
Ri Tal's attempts to steal smiths' techniques for his
own work. Yet his pity ran deeper than his anger; he
knew that Ri Tal was degrading his craft out of
misguided love for it, that his father was sincere in
attempting to regain for his Sil that prestige which
Sartor-ban-i-Tresh knew was lost forever.

But where the potter within Moth pitied his
father, the smith was less charitable; Sartor-ban-ea-
Sar found Ri Tal's attempts at imitating metal-
working techniques mere contemptible opportun-
ism.

It was well past midday. Moth had long since left
the potting compound for the forge. Leaving his
father's house, he had sensed Sartor-ban-ea-Sar
awakening. In the compound his Ri soul alone had
animated his body; in the forge his Tas soul would
reign alone and unchallenged; but as he walked the
winding streets his twin souls fought for dominion.

He walked in silence, Sartor-ban-i-Tresh and Sartor-ban-ea-Sar cooperating to keep their struggle for mastery hidden.

Surely we'll have time to stop and tell Rafti, Sartor-ban-i-Tresh pleaded. She'll be glad to know that the Royal Eunuch accepted all the pots I made for it.

Sartor-ban-ea-Sar ignored the potter. Moth continued on.

When Moth emerged from the compound, Sartor-ban-i-Tresh had been strong, confident. Stolid, pure, and patient, the potter was at first undisturbed by Sartor-ban-ea-Sar's feeble malice and petty assaults; but as Moth approached the forge the potter found himself beset with doubts, his confidence and strength slipping away from him, while the smith's offensive grew ever quicker and subtler, ever more effective against the slower-witted potter, until Sartor-ban-i-Tresh longed for the oblivion he would find in the forge.

Moth was making silver wire. He had hammered the metal into a sheet of thin foil, then cut it into strips; now he was hammering the strips into shape in a V-shaped stone mold.

He heard the slow, heavy footsteps, felt his stomach knot. He looked up. Tas No was standing there scowling at him.

He put down the hammer. "What's wrong, Grandfather?"

"Does the work I give you displease you? Are you *bored,* grandson?"

"No, Grandfather, not at all. I don't understand. Have I done something to anger you?"

"On the day you pulled your soul silver from the

flames I heard a voice."

"I too heard it." He tried to keep his excitement out of his voice.

"The voice said you were destined to become a great weaponsmith. And your soul silver took the shape of a blade."

"Then—"

"A weaponsmith is not just a Master Smith, Sartor-ban-ea-Sar, not just an artisan like your father, no matter how supremely skilled he may be. We are a Sil within the Sil: the Ras Syrr, the Warriors of Sartor's Thirst. For just as Sartor delights in beauty, so He delights in war, in killing and bloodshed. The joy a warrior feels when he falls upon an enemy and destroys him is Sartor exulting within him, and the blades that we forge for His warriors are the tongues with which Sartor Himself tastes that enemy's blood and death.

"Yet there is an aspect of this killing for Sartor's delight that means, not death, but life for the Ras Syrr. A warrior dies and is gone, never to return. But a weaponsmith who forges a blade that delights Sartor is granted life eternal in a realm of undying fire. A life sharp and shining as any sword."

Moth waited for the old man to continue, finally asked, "And how does one forge such a blade, Grandfather?"

"If a smith forges his own death into his blades, the warriors wielding them will achieve heroic feats of arms and Sartor will be delighted."

Tas No paused again, studying Moth's face. "You have it in you to become a great weaponsmith, Sartor-ban-ea-Sar. I have watched you in the forge. The hammer and anvil love and obey you; they whisper their secrets to you. I would not see them reduced to the manufacture of trinkets and pretty rivets for clay pots."

"Then make of me a weaponsmith, Grandfather!"

"I cannot. You are still Ri, still a potter's son. And no potter can work copper, not brittle copper, not ordinary copper, not the secret copper. No potter can become a Ras Syrr and forge his death into a blade."

"Yet the voice said I was to become a weaponsmith."

"True. Were you not Ri—"

"But I have been sealed to the clay, Grandfather! How can I not be Ri? Tell me how!"

"Sartor-ban-ea-Sar, have *you* been sealed to the clay?" Tas No turned back to Moth and stared into his eyes, his face closed, hidden.

He looks so tired, Moth thought. He said, "No, but—but I have two souls, Grandfather. My other soul is sealed to the clay."

"A pity. So long as you remain Ri, you can never become a weaponsmith. And I would be stealing from your father his only son if you were to renounce the clay in favor of the forge."

"If I . . . renounce the clay, I won't be able to make the—things the Royal Eunuchs want. And then Father won't be able to meet Snae Tka's demands. . . ."

"True, grandson. All true."

"If I renounce the clay, the Ri Sil will hate me for it, hate *him* for having put me on the path toward it—"

"Yes. And I love your father as you love him,

grandson. I would not see him harmed."

"Yet—I want to become a weaponsmith, Grandfather. I *must.*"

"I cannot make of you a weaponsmith, Sartor-
ban-ea-Sar. Not while your other soul remains
sealed to the clay.

"But if I—"

"Ask me nothing unless you are sure you want to
know the answer!"

"If I could free my other soul from the clay,
Grandfather?"

"Free your other soul from the Ri without bringing dishonor upon yourself or our Sil, Sartor-ban-
ea-Sar, and I will make of you a weaponsmith."

"How can I?"

"That you must discover for yourself. Perhaps it
cannot be done; perhaps it would require the death
of your potter's soul. But, grandson, before you
think any further on this, consider your father: Ri
Tal, my daughter's husband, a man with only you
for a son. Consider your father."

"Perhaps I could find a way to help him with his
taxes—"

"He would not accept your help."

"Why?"

"Because if you renounce the Ri Sil, you renounce him. Destroy your potter's name and you
destroy his only son. I am prepared to brave his
anger, to live with his hatred for the rest of my life;
I am a smith, and the voices of the forge have told
me what I must do. But you, you to whom the
choice is still open—are you ready to give up your
family, to renounce your father, to never again
know the love of your mother?"

"Grandfather, I—"

"No! This decision is yours, not mine; I want no part of it. I have said what I had no choice but to say, yet it is vile to me. We will speak no more of this until you are ready to learn weaponcraft—or ready to renounce it forever. Do you understand me?"

"Yes."

"Remember, do nothing to dishonor yourself, Sartor-ban-ea-Sar. Do nothing to bring dishonor upon me."

The old man turned away, took a few slow steps, turned back. "And remember too, grandson, that I love your father. I would see him happy if I could."

On the street, his two souls contending within him.

"RiTas Moth!"

Tramu's voice! He spun around, feeling the joy rising within him, uniting potter and smith— But there was only Yeshun, Ri Yeshun now, hurrying toward him.

"Did you hear about it yet?"

"About what?" Moth said dully.

"The Prince. Prince SarVas."

"No."

"He's dead. A lion—"

"A lion killed the Prince?"

"That's what I've been trying to tell you!"

Tas Et's elation blazing like the sun within him, turning his muscles to water, blotting out his thoughts. He felt the fear beginning, felt it cutting the puppet strings that united him to his body.

"Sartor's luck, Yeshun!" He had to get away, find a place to hide while he still could. He ran, teeth clenched, ducked through an alleyway onto another street. No time to get back to his parents' house. He had to hide. He had to—

There. That house. His only hope.

In through the doorslit. To his right the sound of a child crying, a mother soothing it with a rhyme. He darted left.

An empty room, dark, cool. Then the spasms took him and he fell.

⤙❧ Chapter Twenty ❧⤚

It was dark. Tas Et was gone. The dirt floor was cool against his cheek. He tensed flaccid muscles, listened: nothing. He pushed himself up to a sitting position, discovered a blanket covering him.

He froze, listening, his eyes darting back and forth in the darkness. Making as little noise as possible, he got to his feet, started to slip out of the house, then hesitated, returned and folded the blanket.

Once outside, he looked quickly back, trying to fix the house in his memory, then made his way to his father's house.

Ri Tal was waiting for him.

"Father, I—"

"I know."

"Who—?"

"It's not important. A woman once friend to my brother."

"My—secret is safe?"

"For the moment. Her husband will keep silence —this time. But if you keep on—"

"I know. Did—did your friend say what I did?"

"You don't remember?"

"No."

"She told Kuan she found you lying on her floor. She thought you were asleep at first, but when she tried to wake you, you were all rigid, like a piece of wood."

"My eyes. Did she say if my eyes were open?"

"No. Moth—"

"I know. If I don't stop my fits I'll end up in the cage. Like your brother."

"Yes."

"But I can't stop! I can't do anything about them!"

"I don't think you've tried."

"What do you mean, Father?"

"How have you tried to bring your two souls to peace with each other?"

"I can't talk about it."

"True. Then listen to me. You have two souls, your dolthe and your soul-in-silver, and your two souls are always struggling for mastery. It's like a marriage—like my marriage with Kuan. Harmony comes only after the birth of a child."

"A child?"

"Yes. You are Ri, and you are Tas; both dolthe and soul-in-silver dangle from your neck. But you are also RiTas, and you wear no talisman to embody your RiTas's soul."

"Then I have three souls, not two?"

"In a way. And this violence within you will cease when the third soul has a name and a talisman of its own. You must name it, you must devise its proper embodiment, for there is no one else who can do this for you."

"I have to go outside," Moth said. "Far from the compound and the forge, where no one can see me. I need to think about what you've said."

"Make sure no one sees you."

"I will."

He wandered down to the river, turned left, and made his way toward the barley field his mother now worked without his help. There was a half-moon and the sky was clear, so he could see to walk.

He sat down in the center of the field, where the tall grain would hide him. The barley was beginning to bend under its own weight. His mother was late in harvesting it.

He could put it off no longer. Tas Et! he cried within himself. And Tas Et came to him.

First there was the fear. Only flight could save him, but he was trapped in an unmoving skin of ice, his muscles as helpless as worms struggling to escape a jar.

Then the vision: his uncle twisting on the blood-stained stake, the pain-mad eyes staring him in the face. And he was caught up in the spasm, convulsing, choking on blood from his bitten tongue as his body tried to thrust the vision from it, tried to shield itself from the agonies.

Finally it was over and his uncle was only a presence in his mind. He spat blood.

Uncle, each time you come I risk discovery and the cage. I cannot fulfill my oath to you in the cage.

I die on Tvil's stake, nephew: you have not provided me with proper embodiment. I am a weaponsmith, a coppersmith: no soul of silver will contain me.

Then Father was right? You need a third talisman to house you?

Yes. But not like your father wants. I am a smith calling down his death-curse: only a weapon will do.

I can make you a blade of gold or silver—

A lady's blade, perhaps, studded with jewels? No. Only a blade forged from the secret copper can contain me. Nothing else.

Then—

You must cut your ties to the Ri. Or face the cage.

What right do you have to make me do this?

Right? I cannot die until my vengeance is complete. And you have sworn an oath upon your anvil to aid me. You are useless to me in the cage.

What of my father? My father, whom you loved as a brother? If I renounce the clay, I take from him his only son, I take from him his honor, and reduce him to poverty. Can you who loved him do this to him?

I do what I must. Look:

And Moth was looking out of his uncle's eyes, down at Tramu crouching frightened and trembling in the cage, Pyota lying by his side. Pyota's eyes were closed and she seemed to be sleeping, but Tramu was staring up into Moth's eyes.

I have called down my curse on Tvil, nephew. I cannot find rest until my vengeance is complete.

What if I fail you?

Then I must find another instrument.

I am Ri as well as Tas; I am sealed to the clay. How can I renounce it?

You cannot. You can only profane it so that it

casts you out. You can only kill that in you which is Ri.

I cannot.

You must kill every claychild that comes from your hands. Kill the claychildren with a metal blade, a blade you have consecrated to the Earth Mother, so that She will know that it is not Her that you are rejecting.

But to kill Her children—

With a blade of consecrated metal. Only with a blade of consecrated metal. Make it of gold if you can, silver if you must. Every clay vessel to come from your hands must be pierced and killed while it is still soft.

Father needs me.

He cannot have you. Your oath comes first.

I cannot.

It will be better if your father does not learn what you are doing until it is over. Patch the holes you make with fresh clay: your vessels will not revive, but he will not know the difference. You must take care, though, not to profane his potting compound while you profane yourself. The Earth Mother would not forgive you that.

But to kill Her children, like a midwife slaughtering infants—

She is the Mother of All Weapons, potter's son. She eats the bodies of men slain and buried. She understands death and dying.

But they are mine as well as Hers. I cannot kill them without killing part of myself.

Myself. I'm Moth, he realized. Not just Sartorban-ea-Sar or Sartor-ban-i-Tresh. Moth. My father's son, my grandfather's grandson. Me.

I can't kill myself, uncle. I can't.
You must.

"Have you found what you needed to find?" Ri Tal
asked Moth when he returned home.

"No . . ." He paused, swallowed. His tongue
hurt. "Not yet, Father."

"You can't wait any longer, son. I don't want to
lose you like I lost my brother."

"The cage."

"Yes."

"Rafti?"

"Moth! Come in. Are you on the way to your
grandfather's?"

"Yes. I have to help him with something for the
new Necropolis. But I can stay a little while to talk
to you. Are your parents around?"

"Mother's in back. Would you like some barley
beer to warm you for the forge?"

"Yes. Thank you. Your father's not here?"

"He's working in Tas Okar's forge," Rafti said.

"It's all right, the two of us here alone? I know
smith custom is different, but—"

"Very different, yes."

"Good. I wanted to see you, talk to you, but I
couldn't bear listening to him gloating about my
uncle today. . . ." Moth shook his head. "I'm sorry,
Rafti. I shouldn't insult your father."

"He's my father."

"I know."

"But . . . Moth?"

"Yes?"

"I think about Tramu sometimes. I'm sorry."

"Rafti . . ." He reached out to touch her hand. She pulled away.

"Father's right to be angry, after the way they sneered at him, and then let the Nomads steal the sword from them and all. But I'm not angry."

"I'm glad you're not angry. I miss Tramu."

"I don't. I'm glad I'll never see him again; it's just that . . . Moth?"

"What?"

"Do you ever think about your aunt? All she did was marry the man your grandfather told her to marry, and now she's a tongueless slave. Maybe she's dead."

"You're afraid that I—"

"I like you well enough, more than I thought I would," Rafti said quickly. "I like talking to you. But you'll never be the smith Tramu would have been."

"No."

"And look what happened to him."

Moth was suddenly afraid for her. If I fail while trying to avenge Tas Et, he thought, or even if I succeed—what will they do to her?

"Grandfather, I—I want to . . . but I can't, I—"

"Have you done all that needs to be done, Sartor-ban-ea-Sar?"

"Not yet, Grandfather. I need help, I—"

"No! I told you never to speak to me of this again until you were ready, did I not?"

"Yes, Grandfather."

"Then be silent! Your decision is your own; your problems are none of my affair."

"But—"

"Silence!" Tas No spat upon the ground. "You are unfit to work in my forge today, Sartor-ban-ea-Sar. Leave me. Now. If tomorrow you can act as a smith should act, then return. If you cannot, then do not return at all."

"I will return tomorrow, Grandfather."

Tas No turned away, but not quickly enough to keep Moth from seeing the tears glistening on his dark cheeks.

A daysixth remained until sunset. Moth did not have the courage to return home. He could not face his father.

Whom he loved. Whom he had no choice but to betray.

Habit guided his footsteps to the Great Square. He found himself standing before the Potters' Shrine. Perhaps if he . . .

No. He dared not enter.

He hated himself for his weakness.

As he turned away from the Warriors' Wall, he saw Sklar Ton glaring at him from across the square.

He knows about Tas Et, Moth thought. But he said I'd fail. So there's no reason to try. I can just—

He had given Tas Et his oath. And he could not deny the necessities of his own hatred.

The Warrior of the Voice guarding the Tas Shrine told him that the only coin he had was insufficient, and would not let him enter.

He wandered away.

"RiTas! Moth!"

"Hello, Elgar." A weaver's son, slightly younger than Moth, with the features of conquered Drea-

'Est: wide-spaced black eyes, huge pendulous ears, an almost lipless mouth.

"Did you hear about the Necropolis King Tvil's building for his son?"

"A little," Moth said.

"It's going to be right near here, up in the hills."

"I know."

"Did they ask your father to make something for it?"

"Yes."

"They asked my father too. What's your father making? Is it going to be a coffin like he made for King Asp?"

"No. The coffin is going to be gold and copper. Father's making vases. For the Prince's wife's handmaidens."

"For their water-of-life?"

"No. King Tvil had him do that for his father's necropolis, but Father is just making vases for the handmaidens this time."

"That doesn't sound like very much, for a man like him."

"There are going to be seven times seven handmaidens."

"I'd forgotten. Have they chosen them yet?"

"They haven't even found a bride for the Prince. Look, Elgar, I'm in a hurry. I've got to go."

"They didn't ask you to make anything?"

"No. Luck, Elgar."

"Luck, Moth."

Vases. Pretty, useless vases.

Chapter Twenty-One

"Grandfather," he had said, "there is something I must do alone in your forge." And without questioning him, Tas No had gone.

Moth had not eaten for two days and his throat was dry, dust-tickled. It was forbidden to drink water on a day of beginning.

Tas Et had specified the sacrifice: a ground-dwelling shrew, brown like the earth. Moth killed it on the anvil with the triangular sacrificial blade of chipped flint. The tiny animal's blood went to the Earth Mother; its body he burned in the furnace.

From a mixture of beeswax and resin he shaped a slender three-sided blade the length of his hand. He kneaded powdered charcoal and clay together to form the cylindrical core around which he would mold the hilt, then coated it with the wax and resin mixture and joined it to the blade.

Tas Et guided the hand holding the knife as Moth carved the wax blade into its final form. More and more Moth found himself surrendering control, letting his uncle's ghost take over.

He added short branches of beeswax to the form

and coated the whole with a paste containing finely powdered charcoal. Then he carefully pressed moist clay against and around it, so that only the branches protruded.

Some days later, when the mold was dry, he again asked to be left alone in the forge. This time the sacrifice Tas Et had demanded he make was a dirt adder, a small, mildly poisonous, amber-colored snake with a blunt horned nose and eyes of the clearest gold. Though Moth had captured it without being bitten, it slipped from his grasp as he was taking it out of its basket and sank its stubby fangs into his left thumb. He sacrificed it immediately on the anvil, but by the time the furnace fires had consumed its body his whole hand was swollen and painful.

He allowed the sacrificial fire to die, then made a fresh fire of sari-grass charcoal in the furnace and melted gold in a clay crucible. His grandfather had given him the gold without asking the use to which he was going to put it.

Removing the crucible from the flames with a pair of tongs, he poured the molten metal into the clay mold. The wax melted, ran out the sprues; the gold took its place.

When the metal was hard, he broke the mold and removed the golden knife. The branches had to be cut off and the surface smoothed with a file, but even clumsy as he was with his wounded hand, that work was over all too quickly.

He plunged the blade into a bath of urine and plant juices, purifying the golden surface. He was finished.

He had a swollen, discolored hand he could not

take to a physician for treatment, that he would not be able to use normally for twelve days. He had a dagger whose only purpose was to kill that part of himself that made him his father's son.

I prefer to die, smith. I have no desire to take part in your vengeance. I do not wish to see all those I love punished for your hatred.

We swore an oath to Tas Et, potter.

You swore an oath, smith.

My oath is your oath. We are RiTas. Together, not different.

Then kill me, Sartor-ban-ea-Sar. If I do not die, we both die. And you cannot carry out your oath from the cage.

You are me, potter. They cannot make me kill myself. I'll find a way to save you.

There is no way. Kill me.

I cannot. In the potting compound, you wake and I sleep. You must kill yourself.

Sartor-ban-i-Tresh had hidden the blade in his father's potting compound. The ceremonies with which he had introduced the blade into the compound without profaning the enclosure had been both difficult and painful, but Sartor-ban-i-Tresh had performed them successfully: Ri Tal continued to make living vases without realizing that anything had changed.

The presence of the blade had given Sartor-ban-ea-Sar life in the potter's compound. But he refused to act.

And Sartor-ban-i-Tresh could not bring himself to use the blade.

Summoning up his courage, Moth entered the Potters' Shrine. He handed the hooded Warrior of the Voice an auber and prostrated himself three hundred and sixty times before the unfired clay image of Sartor.

Sartor, he pleaded, All-Highest, Merciful Patron, grant me guidance. Help me, tell me what to do.

But no voice spoke from the air, no decision crystallized. The idol's red-brown features remained closed to him.

He left the shrine in disgust. There was nothing for him there.

The image in the Shrine of the Smiths was all of copper, save only the eyes of gleaming gold. Sartor had twelve arms, but only two hands. In one hand He held a beautiful bowl of embossed silver, in the other a golden fan. His other ten arms ended in gleaming blades.

Moth paid the hooded Warrior of the Voice four aubers and knelt before the image. Again he asked guidance, and again his prayer went unanswered.

The days passed, became weeks, months. A bride was chosen for Prince SarVas, to accompany him to Sartor's Royal Realm, where the Kings of Chal enjoyed eternal youth. Moth saw her being driven through the streets in a four-wheeled chariot; she was plump, dressed in shimmery Deltan fabrics, with exquisitely fine features and great round amber eyes. Her name was Daersa. She was the Prince's cousin, and she was ten years old.

Moth thought she looked very proud and very brave.

* * *

Ri Tal invited Tas No to dinner. From the beginning the meal went awkwardly, with short stretches of frantic conversation punctuated with long silences. Carya, usually quiet, spoke a great deal; her conversation was harmless but painfully stupid, and Moth could not help but think how poor a substitute she would make for his own mother.

Ri Tal told Tas No that he thought Moth would have to make himself a third soul talisman. Tas No looked away from him and agreed that it might be a good idea. The old smith drank too much, and Moth and Carya had to help him home.

Ri Tal finished the last of the forty-nine vases for Princess Daersa's handmaidens.

Not all the maidens had yet been chosen. Though rewards were being offered, and the title "King's Friend"—which carried with it the right to wear a copper dagger even if the man receiving the title was not a warrior—was to be bestowed on every man whose daughter was accepted by the Princess, yet more than twenty of the vases Ri Tal had made remained unclaimed.

"Why?" Ri Tal demanded of Tas No. Moth, Kuan, and Ri Tal were sitting with the old smith in the latter's courtyard. "A glorious death, their families enriched and ennobled, eternal life—what more could they ask?"

"Had I died like that, I would never have known you, Tal," Kuan said. "I would never have had a son, nor been able to comfort my father in his age."

"I'm not yet that old." Tas No's voice was weary. He used to be so strong, Moth thought. But now

. . . It's King Tvil's fault. The King and the Nomads.

"A few minutes of discomfort, then eternal life," Ri Tal was saying. "Surely that's little enough price to pay."

"Would you want to be there yourself?" Tas No asked. "Kneeling there in the pit while they piled dirt over you?"

"I? No. I have my pots, my Sil, my potter's chance at immortality. But for a woman—what could her short life have to offer her that could compare with eternal life in Sartor's Royal Realm?"

"Perhaps that would be true of a potter's daughter," Tas No said.

"But you had two daughters once, didn't you, Grandfather?" Moth demanded. "You had a daughter who married, married well; and yet they killed her husband and tore out her tongue and made her a slave. A life well worth the living, a great cause for rejoicing."

"I have one daughter," Tas No said slowly, not meeting Moth's eyes. "And she comforts me in my old age. I am glad I did not have to grow old without her."

❦❧ Chapter Twenty-Two ❦❧

Sartor-ban-i-Tresh picked himself up off the ground of the potting compound.

The blade, Tas Et whispered. Use the blade.

I can't. Not yet.

You must.

"Sartor-ban-i-Tresh." His father's voice.

Moth turned, said, "Father?"·

"Every day I watch your fits get worse. You sit silent and trembling for hours, you flee in terror with no one in pursuit, and when the fits hit you— If you could see the hatred on your face, your body tearing itself apart—"

"I know what I must look like." His voice was harsher than he'd intended.

"I fear for you, son. Yesterday I went to the shrine in the Warriors' Wall and implored Sartor to reveal a way of helping you."

"And?" Sartor-ban-ea-Sar's impatience.

"Nothing was revealed to me."

I'll find a way, potter.

There is no way, smith.

"You can't help me, Father. Don't even try. Only

I can do what needs to be done."

"Then do it. Before I lose you as I lost my brother."

The blade, Tas Et insisted.

No.

"Kuan! What's wrong? You look ill."

"I'm not sick. But Tal, I saw two Nomads today. Here—in Kyborash!"

He took her hand. "But the warriors—"

"Tal, they were *talking* to a Warrior of the Voice. All three of them laughing together."

"They're Kuqui, Father," Moth said. "Here to sell us a piece of sky metal."

"What do they want for their metal?" Ri Tal asked.

"I don't know," Moth said. "But Grandfather says Tas An Sil's fool enough to give them whatever they ask."

"Do you know, Kuan?"

"No. But they shouldn't be here."

Moth's family was eating dinner with Rafti and her parents in the central courtyard of Tas Gly's house when the fit took him. It was sudden, totally unexpected: he was chewing a piece of smoked fish when Tas Et's death agonies exploded in his mind, and then he was twisting on the stake, looking out on the Great Square, down on his wife and son where they crouched in the cage.

Why? he demanded. Why, uncle?

To teach you hatred.

Hatred of you?

Hatred is hatred.

He came out of it abruptly. He was lying on his side, his right leg curled under him, the smell of his urine sharp in the air. Rafti was holding his hand. He kept himself from moving, listened.

"You have no choice," Ri Tal was saying. "Where else will you find Rafti a husband?"

"Better no husband at all than a husband in the cage!" Rafti's mother.

"There are no other young smiths in Kyborash," Ri Tal said.

"Do you think I need you, any of you?" Tas Gly demanded. "Your family— First we're not good enough—not good enough for a tongueless slave! And now you're trying to force your demon-struck son on us!"

Moth squeezed Rafti's hand, felt her return the pressure. He got to his feet, turned to face Tas Gly.

"It is a sickness for which I know the cure, futurefather," he said, knowing already the futility of his words. "The sickness will pass from me, and soon."

"Are you all right, son?" Kuan demanded.

"Yes."

"I am not your father," Tas Gly said. "I will never be your father."

"When his sickness passes—" Rafti began.

"No," Tas Gly said again. He smiled.

"What of your daughter?" Kuan demanded.

"What of my honor? A madman for a son-in-law —what renown your drooling son would bring me! 'There goes Tas Gly,' they'd say, 'you know, the one with the son-in-law who soils himself.' No! Never!"

"You're not a rich man—" Ri Tal said.

"Perhaps not—but I am a proud man. Too proud

to give my daughter to your demon-possessed son! First your brother, now your son, it must be some-thing in your blood, potter, some filthy taint. Do you think I want grandchildren like that? Do you think I'd sell my honor for *that?*"

"What of me, Father?" Rafti asked, her voice a sudden softness after his.

"My daughter's beautiful, isn't she?" Tas Gly asked, turning to Kytra. "As you were at her age."

"She made you little enough money as a hiero-dule," Kuan said.

"True—but her beauty will suffice to make her a valued ornament to Prince SarVas's court."

"Father!" Rafti stared at him, suddenly gone pale.

"No," Moth said. "You can't."

"Can't I? The decision is *mine,*" Tas Gly said. He turned to Rafti. "You are my daughter. You will obey me in this, as in all else. I would rather see you dead than have you bring dishonor upon your family."

"Mother—?" Rafti asked. But Kytra only clenched her jaw, shook her head.

"The honor of my family demands it," Tas Gly said. *"My* family, not yours. We may not be weaponsmiths, we may not eat at the King's tables, but we don't end up spitted like meat, either.

"And you," he added, smiling at Moth, "I'll see you in the cage."

"She is smith-born," Kuan said. "She should not be forced to forsake her proper eternity, not even for the Royal Realm."

"How can we make him stop?" Moth demanded.

"We can't. There is nothing we can do. Were Father still Sil Smith, perhaps. But he is only Tas No now, and Tas An Sil will do nothing. Rafti is Tas Gly's unwed daughter; he alone may decide her fate. But what he does is evil."

"That's all you can do? Any of you? Just *say* it's evil?"

"Both Sil law and the laws of Chal give him the right," said Kuan.

"Then they're evil."

"No, but— No. The law is hard, but only men are evil." She reached out and took Moth's hand. "I liked Rafti. I would have been happy to have her for a daughter-in-law. I'm sorry."

Sartor-ban-i-Tresh took the golden blade and stabbed the soft clay bowl. The blade slid in between his ribs, pierced his heart, ripped through his lungs: suicide.

The leather-hard vase, the figurine he had only begun to shape . . . again and again he killed himself.

I can't—

And Sartor-ban-ea-Sar helped him.

The golden dagger drank; Sartor-ban-i-Tresh died. And with the potter's passing, the one who survived felt all joy, all charity, all hope of warmth drain from him.

Sartor-ban-ea-Sar hid the blade beneath his sil-tunic, feeling its warmth against his side.

Ri Tal saw him as he left the compound. "Son—"

"No longer," Sartor-ban-ea-Sar said. His tears were drying; he felt hollow, numb. An empty husk.

Ri Tal's face went rigid. "I don't understand."

Moth held out the triangular blade so his father could see the damp clay on it. "Sartor-ban-i-Tresh is dead. You murdered him with your ambitions for him."

Ri Tal looked at the dagger. "You could have had honor and eternal life."

"No. I would have died in the cage. As your brother died."

Be kind to him, the dagger whispered. He loved me while I lived. He tried to do his best for me. For us, smith.

Moth reached up and took the darsath from his neck, held it out to Ri Tal. "Here. His body: all that remains of your son. I know you meant him no harm; you did not know the path you chose for him would kill him.

"Here. Take it. Bury him if you like."

Ri Tal took the darsath. Moth turned and walked away.

Thank you, smith, the dagger whispered.

"Make me a weaponsmith, Grandfather. Tas Gly has called for the exorcist, and my fits will not stop until I house my soul in copper."

"You have done what had to be done?"

"Yes."

"And you have brought no dishonor upon yourself or upon the Tas Sil?"

"No."

"Then I can make of you a weaponsmith. Though you will find it more burden than joy."

"Tas Gly—"

"Your initiation as a weaponsmith has begun,

grandson, and he cannot have you tested until it is over."

He handed Moth a stone knife, a small copper bowl. "I will need enough of your blood to fill that bowl. Then I want you to leave the city for the rest of the day, to give me time to notify the Sil."

Moth nodded. He scored a deep, ragged line up the inside of his left forearm with the stone knife, caught the blood in the bowl.

"There was no need to cut yourself so deeply, grandson."

"It doesn't hurt."

"It should." Tas No coated the wounded arm with a poultice of river mud and snarl grass, bound it tightly with scarlet linen.

"Return at sunset," he told Moth when he had finished. "I will meet you outside the West Gate."

Prince SarVas's Necropolis was being constructed less than a half day's walk from Kyborash. A great pit had been dug and chambers of fire-hardened brick constructed to house the Prince and his retinue, his bride and her attendants. Warriors of the Voice were chanting as slaves levered slabs of stone down to cover the rooms; other slaves were heaping soil over the roofed chambers.

Moth watched them work, his wounded arm throbbing with a pain that might have been someone else's. By the time he had to return to Kyborash, only two sloping ramps remained unburied.

The night that caught him just outside the city's

gates was cold, painfully clear. And when he pressed the copper initiation mask Tas No gave him to his face, the chill metal stole the life-warmth from his soul.

◖❀ Chapter Twenty-Three ❀◗

That night the dream began:

Neither sun nor moon to light the landscape, only the stars glinting cold and hard overhead, blind, frozen eyes, staring down at him in mindless hatred, their light illuminating nothing. Yet he can see:

A limitless plain, covered with grass whose dry, brittle blades he crushes underfoot as, turning slowly around, he looks out in all directions from his high place. A plain stretching on and on without end, bounded by no horizon, everywhere the same.

Except here where he stands, a high place, grass-covered like the plain, neither hill nor mountain.

Perhaps he is moving. A cool, dry breeze blows in his face from whatever direction he chooses to regard, ruffling his hair, stroking his bare skin. As if he were rushing over the grassy sea in an invisible coracle that takes its direction from his gaze.

But he has no object for his gaze, no destination. There is nothing but the plain. His momentary exultation fades: his gaze controls nothing.

He is only compelled to look into the wind,

unable to look away from it. And as the wind shifts back and forth, he is compelled to turn with it.

The stars are building a city on the plain. Fingers of cold light reach out from them, and where the light brushes the plain a paving stone, a section of wall, a man's leg appear.

The wind shifts. Moth turns away from the city, gazes out over limitless grassland.

The wind shifts, and he can see the city again, but it is far, far away. No, it is coming closer, he is rushing toward it—

The wind shifts, and there is only the plain.

Shifts.

Shifts again, and he is approaching the city, coming at it from a new angle. He is very close to the city now, looking down upon it.

He recognizes it at last. Kyborash.

Above the city, Sartor's Eighty-four Aspects hang like clouds of bruised shadow.

The wind dies. Fingers of light reach down from the sky through the Eighty-four Aspects, lending them definition as they fill in the final details of the city: the blue godhouse atop the ziggurat, a beggar crouching in the shadow of a wall, two men fishing from a small boat, a bird nesting in an apricot tree.

Moth is moving effortlessly forward, gliding down from his high place like water over a cascade.

He enters the city.

When he comes to the first house, he pauses, looks back over his shoulder. Behind him the plain stretches away to infinity, dry, brown, thirsty. There is no sign of the high place.

He walks the streets of Kyborash, invisible. People pass him, taking no notice of him yet never colliding with him. He can see them speaking to one another, yet he hears nothing, recognizes no one.

When he looks closely at them, he sees filaments of cold light chaining them to the stars.

Some time later he finds himself pausing by a well where a woman is filling a widemouthed jug with water. He glances down at his reflection in the well.

Luminous filaments link his arms, body, legs, head to the stars. He, too, is a marionette. . . .

Awakening, he found Tas No standing over him, his old-man's face creased with worry. The smith was holding a lamp in his left hand; something about the reek of the cheap lamp oil was infinitely reassuring.

"What's wrong? You were moaning, crying out for help. I shook you, but you wouldn't wake up."

"A dream." Moth rubbed his eyes, asked, "Could you understand me? What I was saying?"

"You were trying to escape from something, but you couldn't break free. I was afraid for you."

"Afraid that I was having another fit?"

"Yes. Or that your illness was showing a new face."

"It was a dream, Grandfather. Only a bad dream. Not a fit."

"You're sure?"

"Yes."

Tas No relaxed, tension draining from him like water from a broken vase. "Good. But even so, some dreams are important."

"Not this one. Did Carya . . .?"

"She'll give Kuan the coins at the meeting of the

Women's Mystery tonight. Kuan is sure she can convince Ri Tal that she'd been saving the money for an emergency."

"She won't be able to tell him that again." It was an exercise in duty: he had taken from Ri Tal and Kuan the son whose work would have given them the means to meet Snae Tka's demands, so it was his responsibility to see that the tax collector was paid. And with Tas No's help, he had made a number of gold and silver bowls to sell for them.

But though his dead soul thanked him, there was no joy for him in what he was doing.

"Sartor guard your sleep, grandson."

"And yours, Grandfather."

Moth waited until he heard Tas No snoring again, then got to his feet, dressed hurriedly, and stole from the forge, out through the house and into the street.

Where perhaps Lapp Wur, the exorcist, waited for him. He had put on his copper initiatory mask before leaving the house, but it was a dubious protection now that he had left the routine prescribed for him by ritual.

But he had to do it, despite the danger. Because the ghost of his potter's soul had recognized the plain from another dream. It had been the night of his return from his first clayquest, the night when Sartor was to send him the dream that would determine the shaping of his dolthe, the night before the Seven-Year Festival; and in his dream, a man of clay with a blade of fire-red copper where his right hand should have been had led a horde of Nomads to attack Kyborash.

And that man had been Moth.

Something about the water of the well, the thirsty plain, drew him through the empty streets. There was a bright quarter-moon, and he could hear the river gurgling off to his right. It felt good to translate his tension into movement.

He paused a moment by the well, indecisive, then summoned his courage and bent over it, stared down into it. The light was too dim for him to see · his reflection.

He straightened, looked around. There was no one to see him, but even so he was afraid.

He had to take the risk. Tas Et! he demanded. Uncle! My dream—what does it mean?

Then the fear took him, and the shaking. He saw the stake, felt Tepes Ban slowly stripping the skin from his feet while the musicians played and the King watched and laughed.

Enough, uncle! The pain faded, leaving only presence. My dream, uncle—what does it mean?

It means nothing. Forget it.

The presence faded, was gone.

It means something, the ghost in the dagger whispered. Tas Et was never a potter—he can only understand what a smith understands. This dream was sent to Sartor-ban-i-Tresh by Sartor All-Highest.

You're dead; your dreams mean nothing to me. I am a smith.

Yet you dream my dreams for me now, smith.

Unsatisfied, afraid for some reason to return to his grandfather's house and the safety of the forge, Moth wandered the city. Dawn found him sitting in Ri Tal's barley field. He stood up reluctantly, stretched himself—he was exhausted—and made his way as quickly as he could back to his grandfather's.

Tas No was waiting for him. "If your dream means nothing, why did you risk your life, grandson? Are you an utter fool, to so gamble with everything we have worked for? To throw away what we have bought at such a dear price?"

"The dream meant nothing, Grandfather. But I need the blade to house my soul, I need it soon."

"We leave tonight for the mines. Until then, fast and sleep, grandson."

Sleeping, he dreamed. The same dream, but this time the vision was clear: he saw the chains of cold light binding the people of Kyborash not only to the stars but to one another, and to the very stones of the city.

And when he saw his reflected image in the well, there were a dozen chains of frozen fire binding him to the sky.

He awoke sweating, though it was late in the year and he had slept in the shade of a wall.

In the morning he realized that his left arm had healed completely, with only a faint trace of a scar to show where he had cut himself.

Tell me what the dream means, potter. Why it healed me.

I cannot. I know only that it is important. Sleep again; perhaps you will learn more.

And so he had willed himself asleep, though he feared the dream. And there were more chains, chains not only to the stars but to all those around him, chaining him to the city's stones and bricks, to every man, bird, animal, and tree, and they were all chained as he was to the stars.

Where the stars' luminous chains crossed one another, light pooled in radiant plexuses, and in each plexus one of Sartor's Eighty-four Aspects was limned in terrifying brilliance.

Awakening at dusk, Moth looked up at the sky. At the cold, hateful stars glaring down at him.

Sartor's Nighteyes, watching him.

And still Tas Et told him the dream meant nothing.

❦ Chapter Twenty-Four ❧

Moth donned his mask, left the forge. As he was leaving the house, Carya blocked his way.

"When this is all over," she said, speaking as if to herself alone, "I'll tell him that Rafti doesn't hate him for what happened."

"Silence!" Tas No raised his hand, then lowered it slowly; all contact with a woman during the Tas rituals was forbidden. He gestured, and she moved aside.

They left the house. The people in the streets saw their masks, moved aside to let them pass. No one spoke to them: it was forbidden. The day was cold. Moth grasped his new staff lightly in his left hand.

"He used to be a potter like us, Shuner." A voice behind him: Yeshun. Ritual forbade Moth to take notice, turn around.

"Let him be."

"I'm not speaking to anyone else, just to you, brother. You know, when he took up the Tas I was glad, because I thought he was bringing new honor to our Sil. I was glad to know him then."

"Be silent! He's done you no harm."

239

"But then he threw us all aside so he could be a Tas and have a lovely smith's daughter for a wife. Left his father without the money to pay Snae Tka's taxes, without a son to support him in his old age. We weren't good enough for him, but it seems he wasn't good enough for them, either. Why else would Tas Gly—"

The sound of a blow, a body striking the ground. Shuner's voice: "Let him be, or I'll break your arm. He's done us no harm."

Outside the gate they left the road, traveling parallel to it but not on it. As soon as they were far enough from the road to ensure their privacy, Tas No began to lecture, only the taut control in his voice betraying his tension.

"The best charcoal is made from the acacia tree. The root of the sari grass is also good, as is olive wood, but avoid the sarbatu tree, the duck oak, straw, chaff, and reeds, for they all produce inferior charcoals. The—"

"I know about charcoals, Grandfather!"

"Do you, Sartor-ban-ea-Sar? Do you?" And Tas No continued lecturing as they made their way up through the foothills. Moth tried to listen —something his grandfather told him might turn out to be the secret of surviving the coming ordeal —but his mind kept drifting back to Rafti.

"Do you ever think about your aunt?" she'd asked him. But now it was Rafti who was going to be killed because she'd been given in marriage to the wrong man.

There was a chill hollowness inside him that even anger could do nothing to warm, an emptiness where the person he had known as Moth had been.

Only the golden dagger hidden beneath his siltunic was warm.

They hiked all night and halfway through the day. The sun was bright overhead, but it was almost winter and they were high in the mountains; the air bit, the wind stung.

"We used to use only the blue and green ores," Tas No was saying. "Then a smith reasoned that since certain yellow, gray, and black stones were found a little deeper in the mines from which we took the blue and green ores, perhaps they too could be made to yield copper.

"But when the smiths of that time tried heating the dull-colored stones, they got from them only a glassy black substance. And though they didn't know what it was, they knew it wasn't copper." He paused for breath.

Moth said, "Tell me about the ordeal, Grandfather."

"When the time comes for your ordeal, I'll tell you a story. You will have to prove that you understand it."

"That's all?"

"All I can tell you. Now, when Tas Tyrr—he wasn't yet Tas Tyrr Sil, that came later—had a dream in which Sartor revealed that if he kept the black substance moist for a while he could get it to ripen like cheese, he—"

"What if I turn back now, refuse to go on with this?" Moth demanded, struck by a sudden vision of himself stealing Rafti away from her father, fleeing somewhere with her—

No. There was nowhere to go.

"You cannot. The Sil Council has meant you for

a weaponsmith from the moment you drew your soul silver from the flames: you already know secrets only those to be initiated as Ras Syrr are allowed to know."

"From the moment I drew my soul silver from the furnace?"

"Yes."

"You never told me."

"No. The decision was Tas An Sil's, not mine. I tried to respect your father's wishes."

"Yet the training you gave me—"

"Was to make of you a weaponsmith. Yes. But you could have remained RiTas as your father desired had you so chosen."

"You knew I would not. Could not."

"Yes. I knew."

He had been betrayed. He could feel anger growing, cold and far away, more like something he was observing than something he was feeling.

Control your anger, the dagger whispered. If you had not tried to deny what could not be denied, Rafti might not have to die.

"So when Tas Tyrr soaked it in water, it turned a beautiful green, like malachite," Tas No continued. "And when he tried to smelt it, he found he could smelt it just like the old ores. Which was a good thing, as they were growing scarce."

"And that's why the secret copper's different? Because it's made from this black stuff?"

"No. You'll learn the true reason after your ordeal."

"If I survive it."

"Silence your fears. You call down bad luck upon yourself."

Tell me about the ordeal, uncle, Moth demanded, feeling the spirit's presence. Tell me, uncle.

No. It is forbidden.

By whom, uncle? You're dead; the laws no longer bind you.

Though I die here on the stake, Sartor-ban-ea-Sar, I am a smith; the laws still bind me as they bind you.

"Tell me about a smith's death-curse, Grandfather," Moth said.

"It is forbidden to talk about it outside the Harg."

"The Harg?"

"Where we're going."

"They're not like other mines, then?"

"No."

"What are the mines like where—"

"Be quiet! Your questions will be answered in the Harg, not before."

Tell me about the Harg, uncle, Moth ordered the spirit.

It is forbidden.

Is the Harg like the mines where Tramu is a slave?

Tramu is here, watching me as I twist on this stake.

What are the mines like, uncle? The mines of Nanlasur?

Why are you interested in the mines of Nanlasur? They produce only lead. Nothing fit for the making of weapons.

Tell me about the mines of Nanlasur, uncle.

Only the worst offenders against the Tas are sent

there, nephew. Only those fit for nothing but to be worked to death to repay the Tas for their offenses.

Tramu's there, uncle. Pyota's there.

I see them before me in the cage. Their tongues have been torn out, but I can see the love in their eyes as they watch me—

He's trapped in his own death curse, Moth realized. Frozen in it, like an insect in ice. Is that what the chains are that I see when I dream, being trapped in his dead vengeance?

You, potter! Are you frozen?

No. Tas Et is trapped in his dying. I am dead, and free.

Evening found them on a mountain slope, still far short of their goal.

"I'm sorry," Tas No said. "My old legs can no longer carry me as far and as fast as once they could."

"Then they must have carried you far and fast indeed," Moth said, for once out of sight of Kyborash his grandfather had seemed to regain a little of his former vigor and had surprised Moth with his strength and endurance.

They found a small hollow in the black granite of the mountainside where they could rest undisturbed by the winds. Tas No sprinkled the hollow with the ash from a sacrifice he had performed in preparation for the journey. Then they made rough beds from what leaves and grasses they could find nearby and, wrapping their woolen clothes more tightly around themselves, lay down to sleep.

Riding the wave, prisoner of his gaze. Entering Kyborash. . . .

And now the chains pull him unresisting to the

square where Rafti lies bound to an altar of star-light. No, he wants to scream, no, as Tas Gly leaps and cavorts with the copper dagger in his hand. No! Don't let him, stop him!

His eyes are directed down to his own hands. He sees the luminous chains linking the goldsmith to him: he is the puppeteer, Tas Gly the puppet. Relief washes over him: he can make Tas Gly stop before the jeweler kills Rafti.

But he cannot stop the play of his fingers as he makes Tas Gly yank up the arm holding the knife, for his own fingers in turn are dancing to the commands of the chains that link him to the stars—

And he is a hawk. His feathers black and shiny, his ivory beak hooked and cruel, he has been flying for—how long? A long time, that much he knows, but the beginning of the journey is lost. He had been a man. He is a hawk. But the transformation, the change . . .

He remembers Rafti's death, but it is like something he has been told about, not something he himself has seen. Something that happened long ago.

He flies above an unfamiliar landscape, following a gray hawk, and he has been following the gray hawk since—when? He had been a man, he remembered—No. He had been a man, he remembers staring into the well, seeing the chains *that made him*— No!

He realizes that there has never been a time when he has not flown behind the gray hawk.

When the gray hawk banks right, Moth banks right; when it dips low to the ground or goes into a rapid ascent, Moth is powerless but to do the same.

He sees the ground above which he soars as a featureless brown plain, but with some other sense he is aware of more complex landscapes. Sometimes he knows himself to be gliding low over dense forest, at other times beating his way over desert, then flying over vast oceans, and beyond them once again over the forest. Sometimes his gray guide dips low, flying a circuitous path that Moth knows to be taking them between trees he can sense and not see—

And then, suddenly, inexplicably, a mountain spears the sky.

Moth awoke in terror.

He unclenched his fists. He was stiff, very cold. He levered himself up onto his elbows, got painfully to his feet. His hands were cramped; he rubbed them together, trying to get the stiffness out.

The sky was still black. He began to pace, trying to warm himself.

Potter!

I do not know. But there was a mountain, and we are in mountain country now.

"Rafti—" Too late he realized he had said it aloud.

She still lives. I will know when the time comes for her to go beneath the ground.

The dream, potter. In the dream, I—I did not hold the knife, but I was the one who—

Yes. She dies because of your arrogance, Sartorban-ea-Sar. Because of your cowardice. If you'd helped me die when I should have, she would not have had to die.

She isn't dead yet.

No. But when she does die, she'll die because you killed her.

You did not have the courage to kill yourself either, potter.

No. The guilt is mine as well as yours. But only you survive to bear it, to expiate it.

How?

Ask your dream, smith. I can tell you that much and no more. Ask your dream.

The dagger. If he threw it from him here, in the mountains, where he would never have to see it again, he could rid himself of his ghost's accusations, demands. But he could not do without the warmth, the paradoxical life he felt only in his dead soul's presence. It was as if he were the dead one, warming himself with the voice of the living.

Tas Et, he demanded. The dream—do you still say it means nothing?

This time he was spared the agony, the death scene, felt only the harsh, cruel presence.

It has no meaning. Ignore it.

No longer his uncle. No longer a person. Only frozen vengeance.

Moth continued pacing. A careless step dislodged a pebble that slid, bounced off a boulder before he could catch it, and struck Tas No on the forehead.

The old man's hand went to his head. "Moth?"

"It's all right, Grandfather. I kicked a rock loose. Nothing to worry about. Go back to sleep."

"No. I feel good here in the mountains, even with you throwing rocks at me. I've slept enough."

It took Tas No a while to come fully awake, but after forcing himself through a series of stretches and twists, he took some dry bread from his belt pouch and shared it with Moth.

They resumed their ascent. Clouds were drifting leisurely in from the north, massing overhead, beginning to hide the sky.

Chapter Twenty-Five

The day had grown only slightly warmer when the narrow, switchbacking path down which Tas No had been leading Moth looped back on itself and began to climb.

Moth was sweating. His legs ached and he was short of breath, yet Tas No seemed, if anything, less tired than when they'd started out.

The way led between upthrust walls of close-grained black rock. The walls grew higher, pressing in ever closer, squeezing out the day. It was dark in the shadows, cold.

Tas No motioned for Moth to stop. "Here. Your ordeal. Sit and close your eyes."

Moth sat on the chill stone, closed his eyes.

"I have a story to tell you. You must understand it to survive. It is a very long, very important story, but today I am going to tell you only the parts you need to know to survive the ordeal.

"In the days before the Children of Raburr became the Tas Sil, we were a tribe apart. Only we, of all the peoples in Ashlu, were not subject to the King of Chal, for Sartor had set the smiths apart and we, in our pride, took that to mean that we and we alone need not obey Chal's King.

"The tale of our rebellion is long, but you need not hear it now. It is enough to say that in our rashness and pride we denied Sartor and His husbandman, who in those days was King Ivrat. Our people boasted many Masters of Fire, then as now, and they challenged the King, saying, 'What right do you have to claim dominion over us? What right do you have to claim that only through you is Sartor's will made manifest? Watch, foolish King! Watch, and see what we can do!'

"And as King Ivrat cowered in the safety of his palace, the greatest of the Children of Raburr pulled stars from the sky. Some made their arms very long so that they could tear the stars from the vault of heaven. Others sang such beautiful songs that the stars came to listen, and others pretended to be made of such good meat that the stars were overcome by their hunger and came down to feast. And there were other ways, as many ways as there were Masters of Fire.

"With the light from these stars, the Children of Raburr blinded the lesser kings of Ashlu to the will of Sartor, so that they rebelled against the King of Chal, and forgot they had ever been subject to him. And our people were very proud of themselves.

"But then Sartor appeared to the greatest among the Children of Raburr and spoke to him from his forgefire, saying, 'Foolish smith, you have denied My power, and done that which should never have been done. For this you and all your people shall be punished.'

"But the greatest of all the Children of Raburr

—a man famous in all Ashlu then, though his name has not survived—answered Sartor boldly, saying, 'We have challenged your King and won. Why should we fear you?'

"And Sartor told him, 'You have only done that which it was My will that you should do, nothing more. I, Sartor, wished the lesser kings to rebel against My King so that there would be more fighting and more bloodshed to quench My great thirst.' For though Sartor loves beauty, He delights in war and bloodshed above all else.

"But the greatest of the Children of Raburr denied Sartor yet again, and called Him a false god.

"Then Sartor made to him this challenge: 'If, great smith, you have truly made the lesser kings to rebel against My King of Chal, then the power must be yours to bring them back to him. Do so, and I will admit Myself defeated.'

"'Why should I undo what I have done?' the greatest of the smiths demanded.

"'Because I say that you cannot,' Sartor told him.

"So all the sixty times sixty Masters of Fire of the Children of Raburr stood in a line and tried to take the stars with which they had blinded the lesser kings and return them to the sky. Some sat and sang, some swallowed arrows and made them come out of their bellies. Some swallowed feathers and turtles, and some swallowed whole trees. But they could not take the stars from the eyes of the lesser kings.

"Then Sartor told the Children of Raburr, 'You have rebelled against Me, though you are nothing in My eyes, and for that shall I punish you. No more shall you be masters of your own fate; no longer shall you be great and free.

"'Henceforth shall you be subject to the King of Chal, to live and die at his command, and all your mastery of fire shall be used only in the making of weapons with which his warriors will slay those whom you, in your pride, thought to raise up against him.'

"Of the sixty times sixty Masters of Fire, Sartor killed all but only twelve. And these twelve he sent to beg the pardon of the King of Chal. King Ivrat granted them his pardon, for he knew that such was Sartor's will, and he made them to be the Tas Sil.

"You have heard what you need to know, Sartor-ban-ea-Sar. Think on it while you count to sixty twelve times, then open your eyes and follow the path I will have taken. You will not see me again until you have survived the first ordeal.

"Sartor's luck be with you, grandson."

Soft footsteps, then silence. Moth was alone.

He examined the story while he counted, pulling it apart like a riddle for hidden meanings, but could come to only one conclusion: the tale was a warning not to try to defy the King. A warning that was meaningless unless, somehow, they knew about Tas Et's ghost.

Are they warning me against your vengeance? he asked Tas Et. But the spirit kept silence.

Perhaps they knew a way to release him from his oath. Yet he knew himself empty, the hollow shell of a man, with only his uncle's hatred to fill him; take that away, and he would have nothing left.

He finished counting, opened his eyes. Tas No was gone, as Moth had been sure he would be.

He got to his feet, began picking his way forward through the shadows. The path was beginning to twist, loop, coil back upon itself; in places the rock underfoot was as slick as faience. He kept one hand against the stone of the wall to keep his balance and maintain his sense of direction.

The air was growing warm. A raw, dry stench, faint at first but growing stronger with every step he took, hung in the air.

The stone was almost hot to the touch. There was no light. He slid his feet cautiously forward, unwilling to risk more normal strides.

And then his right foot was out over emptiness. He drew it back, retreated a pace, knelt and explored the floor of the passage with his hand:

Broad steps leading down into the hot, egg-smelling darkness. He crept down them, his hand always against the wall, testing each step before resting his weight on it.

Sixty steps.

Six times sixty steps.

Sixty times sixty steps down into the hot darkness: a great chamber carved from the black rock of the mountain, a doorway cut in its far wall.

Between the foot of the staircase and the doorway was a river of burning rock.

The river was too wide to leap. A bare-chested smith was standing in midstream, seemingly no more troubled by the lava flowing around his belly than he would have been by the waters of the ditches where Moth had once pulled reeds.

"The ordeal is this," he called to Moth. "You must cross."

Chapter Twenty-Six

The lava flowed like sullen mud from a cleft in the right wall out into a straight-sided channel and across the chamber, only to disappear into another cleft in the opposite wall. The walls were smooth, shiny black; the molten rock gurgled, stank, lit the rocks a dull orange.

Moth's skin was dry, beginning to crack. He felt dizzy. But the smith standing in midstream was not even sweating.

Perhaps all I have to do is what I did when I took my soul silver from the furnace. Call upon my hassa. That's why he isn't sweating.

But it was too easy, and it had nothing to do with the tale Tas No had told him. It would prove nothing.

The smith was grinning at some secret joke. Looking at him, Moth knew there had to be some obvious trick to the crossing: he would not have been smiling like that if he'd expected Moth to fail and die.

Perhaps this ordeal was only a matter of form, like his initiation into the Ri. Tas No had not seemed overly worried. Yet something about that felt wrong. . . .

He backed away, retreated up a few stairs. The heat diminished a little. He sat cross-legged on a hot stair, arranging his siltunic beneath him for protection. Closing his eyes, he turned his attention inward and found his hassa, the thread-thin canal of ascending flame pulsing with every breath he took. It was easy to master it, to bend it to his will, feel it dance and expand. . . . The feeling was pure intoxication, a giddy excitement—

He stopped, damped his hassa's fires. It was painful to return to his normal state, to the heat that was slowly roasting him like a piece of meat, but he had to clear his mind.

There was danger in this too-easy mastery. The Masters of Fire had all been destroyed by Sartor, save only twelve. And those had survived by submitting to the King of Chal. But how was he supposed to submit to the King *here?*

Was he supposed to pledge fidelity here, before this smith? But to what point? Yet if the only thing involved was mastering the heat of the lava, why was there a smith standing in the stream?

The smith was the key. He was clearly a Master of Fire, so—

No, his dagger whispered to him. You miss the obvious. The man has red hair; he is a smith. The smiths became the Tas Sil after they submitted to the King of Chal.

So?

You, too, are Tas. You will survive this ordeal not by proving yourself a Master of Fire, but by proving yourself a member of the Tas Sil.

Thank you, ghost.

Moth rose and walked to the burning river's edge. "Guardian," he said, "I am Sartor-ban-ea-Sar of the Tas Sil. Do you have a name?"

"I am known here only as Tas," the smith said.

"What would the Sil have me do to cross?" Moth asked.

"You need only ask and accept my aid. Do you ask it of me?"

"Yes."

"Good. But, young Tas, it is not enough to want to accept my aid. It is not enough to say you accept it. You must have total faith in me, and in what I teach you to cross unharmed. Doubt me even for an instant, and you die. Do you understand?"

"Yes."

"Understanding, do you accept?"

Moth thought for a moment longer, nodded. "Yes."

The smith waded toward him, stepped out of the river onto the bank. Liquid rock ran sluggishly down his legs, pooled at his feet.

"Close your eyes."

Moth pressed them tightly shut.

"Turn your gaze inward, concentrate until you can see your hassa dancing and weaving within. . . . Can you feel it now, feel its beauty, its strength, its eagerness?"

"Yes," Moth whispered.

"What color are the flames?"

It was hard to put a color to them. "Red," he said finally.

"Correct. Now, reach out, take my hand. Good. Feel the heat passing from my hand into yours, feel it as it becomes yours. . . ."

Stars blazed through Moth's closed eyes, piercing him, filling him with cold brilliance.

"Can you feel our hassas entwined, see them weaving and dancing as one?"

"Yes."

"Open your eyes. Can you still see them?"

"Yes."

"Concentrate. The flames are changing color. What color are the flames?"

"Orange. Orange and yellow."

"Good. Now, walk with me. As we walk forward, concentrate on our hassas as they dance and weave. If you have faith, you will feel them, you will see them, and they will keep you from harm.

"Now, take the first step." The smith's hand was dry, reassuring in his. Moth gripped it tightly. "What color are the flames?"

"White."

"Good. Walk with me. The flames are turning blue. Concentrate on them, and we will cross in safety."

Moth stepped forward into the molten flow, concentrating on the twin serpent-columns of flame. The lava hissed, bubbled as he stepped into it, boiled. Was gone.

He stood in an empty riverbed, blinded to all but the twining hassas by the white-hot cloud that filled the chamber.

"Remain unmoving until your hassa burns green."

Moth waited until the green crept from the smith's hassa into the ascending turquoise of his own. He felt the change; the secret of the smith's mastery was suddenly obvious.

"Your hassa burns green: you have a weapon-smith's mastery of fire. Release my hand."

Moth let go.

"You must cross the rest of the way alone, trusting in what I tell you and not deviating by so much as a handswidth from the path I give you. Now. Go."

Moth walked cautiously into the white-hot darkness, now sliding left, now going right, now stepping straight ahead. Before and behind him things slithered and hissed, but he refused to allow them to frighten him, and crossed in safety.

On the far shore, he allowed his hassa to sink from green to blue, from blue to white.

The air rained lava. The molten rock flowed down a gentle slope in the floor of the chamber that Moth had not noticed before and rejoined the lava humping sluggishly out of the cleft in the wall that was now to his right. The channel was full again in a moment, but Moth had had more than enough time to study the great coiled shapes that lived on the riverbed before the lava hid them.

The air was clear of all but a little drifting ash; he allowed his hassa to sink the rest of the way through yellow and orange back to red, then stilled its dance.

"Your grandfather awaits you, Sartor-ban-ea-Sar," Tas said. He was once again standing in midstream. "Continue on, and welcome!"

Moth crossed the chamber, stepped through the archway. The ordeal had been too easy; all he'd had to do was follow instructions. He didn't trust it.

A number of right-angle bends later, the air smelling sweeter with each turn, the corridor led him out onto a tiny terrace of white marble. On either side of him stood a greening copper statue of a smith holding a sword; a flight of steps led down to the ground below.

He was in an immense closed valley, its floor bright with countless greens both soft and vivid, the vertical walls of black stone enclosing it seeming less to confine than to shelter and protect it. A river sparkled in the near distance. The few clouds scattered across the blue of the sky were too small to block the noon sun; in the golden sunlight he could see groves of broad-leaved trees heavy with unfamiliar red fruit, tilled black fields green with the beginnings of some new growth, shade trees lining the river's banks.

There was a pavilion a little to the right of the foot of the stairs, a graceful round structure of dark woods inlaid with copper and gold.

The landscape had an almost feverish intensity to it, as though there were some trick of the air or light that made even the warmest and gentlest of vistas vibrate with crystalline clarity.

It was the loveliest scene Moth had ever seen. The air was warm, springlike; in the silence he could hear the river's muted song, the briefer melodies of the birds.

Perhaps here he could regain all he had thought forever lost. He made his way down the black stairs, the valley's beauty warming him like wine.

I hate this place. Beware it, smith.

Why?

The Earth Mother is not here. The very rocks cry

out in loneliness for Her. And where the Goddess is not, no Ri should be.

What do you have to fear, ghost? You're already dead.

Inside the pavilion he found Tas No sitting on a bench fashioned from an unfamiliar white metal into an intricate pattern of birds and coiling serpents. The old smith was sipping hot tea from a goblet of the same unfamiliar metal, his face flushed and happy-looking; at his feet a redheaded man with the body of a man of the forge but dressed in a robe of green linen was kneeling to feed a tiny fire in a shallow copper bowl with wood chips and what looked like pieces of dried meat.

Grandfather looks younger, Moth thought. As though he's regained what he had lost.

"Sartor-ban-ea-Sar!" Tas No leapt up, embraced him, kissed him on both cheeks. "Sit with me, grandson, as I once sat here with my father, and as he once sat here with my grandfather. I have waited so long for this!"

The red-haired man poured some dark tea from a pot into another goblet of the white metal, and handed it to Moth. Moth glanced at him, sipped the bitter, brackish liquid.

"Then—it's over?"

"Hardly, though you've survived an ordeal that kills many candidates. But I had no fear for you."

"It was easy. Tas told me everything."

"Perhaps you found it easy, grandson. But the fireworms would have stripped your flesh from your bones had you tried to cross with a hassa any color other than green, and even then they would have devoured you had you deviated from the proper path. Because you asked Tas's help, your crossing was easy, but do not be too contemptuous of the insight that led you to seek his aid. Many who come to the ordeal are too stupid or too proud to ask. They die."

Thank you, ghost.

The answer was there within you, smith. I merely helped you see it sooner.

"What must I do now, Grandfather?"

"There are secrets to be learned, things that can only be spoken of here in the Harg. I will help you when I can. Thlal"—he indicated the redheaded man with a nod—"will be your servant while you are here. He is under a vow of silence that prevents him from speaking of his own will, but he can answer any questions you put to him that are proper for him to answer."

A soft breeze was blowing through the pavilion, rustling the leaves of the trees outside.

"When you have learned what you need to know," Tas No continued, "and done that which you need to do, you will make yourself a blade of the secret copper. And having made it, you will face the final test."

"Which is?"

"I cannot tell you yet. But ask Thlal a question: he is here to answer you."

"Thlal, tell me the secret of the smith's death-curse."

The redheaded man turned to him, smiled, went back to feeding the fire.

"He cannot answer you, so he says nothing. Ask him another question."

"Thlal, what is the final test?"

Again the man smiled at him and said nothing.

"Ask him, rather, what he *can* tell you about the final test."

Feeling impatient and somewhat foolish, Moth asked, "Thlal, what can you tell me about the final test?"

"Only this, Sartor-ban-ea-Sar: you will know it when its time comes. And should you fail it, you will not have to die for your failure, but will become as I am now until you find it within yourself to succeed."

His voice was that of a smith, but gentler; somehow Moth found it difficult to imagine him angry. And there was a quietness to his expression that Moth had never expected to see on the face of a redheaded man.

More to hear Thlal speak than out of any immediate desire to have his question answered, Moth asked, "What is your life here like, Thlal?"

"It is . . . very peaceful, but—incomplete."

"I don't understand."

Thlal smiled, looked away.

"What would you advise me to do next, Thlal, if I am not to end up—incomplete—like you?"

"Listen to your mentor. Do as he says."

Moth turned to Tas No. "Grandfather?"

"For the moment we will sit here on this bench and you will listen to me, Sartor-ban-ea-Sar, while I reveal to you the first of the Great Secrets. This can be spoken of here, and nowhere else. Listen:

"There is no secret copper. Its existence is a lie, a lie we have put about to hide the fact that we have a far greater secret. The secret of the Marriage of Metals."

Marriage. Moth thought of Rafti; metal marrying clay and the clay dragging her down, pulling her beneath the ground to rot in SarVas's Necropolis. . . .

"Beyond this valley lies a second valley, and it is in this second valley that we dig our copper. It is excellent copper, but there is nothing strange or different about it. It is just very good copper.

"But in the valley we are in now, there are no mines. There is only the river, the Syrasse, flowing from a cavern high on the cliffs. Yet from the Syrasse we take the bridestone, and from that ore we extract bridesmetal—the metal from which the bench on which you are sitting is made, the metal of the goblet you hold in your hand.

"When the bridesmetal's marriage to her copper husband is consummated in the flames of the furnace, the metal you know as the secret copper is born. And that is our secret, ours and ours alone.

"You've seen the warriors of the Delta, tall and proud with their blades of copper? Laugh at their pride, Sartor-ban-ea-Sar, for their blades are made of copper stolen from slain Chaldan warriors, and they have only enough of it to put on a brave show for us. In their home cities they carry blades of copper little harder than lead, or so brittle it would shatter in any serious fight!"

He's so excited, Moth thought. As though he's forgotten the Festival ever happened. It must be the light or the air here; whatever it is, it's part of him too, it's in him just like it's in everything else here.

Once, Tas No's delight would have meant something to him. But now it changed nothing.

ᏚᎾᎪᏒ Chapter Twenty-Seven ᎨᏬᎾᎪᏒ

Sartor-ban-ea-Sar stood on the river shore, a shallow wooden bowl inlaid with white bridesmetal in his hands. From a wooden bench nearby, Thlal and the slave who had been renamed Moth watched.

Thlal was impassive, calm as always; the slave named Moth was tense, hidden, inward-looking; but Sartor-ban-ea-Sar was smiling. He had been smiling and laughing for two days.

Still grinning, he repeated the appropriate prayer, then bent down and filled the bowl to the brim with gravel. Shaking it gently to settle the earth it contained, he repeated the prayer a second time, then waded out into the stream.

The water was refreshing, cool but not cold. A fog thick and white as doves' wings veiled the surrounding cliffs, bleached the vivid greens of the trees and bushes to softness, and leeched all solidity from even the nearby Thlal and Moth; yet the valley remained as warm as Kyborash in late spring.

Pebbles shifted under his feet as he made his way to the center of the river. The water was shallow, only a little higher than his waist.

Holding the large bowl awkwardly in his left hand, he picked from it the biggest pebbles and chunks of rock, washed them clean in the river, then examined them carefully before tossing them away.

Lowering the bowl to the water, he let the gentle current carry away some of the soil and twigs. He lifted the bowl again and raked his fingers through the remaining gravel, pulling the largest rocks to the surface. One by one he washed them, examined them, and threw them back. After he had examined most of the bowl's contents, he broke up the remaining clods of earth and lumps of clay with his left hand, then lowered the bowl to the water again.

The bowl was a little over a third full of small pebbles and sand. Holding it tipped away from his body, he began to shake it slowly, quickening the motion slightly at the end of each circular stroke. The water climbed the bowl's walls, rolled over the rim, carrying with it excess gravel and soil.

Nearby, veiled by the fog, other smiths were also questing for bridestone. He could hear them splashing around, chanting their prayers in low voices.

Most of the gravel was gone. Without interrupting his circular motion, Sartor-ban-ea-Sar set the bowl to spinning. The remaining chunks of rock began to space themselves out around the rim, the lighter sands racing on ahead, the heavy gold lagging behind, the bridestone in the middle.

He brought the pan to a stop, but he had been too clumsy, and the separation he had worked so patiently to achieve was lost. He tried again, failed again.

He smiled. Tas Et! Guide my hands!

It was not a request.

This time he was able to remove the gold with ease. Another try, and he had most of the other excess matter separated from the bridestone.

Thank you, uncle. I begin to get the feel of it.

The ritual called for him to thank Sartor All-Highest, Sole Patron of the Harg, aloud at this point. He did so, then transferred the brown, fibrous masses of bridestone to the pouch he wore around his neck.

He returned to the shore, scooped the bowl full again.

The sun had been shining brightly two days previously, when he and Tas No had followed Thlal down to the river. Their path took them across numerous tiny bridges of smooth carved woods beneath which clear streams ran; every sixty paces they passed graceful benches wrought of golden serpents and jewel-eyed birds.

They soon came to the fields and orchards where slaves were digging, tilling, weeding, pruning. They were all male, thin for the most part but not starved-looking, and though all of them had been branded and many bore old scars, none of them showed signs of any recent ill-treatment.

Moth's attention was caught by a young, dark-haired man who was pruning a fruit tree. The man was almost as muscular as Moth, though not quite as tall, with a pale squinting face; he wielded the pruning pole with the stone blade at its tip with obvious vigor, and Moth could hear him humming to himself.

They seemed well treated here, well trusted for slaves. Moth only hoped Tramu was being treated equally well.

Considering what Tas Et had told him of the mines at Nanlasur, it seemed unlikely.

If I ever get enough influence in the Sil to have you brought here, I will, Tramu, Moth told himself. I promise.

The banks of the river were lined with trees: gnarled giants with gray-green needles and trunks sticky with sap extending their branches in great fan shapes over the clear water and land alike; stout, smooth-skinned trees with green bark and leaves that were emerald above, rust mottled with gold below; and delicate, narrow-leaved trees with forking trunks and tapering boughs bright with clusters of red berries. Fisherbirds and tiny purple songbirds were everywhere.

Redheaded men were wading in the river. Most of them were young, but some of them looked as old as Tas No.

"Are they questing for bridestone?" Moth asked Thlal.

"Yes."

"Are they here to become weaponsmiths, too?"

"In a way. Like me, they came here to become weaponsmiths but failed their final ordeal, and so remain here. We gather bridestone for the Sil."

As they continued upstream the river grew wider, eventually forming a narrow lake surrounded by pavilions and low wooden buildings. At the center of the lake a great circular structure, all ancient gray stone, rose from the water. Graceful wooden bridges arched to it from the shore.

"The Tower of Three Levels," Tas No said. "The Heart of the Tas Sil."

"It looks ancient," Moth said.

"It is," Tas No said. "The Harg was ours when we were only the Children of Raburr. It was in the Tower of Three Levels that the twelve surviving Masters of Fire pledged themselves to Sartor and vowed to serve the King of Chal. Chal has protected us in turn: It was because the King of Drea'Est dared try to take the Harg from the Tas Sil that King Delanipal made war upon them and overthrew their city.

"For the Tas Sil needs the Harg, grandson. In all of Ashlu, only the Harg is held by Sartor alone, without taint or contamination. And as the Harg is the Body of Sartor in Ashlu, so the Tower of Three Levels is His Heart and His Life. Only in the Tower will He make of a smith a weaponsmith, of a Tas a Ras Syrr."

They had come to a low oval wooden building. "I'll leave you here," Tas No said. "Thlal will tell you what to do. You must be cleansed before you may enter the Tower. The Heart must remain inviolate."

Moth nodded.

"When you finish, put on the new clothing that you will find waiting for you. You must retain *nothing* of your old clothing, and *nothing* that you may have with you. Keep only your soul silver, and that you must wear during your purification, for though it is itself pure, yet it too must be cleansed.

"My purification will be somewhat different

from yours, and will take place elsewhere. I will return for you afterward."

Thlal taught him the appropriate prayers and explained the ritual sequence of hot and cold baths, then remained outside while Moth entered the windowless oval building alone, closing its heavy wooden door behind him. The interior was large, empty, constructed of smooth blond wood; a lamp burned on the far wall, by a second door. In the center of the tiled floor were two pools, one churning with cold water piped in from the river, the other still, but steaming.

A scarlet siltunic and linen undertunic hung from a notched post. Moth began to remove his clothes, looking around for someplace he could hide the dagger.

No! Keep me with you! Do not abandon me here!

Why, dagger? Nothing can harm a ghost. You're already dead.

I am dead, but I am Ri: I am of the Earth Mother, and it is to Her that I must return when I fade. But She is not here; this place has been wrenched from Her by violence, and it is Hell to me. Abandon me here and I suffer for all eternity. Even its touch is agony—and I am you, smith.

You were once me, ghost. I will not abandon you.

And the stake is driven through him, and he hangs there, staring at his tongueless wife and child.

Enough, uncle! Spare me!

"Ah, if only you could make them sing for me, Ban!" he hears the King say.

"Perhaps in time, King of Kings. Life is long and the art is never-ending; who knows what perfections may await us?"

Moth found himself on his knees, picked himself up.

Nephew, you profane the Harg! You have sworn oaths to me and to the Tas Sil: I forbid you this, as your name is Sartor-ban-ea-Sar. I forbid you on the oath you swore on your anvil!

Moth had lost Tramu, Pyota, Tas Et himself. Rafti. And now his other self. For the second time, his other self.

No. He would not.

Why, uncle? What harm would I do?

Nothing of Earth can be permitted to enter the Tower! Nothing!

Why, uncle? What would happen?

Upon the sanctity of the Tower depends the safety of Chal.

How so, uncle?

When the Children of Raburr submitted to Sartor in the Tower of Three Levels, Sartor said to them, "Of you, Masters of Fire, I make the Tas Sil. You shall be the strength of Chal, and upon you I place the burden of its survival. So long as you remain faithful to Me and Mine, for so long shall Chal survive, and your people with it; but should you break faith with Me, I will cast down all Chal, the King and the lowliest slave alike! And then, O Masters of Fire, for whom would your blades drink the life to feed your eternity in My Realm of Eternal Fire? For if Chal is My Body, and your blades are the Teeth in My Jaw, yet the King of Chal is the Life of that Body, and when the Life is fled does the Body crave nourishment, does the Jaw bite?"

Moth's rage was a bright-fanged copper serpent within him, but cold, so cold. So, uncle, he asked, with the fall of the King of Chal, the Realm of Bright Fire falls also?

Yes. Of course. Only in the service of the warriors of Chal can we earn our smith's immortality.

You have sworn me to the destruction of the King of Chal!

Dying here on Tvil's stake, I swear vengeance on him and on all those who love him.

Yet your vengeance will destroy Chal, uncle!

No. Never. Only through Chal do we possess our smith's immortality.

And Tas law forbids me to take the dagger into the Tower of Three Levels?

Yes. Upon the Tower's sanctity depends the safety of Chal.

Moth found himself empty of everything but laughter. He'd lost his family and friends, his wife to be, the Sil to which he'd been born; he'd murdered the self that had been his only warmth and life, and for what? For an oath to something less than a dead man—an oath whose fulfillment would destroy his only remaining chance for immortality.

And it was funny, because none of it mattered anymore. Not his bones of ice, not the death waiting for him when he tried to carry out his uncle's vengeance, nothing. He was pure and empty, like a breeze playing over a mountain snowfield, and he knew himself free. He could kill himself, he could throw away the dagger, he could violate his oaths.

But he would not.

I will honor my oath to you, uncle. Not out of duty, nor out of fear, but to gratify myself with hatred and vengeance until they destroy me. Until they destroy both of us. But I will not let the only soul I have that can take joy in warmth and love spend an eternity of suffering.

You cannot take the dagger into the Tower!

I can. I will.

Your oath—

My oath, uncle, demands the downfall of the King of Chal. What better way to bring it about than by profaning the Tower?

If Chal falls the Realm of Bright Fire is lost forever. I forbid you to profane the Tower!

Who are you to forbid me anything, smith's curse, blasphemy? I will profane the Tower, the better to fulfill my oath to you.

Laughing, he cleansed himself in the pools and dressed in the new clothes. He hid the golden dagger beneath them and left the building by the second door.

Tas No was waiting with Thlal, a great smile on his face. Moth smiled back at him, feeling a joy like singing ice within.

Together the three crossed the bridge to the Tower. Nothing happened at the threshold, nothing happened as the smiths inside greeted them, nothing happened as they sat and shared a meal of raw fruits and soft-cooked grains.

After the meal was over, Sartor-ban-ea-Ndrur, the Tower Sil, took from Moth his usename in a ceremony held on the Tower's lowest level, beneath the waters of the Syrasse, where the eternal flame of the Tas burned in a furnace of precious stones. When Sartor-ban-ea-Ndrur had taken from Moth his usename, he demanded that Sartor-ban-ea-Sar choose a slave to bear it for him. And so, not questioning, he acquired the black-haired man whom he had seen humming to himself as he pruned the fruit trees.

That night, as he and his slave slept in the flickering warmth of the room beneath the river, the dream came over him again:

Riding the wave.

Entering Kyborash.

Tas Gly cavorting with the knife.

And the mountain spears the sky, a towering slag heap all pocked gray stone and black obsidian. Old and cruel, dead and deadly.

The gray hawk circles the mountain, Sartor-ban-ea-Sar close behind. They spiral upward, climbing on untiring wings until they soar above it. Sartor-ban-ea-Sar can see that it is hollow, a cone, with fires pulsing red and orange within.

The lead hawk's feathers catch the fires as it dives and is gone, swallowed up, eaten, and Sartor-ban-ea-Sar, helpless, banks and shoots down into the flames, hearing the sound of a laughter not his own—

Only to awaken to the sound of his own cold laughter.

Outside the Tower the valley was hidden by silver-winged mists. Strange mists, he heard one of the green-clad smiths tell another, in a valley where the sun always shined. But he liked the cool obscurity, the drifting veils, the moisture on his skin. If this was Sartor's vengeance on him for his blasphemy, he was well pleased with it.

I will not abandon you, dagger, he promised. Nor Rafti, Tramu, Pyota—none of you. If I cannot save you, I will do what I can to avenge you.

He knew it was a fatal promise, but death was Nothing, dying the beginning of Nothing, the end of pain.

And now, as he stood in the Syrasse questing for the bridestone to which he would marry the copper for his weaponsmith's dagger, it was a continual amusement to him to realize that his blasphemy had called down no punishment, and that though it was not yet late afternoon, Sartor had already seen fit to grant him enough bridestone to fill his neck pouch almost completely.

Thank you, Merciful Patron, he thought, laughing. And he laughed again, long and loud, so that Thlal and the slave named Moth stared at him from the shore, when he took from his bowl a mass of gray crystals the size of his right fist. Bridestone, as miraculous a find as the white clay from which he had shaped his darsath.

See, uncle? Sartor rewards me for my blasphemy!

You must examine the rest of your gravel before you pour it out. To discard it would anger Sartor.

Blind. Blind as Sartor. But he washed and examined it, found four smaller crystal masses, one red, one yellow, one black, and one brown, in the bowl, all with the proper luster, the proper weight. All bridestone.

Already more than he would need to make himself his dagger.

Chapter Twenty-Eight

The line leading into the tunnel went slack: the slave named Moth had passed out again from breathing too much smoke. The line was tied around the slave's waist; Sartor-ban-ea-Sar signaled Thlal to pull his namesake from the tunnel while he himself ran into it with the tarred bucket full of water and vinegar.

The horizontal mine shaft, the adit, was about ten bodylengths deep, and dark. The thick smoke from the fire-setting would have extinguished any torch, so he carried none. Sartor-ban-ea-Sar scraped himself repeatedly and knocked his head against the low ceiling, even though he was running almost doubled over; twice his feet got entangled in the rope with which Thlal was dragging Moth out of the smoke.

Then he tripped over the body of the slave himself, and knew he was nearing the shaft's end. His lungs were bursting; he could feel the heat, see the faintly glowing embers of the fire Moth had set against the far wall of the shaft. He dashed the contents of his bucket against the hot rock, heard it crack, then had to take a breath and choked. Coughing, he ran back up the tunnel to Moth, dragged him the rest of the way out.

They waited until the smoke had cleared. It took a long time, for unlike the shafts in the lower valley where slaves delved copper for their Tas masters, the adits here in the upper cliffs where the Tas themselves delved the copper they needed for their rituals had no provisions for ventilation. When the smoke was gone Sartor-ban-ea-Sar examined the wall where the fire had been set: it had cracked, but not enough.

Twice more the fire had to be set before enough rock had been loosened for Sartor-ban-ea-Sar to attack it with his stone chisel. Daysixths of hard labor later, the stone hammer heavy in one hand, the stone chisel in the other, his wrists aching, he could finally see by the light of the torch his slave held for him that the leather sack was once again full of the malachite-bearing rock.

Not for the smiths themselves the digging of yellow and gray ores from the deep veins; no, for them the rich shallow veins, the soft stone and green malachite, the blue-green turquoise and chrysacolla. But even so Sartor-ban-ea-Sar needed more ore, much more, and so the whole process began again.

Finally, he could rest. He gestured Thlal and Moth away, sat down on a rock. His head ached where he had struck it against the roof of the tunnel. He rubbed at it, looked at his hands and legs: he was covered with scrapes and bruises, small cuts that had refused to close or scab over, that still oozed blood and infected yellow pus. And there were more every day.

Why isn't my body healing, ghost? Is it because I'm here, in the Harg? Because we profaned the Tower of Three Levels?

I don't know why, smith.

When, three days before, he had returned to the Tower of Three Levels with his miraculous take of bridestone, the smiths had been overjoyed for him. They had crowded around him, congratulating him and kissing him on the cheeks, and he had stood smiling and laughing with them, happy on the outside, cold and free and contemptuous on the inside.

"You have been granted a truly miraculous gift," Sartor-ban-ea-Ndrur had told him. "Far more than you will be able to use. What do you intend to do with the rest of it?"

"What do you suggest?"

"Thlal needs bridesmetal of his own if he is to attempt the final ordeal again."

"Then he is welcome to all that I myself do not need." It was the right thing to say. Thlal and Tas No beamed; Sartor-ban-ea-Ndrur smiled; and even Tas Et said, Nobly done, nephew.

What about you, ghost? No praises?

You give him something you neither want nor need, smith. In what way is that praiseworthy?

I agree with you, potter. It is not worthy of praise. But it is pleasant enough that these smiths do not share your opinion.

That evening Tas No told him, "The bride must be readied for her marriage," and taught him how the bridestone was to be smelted. Most of what Tas No told him Sartor-ban-ea-Sar had already learned in bits and pieces at other times; most of what he was to do he had already approximated in some way in his regular work in the forge. And he would not have to build the furnace or ignite and quench the wood from which the charcoal was to be made: all that had been done for him.

He knew the thing would be easy, and quick.

It was. The furnace, built of stones and lined with clay, was set at the edge of a depression in the ground. Inside it, bridestone was mixed with billets of pistachio-wood charcoal. Sartor-ban-ea-Sar struck the fire and tended the operation while Thlal and Tas No worked the blowpipes; when there was nothing else that needed doing, he too blew on the flames.

Moments after the flame had been struck, it began to rain.

The molten bridesmetal settled to the bottom. The waste slag remained at the top until Sartor-ban-ea-Sar pulled the stone plug and allowed the slag to empty into the ring-shaped trough dug to receive it. Rain hissed on the slag as it cooled. Then Moth lifted it from its trough with a hook while Sartor-ban-ea-Sar lifted the hardened bridesmetal from the bottom of the furnace with a long rod.

He had recited aloud the prayers the others expected to hear, ignored those he was supposed to repeat silently. Neither Raburr nor Tas Et had animated the furnace flames; his tools had been lifeless stone and metal. And though it had been sweaty work despite the rain, it had still been easy, easy, so easy and so soon finished.

Then, accompanied by his grandfather and the slave bearing his name, he had followed Thlal through the torchlit tunnel to the second valley. The tunnel sloped gently downward. It was very long, perfectly straight; its smooth walls of purple stone occasionally glimmered in the torchlight with huge crystals.

They emerged onto a hillside. Thlal paused a moment before leading them on, and as Sartor-ban-ea-Sar stared down at the mines he felt the giddy lightness leave him forever:

What was his icy freedom, his resolution to free or avenge those he loved in the face of his knowledge of certain extinction, compared to *this?*

The sky above was dark with clouds or smoke, it was impossible to know which. Uncountable holes had been dug into the black and purple cliffs: the valley looked as through wasps the size of men had nested in the bruised flesh of a giant. And from the holes black smoke rose, mingling with the smoke pouring from the dozens of glowing furnaces, adding to the cloud above.

There was a smell like eggs burning, and freezing rain fell. The wind blew gritty ashes into their eyes.

He'd wanted to free Tramu and Pyota for a life built on *this:*

Redheaded men with whips tipped with jagged metal, laughing. Slaves with hair of all colors, sweating, straining, bleeding. Men, women, children bent beneath inhuman loads, attacking the naked rock with stones, scrabbling away at it with bleeding hands. Falling. Bleeding. Being dragged unconscious from the tunnels, their skins scraped from their bodies by the jagged rock.

Lying dead. A pile of bodies off to the right. One of them a young girl, a lone carrion bird perched on her face, ripping away at it with its hooked beak.

Redheaded men, laughing, with whips tipped with jagged metal: the truth that rendered his freedom meaningless.

Tramu and Pyota at Nanlasur. He had thought to help them by bringing them here.

Laughing. He had been laughing.

To be a giant, blot it all out with his massive heel, crush it all underfoot like some loathsome insect, and himself with it—

But he had followed Thlal down into the valley, his grandfather prattling on unmoved at his side, the close-faced slave named Moth just a little behind him, and he had breathed the air thick with the stench of pain and burning, and he had done nothing. Now it was he who was the insect, the jointed worm burrowing through the Earth Mother's ravaged flesh. A privileged worm, crawling through the choicest of the bruised rock, spared the flooding, the disease, and the whips, spared the bleeding hands with the nails scraped away.

As free as a worm could be. Never to be anything else. But free to turn and bite his fellow worms, to tear their scaly heads from their bodies and see the purple blood come gushing out.

Free to kill them and watch them die.

Yes.

❦ Chapter Twenty-Nine ❦

Last night he had stood in the Tower of Three Levels, in the chamber beneath the water, with a rictus of feigned ecstasy on his face as he pretended to hear the voice that was to have spoken to him from the undying flame, pretended to feel the same joy that Thlal had felt as he disemboweled his own slave and at last hacked his way into the Ras Syrr; and with the dagger he had forged Moth killed the slave who bore his usename, and so took it back for himself. Now, sleeping in the room on the Tower's third and highest level, to which his new status entitled him, he dreamed:

The plain..Kyborash. Tas Gly. Flying above the unseen landscape.

The mountain spears the sky, and the lead hawk's feathers catch the fires as it dives and is gone, swallowed, eaten up. Moth banks and shoots down into the burning, hearing the sound of laughter not his own.

He falls through the burning, through the laughter, through the pain and the face of the slave named Moth as it coughs blood and grows slack. He falls through, and emerges onto a cold plain —the same plain, perhaps, where the dream began, but white now, ice-covered, every blade of grass sparkling and rigid.

There is a campfire, and the campfire is the fire in the mountain. By it sits Casnut, and perched on his shoulder is the gray hawk. The gray hawk looks at Moth now with golden eyes, and together the hawk and shaman laugh, and their laughter is the campfire, is the fire in the mountain, is the mountain itself.

Tas Et sits by the fire as well, but his face is turned away from the flames and he gazes out over the icy plain, where there is nothing but the sparkling cold. From his back a stake protrudes; his dripping blood has crystallized and ugly red-black jewels lie heaped around him.

"Welcome," the shaman says, without ceasing to laugh. "Welcome. We have been waiting for you a long time."

He tries to run. He knows it is expected of him, that he try to run, but he cannot: he is chained to something in the far distance with chains of silver and ice. As he struggles to free himself, the chains yank on hooks imbedded in his lips and throat, and he hears himself say, "I am coming for you, Moth, and you will be mine, as you have always been mine."

The voice is known to him, though he cannot say whose it is, or why he fears it as he does.

He would scream if he could, but he cannot.

He can almost see the Power coming for him from the far horizon.

And the shaman laughs and laughs.

Awakening in the shifting darknesses of the Tower's highest level, hearing the gentle rain on the stone roof, Moth pulled himself heavily to his feet and staggered past the tiny fires burning before the bridesmetal statues to one of the great window holes, looked out through the grill of crossed blades.

The wind blew warm and damp on his face. A sliver of moon appeared through a hole in the clouds, brought a dead sparkle to the river, disappeared.

But the moonlight had been bright enough for him to see that all the cuts and scrapes that had covered his hands and arms were gone. He ran his hands over his arms and legs, body, everywhere there'd been a cut or scrape or burn or bruise, and found the skin smooth, unmarred, as though there had never been anything wrong. The dream had healed him—just as, he realized, it had healed the arm he had slashed open to get the blood Tas No needed on that first night the dream came to him, the night he'd begun his initiation as a weaponsmith. So it had nothing to do with the Harg, or with his profanation of the Tower.

But those two times were the only times his body had healed itself at all since the dream had begun. As if the dream were feeding on him, had stolen his ability to heal himself for its own and left him nothing.

Tas Et. What do you know of Casnut, the campfire, the icy plain?

Dying here—

No! The campfire, the plain! I saw you there,

uncle, with the stake through you and your blood a pile of frozen rubies.

I die here on this stake, nephew. With the last drop of my blood I curse King Tvil.

Tas Et knew nothing of the dream, and it was no part of the Tas mysteries, nothing he could ask Tas No about.

The copper dagger was hidden in a leather sack on a cord tied around his waist, where it would remain until he was able to set it in a place of honor in his own forge. He held the sack up to his face, traced the metal through the thick leather with his fingers, remembering:

The slave named Moth had been dying, blood dribbling out of his slack mouth, when the face had suddenly firmed and Tas Et had stared out of it at him, whispered, "Thank you, nephew." As the life went out of the slave, the dagger in Moth's hand had grown heavier, and within it he had felt his uncle.

"Sartor has tasted your life's blood, grandson," Tas No had said, blood-spattered and grinning as he faced Moth over the slave's body, and Moth knew that though the crime had been his, he would never forgive Tas No for the loose-lipped delight his grandfather has taken in it. "Your life is His now, your blood His and His alone to drink.

"For that Sartor grants you nothing—you have always been His, to do with as He desires. But He has tasted your blood and He will no longer be satisfied with less than all of it. That is your smith's death-curse: at the moment of your dying you can call down Sartor's wrath on anyone who tries to rob the All-Highest of the blood He covets."

But that didn't explain Tas Et's attempt to avenge himself on Sartor's King. It didn't explain the dream.

Unless the Power coming for him across the frozen plain was Sartor? But the voice was known to him, though he could not recognize it, and he had never heard Sartor's voice. And Casnut? What could a Nomad shaman want with *him?*

Dagger?

I can tell you nothing. You have become too much of this place.

No. I reject the Harg, potter. I hate it as much as you do.

When you killed your name, you killed that part of you that was still me.

I had no choice. We would have been trapped here forever.

You had a choice.

I am not a part of this place. I felt no joy, heard no voice from the flames. The slave would have died anyway, and I did what I did so we could escape.

You listened to a voice telling you to kill an innocent man. Does the fact that the voice was your own make you any less guilty?

To get out of here. To get *you* out of here, potter. And I had to have a proper dagger to hold Tas Et.

Did you? He obeys you, now that you no longer fear him; you could have kept him from causing you any more fits. You chose to kill.

What other choice did I have?

You could have chosen to stay here like Thlal while you looked for another way out.

And if there is none?

Then, and only then, would you have had to choose between killing and dying. And you could always have chosen to die.

What of you, ghost? You would have been trapped here forever.

Perhaps, smith, that would have been my choice. You did not ask me.

↝ Chapter Thirty ↜

The first person Moth saw when he reentered Kyborash was Tas Gly. The ferret-eyed jeweler wore a siltunic of crimson shot through with gold threads, and on his chest was worked a golden eye; at his waist he wore the jeweled copper dagger that proclaimed him King's Friend.

Seeing him standing there rooster-proud, Moth knew there was no hope of persuading him to spare Rafti.

Tas Gly had been talking with three Warriors of the Hand. When he saw Moth and Tas No, he pointed to them and said something. The smallest of the warriors hurried off while the other two, big men with breastplates and helmets of gold, accompanied the little smith as he swaggered over to Moth and Tas No.

"You've returned from the mines a man and a weaponsmith, Tas Moth," Tas Gly said, positioning himself with the two warriors so as to block their way. "Let me be the first to congratulate you."

"I have no need for your congratulations. Let me pass."

"Yet nonetheless I congratulate you, for, as one myself about to become a weaponsmith, I have the greatest respect for the honor involved."

"You, a weaponsmith?" Tas No demanded. "Never!"

"It is true that for many years my virtues were unjustly neglected, old man, but now that Tas An Sil decides such matters, I have at last been granted the recognition I deserve. And to recompense me for the years of unmerited humiliation I suffered, the Sil Smith himself sponsors me."

"Tas An Sil has always been a skillful smith," Tas No said. "It is a pity that the slowness with which he works has kept him so poor."

"You dare imply—"

"I imply nothing. But a man so long poor would be the first to recognize the distinction your new-found wealth obviously reflects. Shall we go, grandson?"

"Won't you consent to wait a little longer?" Tas Gly said. "Syrr Dalma will be back with Lapp Wur in moments, and he's been waiting for your return with such eagerness."

I'll see you dead, Moth thought.

He earned his copper dagger the same way you earned yours, his ghost told him. By killing an innocent.

"Ah! Lapp Wur!" Tas Gly said when the exorcist arrived, accompanied by the third warrior. "Reverend exorcist, I accuse this man, Tas Moth, of sorcery! He has entered into alliance with unclean foreign spirits and with them he has tormented me awake and asleep! His spirits have tortured me with piercing nails, and threatened to kill my wife and myself if we do not abjure Sartor and pledge ourselves to treason against the King of Chal!"

"He lies," Moth said. "Not a word of it is truth."

"You deny the charges, then?" Lapp Wur asked. He was a bent man, small and twisted. His siltunic was black, his right eye blind and milky.

"Yes. I deny them utterly."

"The charges, unfortunately, are too serious to be dismissed without investigation. I'm sure you understand. You must be examined and judged; the demons, if any, must be made to speak."

To the three Warriors of the Hand the exorcist said, "Bring him."

Lapp Wur's assistants had stripped Moth naked, taken from him with his clothes both the golden dagger and the copper blade housing Tas Et. They had bound him with ropes of nettle fiber, then examined his body for telltale scars or other clear signs of sorcery—a third nipple on his chest, a wound of such and such shape on his thighs or back—but found none.

Lapp Wur drew a circle in the dust of the floor around Moth, another around himself. He raised his hand and intoned:

> May the wicked demon depart!
> Sartor, Spirit of the Heavens, conjure it!
> May the demons seize one another!
> Sartor, Spirit of the Earth, conjure it!
> The propitious demon, the propitious giant,
> May they penetrate his body!
> Spirit of the Heavens, conjure it!
> Spirit of the Earth, conjure it!

Sartor, Lord of all Countries, conjure it!
In the name of Sartor All-Highest,
In the name of His King of Chal,
May the wicked spirits depart!

His voice had been that of a seller of songs exalted
by his singing; now he turned, spat: "Demon!
Confess your crimes!"

"There were no demons. There were no crimes,"
Moth said.

"You deny the accusations?"

"Yes. I had two souls for a time, reverend exorcist, but they were both mine. I was initiated into
both the Ri Sil and the Tas Sil. The two souls could
not live together; they fought, and eventually my Ri
soul died. There were never any demons."

Tas Et and the ghost in the golden dagger were
somewhere hidden from him, in another room. He
could have called on them; he dared not.

It was strange to be alone.

"You say they fought, and the Ri soul died?"

"He killed himself."

"He was not murdered by the Tas soul?"

"No. He could not bear to live and took his own
life."

"How?"

"I cannot tell you. It is a Sil secret."

"Indeed. And which soul was it that tormented
Tas Gly?" asked Lapp Wur.

"Neither soul, reverend sir. The man hates me,
and lies."

"Why should he lie?"

"To injure me, from hatred of my family."

"Ah. And why do you say he hates your family?"

"Because, reverend exorcist, he believes my uncle refused Rafti, Tas Gly's daughter, as bride to my cousin."

"Your cousin?"

"Tramu, son of Tas Et."

"Yes. And this girl—is she the one you were to marry?"

"Yes."

"Why?"

"They could find her no other husband."

"Why would your family have had you marry her, if they had refused her once before?"

"They could find me no other smith's daughter for a wife."

"Then why did Tas Gly accuse you of sorcery?"

"He knew I had two souls and—"

"How did he know?"

"He saw me when they were in conflict. He saw me fighting myself."

"And?"

"He saw the opportunity to rid himself of both his daughter and myself by giving her to the King for Prince SarVas's Necropolis. But he needed an excuse to break off our marriage, and so accused me of sorcery."

"You deny you are a sorcerer?"

"Yes. I deny it utterly."

"Yet you think he did wrong by giving his daughter to the King?"

"No, though I was— No. Though I cared for her, and would have been happy to have her for my wife."

"And it was after he told you that he was giving his daughter to the King that you sent your spirits against him?"

"No. I have so spirits."

"Then who sends spirits to torment him?"

"He lies. No spirits torment him."

"How do you know? Have your spirits told you he is lying?"

"I have no spirits. I have done nothing to harm him."

The questioning continued without cease for three days. When Lapp Wur found it necessary to sleep, his assistants took over; when Moth lost consciousness, he was slapped awake.

"I am a gentle man," Lapp Wur told him on the evening of the third day. "The kindest man, I believe, ever to hold this position. Without harming you I have determined that either you are possessed by one of three demons—by Ishin-Shulgit, by Luzgalzaggrisagon, or by Urnigulul—or you are the innocent man you claim to be. And you cannot complain of the treatment you have had from me."

He's afraid of my smith's death-curse, Moth realized. "No," he said.

"Good. Now, if you are to be cleared of the charges against you, I will have to invoke and attempt to drive forth first Ishin-Shulgit, then Luzgalzaggrisagon, and finally Urnigulul. Should any of them answer my summons, I will know you to be guilty; if none of them manifests himself, you will have shown yourself to be innocent. This is, as I am sure you will understand, necessary. Yet the procedure will prove somewhat painful, and though I do not need your consent, I would be much happier if you gave me your permission to do to you that which I must do anyway. So will you, Tas Moth, consent to my examination?"

Moth looked at the assistants heating their tools over the coals of a small fire. Their fires would burn him, he knew; if he broke Tas law and tried to use his mastery of fire to protect himself, the exorcist would take it as proof of possession.

"I give you my consent, reverend exorcist." After all, he had no real smith's curse to call down on anyone anyway.

Two weeks later his wounds were still open and suppurating beneath the cloths with which Carya had bound them, still as painful as they had been just after Lapp Wur and his assistants had inflicted them, despite Carya's salves and poultices. His legs were incapable of carrying him the half day's walk from Kyborash to the Necropolis, so Tas No hired a litter.

Moth watched as the six chanting Warriors of the Voice carried Prince SarVas's golden coffin down the ramp into the tomb.

"Now they carry him into the chamber, the chamber that is his alone!" the Sil Herald chanted for the benefit of those outside the tomb. "Now they lay him on his bier, his bier with the legs and claws of a lion. Now they drape his coffin with the skin of the lion who slew him, the lion slain by King Tvil his father!

"Beside him lie his weapons: his sword of copper, his arrows tipped with heads of copper, his copper dagger, his spears with their heads of copper, his copper dagger, his spears with their heads of reddest copper! Beside him is the boat of lapis lazuli that will carry him into Sartor's Royal Realm!"

Four tall men in brown siltunics edged with red and gold descended the ramp into the tomb. Each carried a wooden harp with a sounding box fashioned as the head of a bull with eyes and beard of lapis lazuli, and each harper was crowned with a thin circlet of gold.

"They take up their positions at the feet of the Prince, in the chamber that is his and his alone! They begin their song as Sartor's warriors seal the chamber!"

Somewhat later the six Warriors of the Voice emerged from the tomb. A seventh took up position at the head of the ramp, and the Warriors of the Hand who formed the Prince's retinue began to make their way down into the tomb, each pausing first to drink sleep from a copper cup held out by the seventh Warrior of the Voice.

The warriors of the retinue wore siltunics of blue wool and breastplates and helmets of red copper. In their right hands they carried their swords; in his left each held something that had been precious to the Prince: an ivory gaming board, a golden onager, a small box of inlaid wood.

"They take their places in the outer chamber!" the herald cried. "On their sides they lie; their thoughts grow heavy and they sleep, to awaken in Sartor's Royal Realm!"

King Tvil sacrificed the white bull with his own hands. It was carried down into the chamber where the warriors slept. The tomb was sealed with slabs of white stone. Earth was heaped upon it.

The Princess Daersa walked slowly down the second ramp. Her head was held high; her eyes were calm. She was dressed all in cloth of gold; around her neck she wore a collar from which dangled ropes of green pearls and long strings of cylindrical beads of lapis lazuli, carnelian, gold, silver, copper, amber, and jade. Her hair was completely hidden by an immense headdress of lapis lazuli beads on which tiny copper and gold birds sported.

"She enters her chamber!" the Sil Herald cried. "In her left hand she holds a mirror of copper, in her right a golden cup! She regards herself in the mirror, she drinks from the cup! On her bed she lies; she covers herself with a robe of white eagle feathers! Her eyes grow heavy! She sleeps, she sleeps, to awaken in Sartor's Royal Realm! The Warriors of the Voice wall up her chamber!"

The warriors emerged; the handmaidens began to descend the ramp. They were robed in red; headdresses similar to the Princess's, but simpler, hid their hair. Their faces were painted green and gold. Each wore a golden ribbon on her left arm.

Moth tried to pick Rafti out of the procession but could not recognize her. The handmaidens all moved with the same studied deliberation, the same formal grace; none hesitated or betrayed any trace of fear. They drank from the copper cup and went beneath the earth.

I would rest here, fade with Rafti, the golden dagger said. Thrust me into the ground and leave me here.

Moth thrust the dagger into the ground, felt the warmth drain from it. He was alone.

The tomb was sealed, its entrance buried. Moth was carried back to Kyborash.

When he finally fell asleep that night, the dream came to him again at last, and when he awakened the next morning the pain from his wounds was better, the wounds themselves almost healed.

ᐇ Chapter Thirty-One ᐇ

Moth was cold-raising a bowl. Taking a flat disk of silver, he held it at an angle on the slightly concave end of a prepared stump; then, using the smooth-ground end of a sheep's legbone, he hammered it until it had become a shallow saucer.

He took the saucer and placed it against the flat end of the stake. Hammering all the way around, he formed an angle; more hammering, and his bowl had a flat bottom.

A second angle, partway up the bowl's sides, making them vertical. Yet a third angle, curving the lip inward. Moth pounded the angles out into smooth curves with the bone, then rubbed the outside with a fine soft henstone to smooth away roughness.

A final burnishing with a piece of agate, and the bowl was finished. He picked it up, looked at it. The slightly irregular surface reflected light in soft patches.

A good piece of work, Tas Et told him from the dagger. *It should fetch a decent price.*

I need it.

297

For your exorcist?

To get him to examine Tas Gly, yes.

I will not haunt him for you.

You will.

No.

What if I find a way to use him against the King?

How?

I don't know yet. But I will.

The dagger was mounted on a post set by the furnace, where Moth had put it as soon as he'd recovered his health and had been invited by Tas No to share the old man's forge, not as an apprentice, but as an equal.

The first months of winter had been spent working metal in the forge during the day, drinking barley beer with Carya and Tas No at night. Snae Tka was unaware of the skills Moth's ability to draw on Tas Et gave him, and by selling some of Moth's finest work and passing off the rest as Tas No's, Moth and Tas No had been able to keep him ignorant. So the taxes Snae Tka assessed, which would have been ruinous had he been only a thirteen-year-old barely master of his craft, left Moth not only enough money to help Tas No and, secretly, Kuan with their taxes, but enough to put some away toward his two revenges.

When Tas Gly had left for the Harg, Moth had hoped the fireworms would devour him. But two weeks later Tas Gly had returned a weaponsmith —and that could only mean, Tas No had admitted, that Tas An Sil had been paid to reveal the secret of the river of burning rock to him, since the arrogant little smith would never have been able to cross it without help.

And so now, night after night as he sat and drank beer with Carya and Tas No, Moth schemed and planned. It was a game he played with himself: the object, Tas Gly's humiliation and death; the rules, that Moth must achieve it in such a way as to not only leave himself blameless but also advance him in the pursuit of his other goals—freeing Tramu and Pyota from the mines, if they still survived, and carrying out his uncle's vengeance.

For enough money, Lapp Wur would be willing to bring an accusation against Tas Gly; and if Tas Et could be convinced to help, it would be easy to prove Tas Gly possessed. The money was slowly accumulating, and night after night Moth attempted to find an argument to convince Tas Et that Tas Gly's death would advance the spirit's vengeance.

Those nights he spent with Carya and Tas No . . . Tas No he still perhaps loved in a way, but he had never forgiven the old man for what he had revealed of himself at the Harg, never forgiven him for the hypocrisy that masked his weaponsmith's ferret soul. But though Carya was no more interesting than before, though her conversation was no more elevated and her intelligence no more penetrating, yet there was about her an innocence that Moth would have cherished had he still been capable of cherishing anything.

It was because she was a woman, and ignorant. It was not that women were inherently any better, any kinder or more honest than anyone else. No doubt she would have killed the slave and lied to herself about it just as her husband had, as Moth had, if she'd been given the opportunity. But she was shut

away from responsibility, kept from knowledge; she
had the purity of unsuspecting ignorance that Moth
himself had lost, the warmth that had gone from
him when his potter's ghost had abandoned him.

She had sensed his loneliness, his emptiness, as
Tas No had not. "A young man needs a wife, and if
not a wife, a woman," she had said. Twice Moth
had taken her advice and visited the veiled girls
and women who served the Siltemple as hierodules,
finding in them the same innocent calculation, the
same ignorance, that he admired in her; finding, as
well, that they were no more able to comfort him
than she was.

The silver bowl had been a simple piece of work,
demanding more patience than skill. A piece for
Snae Tka, or perhaps for the Sil, in return for more
metal.

It was late afternoon, too late to do anything with
the bowl. Moth cleansed himself, going through the
ritual purifications not for his own sake but for his
grandfather's, and left the forge for the house.

Tas No was out arranging the sale of one of the
pieces being kept secret from Snae Tka. Carya
served him beer and sat with him. Moth took a
chill comfort in her presence, but had nothing to
say to her. She sat silent, watching him. She seemed
nervous.

Sometime later she got up and left the room, only
to return immediately.

"Moth?"

"What?"

"There is someone here to see you."

"Who?"

"She's waiting in the courtyard."

Kuan was there, veiled as a hierodule. "Moth."

"Yes."

"Son." Above the veil her eyes looked old.

"No longer."

"Still. A son remains a son, whatever he may think. But your father—" She hesitated.

"Do you need more money? You should have told Carya. You shouldn't have risked coming here."

"No. No more money, Moth. Tal would not believe I had any more hidden away. It would shame him too much to learn that you were helping us. I could not bear it."

"Then . . . ?"

"We're leaving, Moth. Tal has asked to be given charge of the Sil's affairs in Chal again. No one will know his history there, and Snae Tka cannot follow us."

"And he won't have to be reminded of me there. Say it: the truth will not hurt me."

"Yes. He won't have to pretend not to see you when he passes you in the street."

"When are you leaving?"

"In three days. On the barge."

"Do you need money?"

"No. I told you, no. And it will be better if Tal does not see you again before we leave."

"Very well. Sartor's luck to you both, mother once mine. Perhaps it is best that you go. I wish you the happiness I could not bring you."

"Luck to you too, son." She raised her hand as if to touch his face, then dropped it and turned away.

He watched her walk away. Should I feel sad? he wondered. Should I want to cry, feel as I do when I go out to the Necropolis and hear my ghost whisper "Go away" from the warm earth?

But even at Rafti's tomb he had been unable to cry.

It would be easier with them gone.

ᕋᕘᕏ Chapter Thirty-Two ᕕᕉᕋ

When Tas No returned from the market with the money he'd obtained for the copper blade Moth had given him to sell, he said, "The Royal Eunuch —the one who rescued you at the Fair—was there today. I saw it coming out of the Siltemple. It wants to come talk with you here in the morning."

"Why?"

"I sold it the knife you made. Perhaps it wants more. The knife was a fine piece of work. But —Moth?"

"What, Grandfather?"

"The way the Warriors of the Hand and Voice were looking at us while we were talking, I . . . You know how high taxes have become."

"You think we're going to have another war."

"I think so. Against the Delta."

"So people will think I'm a traitor if I deal with this Royal Eunuch?"

"They might. People are suspicious of everybody who has anything to do with foreigners now, after the way Bigandzin fell. It's too easy for a few people

303

to betray an entire city."

"But Kyborash, Grandfather? Me? It's not as if I were a Warrior of the Hand, or a gate guard, or someone else who could open a gate for them at night." Yet, why not? Moth had already sworn vengeance on King Tvil, profaned the Tower of Three Levels upon whose sanctity the survival of all Chal supposedly depended: he was already a traitor. It would serve no purpose to betray Kyborash to the Deltans now, but perhaps someday, when things were different . . .

All the more reason to maintain and strengthen his association with the Pink-Eyed.

"Of course not," Tas No said. "We're too far from the Delta, anyway. But people talk. And some people already think Tas Et betrayed Chal."

"I know." There was something there, hidden in his grandfather's words, something he had to think about later. "And since we're of his family, we're not to be trusted. Don't worry, Grandfather, I won't do anything to bring suspicion down on either of us."

"Thank you, grandson."

That night as he lay on his pallet fighting off sleep he examined the idea.

If he were chosen as the Royal Weaponsmith and entrusted with the Dying and Reborn Sword the way Tas Et had been, he would have the means of carrying out Tas Et's vengeance on King Tvil. But who would trust the blade to a dapple-haired half-smith whose uncle had lost the last sword and killed the King's father? No one.

Except—he did not really have to become the Royal Weaponsmith. It would be enough to be chosen as one of the Royal Weaponsmith's assistants. A blowpiper would have a chance to profane the blade. Even Tramu would have been able to do it.

Tas An Sil would undoubtedly appoint himself Royal Weaponsmith. But he would never choose Moth, even as a blowpiper, unless—

Unless he had a good reason to do so. And for Tas An Sil, as Tas Gly's initiation as a Ras Syrr showed, money would always be a good enough reason.

So there it was. He would need a great deal of money, far more than he'd ever be able to save doing what he was doing now. He'd have a little more now, of course, with Ri Tal and Kuan leaving, but—

And then he finally saw it, the solution to both his problems, the means of accomplishing both his uncle's revenge and his own. He'd been circling around it, coming closer to it all the time without realizing it.

Tas Et!

What, nephew? the copper dagger answered from the forge.

Tonight, now, you will visit Tas Gly and torment him. You will share with him your agonies on the stake, but you will not let him see with your eyes, you will not let him hear your voice or know who you are.

Why? In what way will this further my vengeance?

I need to gain enough wealth to buy a place among the blowpipers helping forge the Dying and Reborn Sword at the next Seven-Year Festival.

Then I will ensure that King Tvil is never resurrected.

How will haunting Tas Gly help you do this?

At the next Fair I will sell him to the Nomads as a madman. The money from his sale will help buy me my place among Tas An Sil's blowpipers.

Good. Fitting, nephew.

Yes. Uncle, do you remember the campfire, the frozen plain where you sit with Tvil's stake through your back? You gaze out over the waste and Casnut laughs.

Your words have no meaning. Take me and bury me in the dirt behind Tas Gly's forge.

See that he suffers, uncle.

I will.

Later, lying sleepless on his pallet, Moth tried to still his fears of the Fair.

If Casnut was Judge, would Moth be able to keep hidden from him the use to which he would be putting Tas Et? Even if he did find out, would he interfere, so long as Moth took care not to break Fair law?

But there was another, more disquieting level to Moth's fears: with Moth, Tas Et, and Casnut all together at the Fair, the circumstances of Moth's life would be drawing perilously close to those of his dream.

The dream had already stolen his body's ability to heal itself. If dream and reality converged, would he be able to keep the rest of his waking life his own? Or would the dream steal that from him too?

Did he awaken? Moth asked the dagger. Was he terrified?

He screamed when he felt the stake, nephew. He screamed all night. He has no strength; he should never have been allowed to become Ras Syrr.

Did anyone hear his screams?

Only his wife. She threw blankets over him to silence him.

Good. We do not want him discovered and put in the cage, uncle; we need him free to attend the Fair. Wait until he's alone with his wife tonight before you visit him again. And—whisper to him that you are Rafti's ghost and that you will torment him until he gets you what you want from the Fair.

Why should I say that?

His guilt will keep him from asking for help if he believes it is his own daughter haunting him.

What should I say I want him to get at the Fair?

Tell him you will reveal what you want from him only when he is already there.

"So you would like to buy a dozen blades of . . . exceptional quality?" Moth asked the Royal Eunuch.

"Yes. You do fine work indeed, for one so young." The purple silk fluttered with the words. "The work you did for me in the past was very good, in its way, and the blade I bought from your grandfather yesterday was an excellent piece of work, quite beautiful. Though not, of course . . . exceptional."

"Ah. Some more wine?" Moth poured it, thinking, Your voice is the same, you look and act almost the same, but—you're someone else. I'm not sure how I know, but I know. Why are you pretending to be the one I knew?

"Thank you. As a demonstration of the trust I place in you, and as a sign of the friendship I hope to see growing ever closer between us, I will pay you three times the sum we discussed—one third of it now, in advance, the remainder when I receive the blades."

"Your trust honors me," Moth said. "Yet though I, personally, have always had the same sort of trust in you, you must have noticed that my people have been suspicious of anyone from the Delta lately . . . ?"

"There has been a certain tension."

"Exactly. So I would feel better if it was not known that we are doing so much business together. If, for example, rather than returning here, you were to meet me two months from now, at the Fair."

A short trill of laughter. "I may not be able to attend the Fair in person this year. But, from what you say, that might even be preferable. I could have someone meet you there."

"Good. Yet another thing has just occurred to me. It would undoubtedly look better for both of us if your representative were to make a public commitment to buy, say, some vases or bowls from me."

"Shall we say two dozen vases, half in gold, half in copper?" said the eunuch. "To be delivered to my representative at the Fair?"

"That would be excellent."

Moth dreamed that night that beside him on the frozen ground of the plain was a white-glazed jar

with a sealed mouth. Inside the jar a baby was
crying.

Lapp Wur led Moth into the sesame-oil-scented
interior of his house. There Moth found nine of the
exorcist's former victims, men who had developed
an attachment to the milk-eyed man during their
interrogations, sitting and drinking wine: a shabby
court, diffident and exalted, with Lapp Wur as its
center, shining brighter to his scarred and maimed
devotees than the King of Chal.

"Tas Moth!" called a man with a sweet voice. He
was missing two fingers on his left hand and his
cheek was scarred.

"Alrabanas," Moth said, embracing him. "I had
not realized I would find you here."

"I come often. The reverend exorcist has need of
a seller of songs to entertain his friends. And I—I
have not been in much demand since the day when
the spirits within me began reviling people. But the
revered exorcist helps me fight them, and someday,
perhaps . . ."

"Perhaps he'll be able to do well again at his
singing," Lapp Wur said. He smiled apologetically.
"If my efforts to drive the demons from his body do
not scar him so badly that he frightens away his
potential clients."

There was a moment's silence. "Some wine, Tas
Moth?" Alrabanas asked finally.

"Please."

⊶ Chapter Thirty-Three ⊷

He falls through the burning laughter and emerges on the plain of white içe.

There is a campfire, and the fire is the flame in the mountain. By the fire Casnut sits with the gray hawk perched on his shoulder, laughing.

Tas Et also sits by the fire, his face turned away, the stake protruding from his back. Between Casnut and Tas Et, a graceful white jar like the one whose neck Ri Tal had once forced Sartor-ban-i-Tresh to ring with nettle fibers rests on the frozen ground, and from within the jar comes the sound of an infant crying.

"Welcome," the shaman says. "Welcome. We have been waiting for you for a long time."

As Moth tries to run, the thing in the far distance to which he is chained yanks at the hooks imbedded in his lips and throat, and he hears himself say, "I am coming for you, Moth, and you will be mine, as you have always been mine."

And the voice is known to him, though now, awakening, he cannot say whose it is or why he fears it as he does.

He shook his head to clear it, stood up. It was the morning of the Fair, two weeks before his birthday and six days before the date for which Kel Vaq Sil had proclaimed the Spring Inundation.

Will Casnut be the Judge this year? If he is, will he try to stop me? Do I dare try to learn from him what my dream means?

He shook his head again. Even if Casnut knew, he didn't dare ask him.

Does Tas Gly have the swords ready? he asked Tas Et.

Yes. He has arranged to accompany Syrr Aol.

He does not suspect?

No. He is too cowardly to open the sack. He fears me too much, nephew.

With good reason, uncle.

Moth washed himself, dressed in his finest sil-tunic, and splashed scent on his hair, then took the sword he had ready for Syrr Paurr and carried it through the still-dark streets to the Great Square.

When he passed Tas Gly's new house, it was the matter of an instant to remove the loose brick in the wall, retrieve Tas Et, and replace the brick.

"Beautiful work," Syrr Paurr told Moth when Moth showed him the sword. Moth agreed that it was a sword he could be proud of—though it was not, in fact, nearly so fine as the swords Tas Gly would be delivering to the eunuch's representative. He had had only so much bridesmetal.

Is he coming, uncle?

Yes.

Moth put the copper coins Syrr Paurr paid him in his belt purse and pushed his way through the crowd.

"Lapp Wur!" He made himself heard over the braying onagers, the protesting oxen, the foreigners yelling in tongues he did not understand. "Reverend exorcist."

"Ah, Tas Moth. It has been too long since you last graced my home. Sartor grant you luck today."

"May he grant it to you as well, reverend sir." The milky eye disturbed him with its stare. He glanced away, suddenly saw who was in the cage.

"Alrabanas! What happened?"

Alrabanas looked miserably at him, grimaced, and shook his head.

"Unfortunately, he is unable to answer you," the exorcist said with grave dignity. "The spirits I thought were driven from him have returned to stay, and do not allow him the use of his tongue. And the blasphemies they utter make it impossible to let him remain free. Yet sad though I will be to lose his companionship—for I have long counted him a friend—yet there is some consolation in the knowledge that he will fetch a good price for the Siltemple."

Moth could feel Alrabanas's pleading eyes on his back as he walked away.

Dawn had come, mist-veiled but bright, striking harsh gleams from breastplates and shields, helmets and blades, softer lights from jeweled swordhilts and ear ornaments, from the collars of Deltan merchants heavy with jade and garnets, from the harnesses of the horses that pulled the warriors' chariots and the white quartz sewn to the siltunics the Warriors of the Voice wore.

It was time to find Sklar Ton. The trader no more wanted to accompany Moth than Moth wanted to ride with him, but the Siltemple had assigned them to each other, and Sklar Ton had no choice but to obey his orders.

Moth found him already seated on his cart, Snae Golgin beside him.

"Sartor's luck," Moth said. He climbed into the back of the cart, sat down against a wicker hamper.

"Sartor's luck," Sklar Ton said, keeping up a pretence of civility. His hatred was based on knowledge gained through prophecy; if the Siltemple ever learned he'd been prophesying without their approval, he'd end up in the cage.

"Sartor's luck, Tas Moth," Golgin said, smiling back at Moth. At fifteen he was as fat as he'd been as a boy, but beneath the fat was strong muscle, and though he acted the part of everyone's friend, he was no more to be trusted than Snae Tka, his father.

They'll hate you as much as they do him, Moth thought. "You were more heavily loaded the last time we made this trip together," he said, turning to Sklar Ton.

"Yes. I was. I had to pay a great deal to get your father what he wanted."

He doesn't want Golgin to learn how he feels about me, Moth thought. But he'll still be watching me. And so will Golgin—he's here to make sure he gets his taxes. I'll have to get away from both of them when the time comes to seil Tas Gly.

Moth leaned back, closed his eyes.

Tas Et? Where is he?

To your right. At the far end of the square. The sack is already in Syrr Aol's cart.

There will be no trouble with the Warriors of the
Voice?

None. Tas Gly has paid Syrr Aol well.

Good. Torment him, uncle. Not enough so those
around him suspect. Just enough to ready him for
today.

I am already doing so, nephew.

Moth opened his eyes, glanced casually right, saw
Tas Gly sitting upright in a cart with three Warriors
of the Voice. The pinched-faced smith was resplen-
dent in his siltunic of gold-shot crimson with the
golden eye of the King on its chest, but he looked
tired, old, his skin stretched tight over the bones of
his face.

Moth couldn't keep himself from smiling. He
closed his eyes, pretended to rest.

"At last," Golgin said as the cart jolted into
motion. Moth opened his eyes again. "I was afraid
we'd never get started."

The caravan made its way down the Avenue of
King Delanipal the Conqueror, out the West Gate.

"There are more Deltans here than I remember
seeing before," Golgin said to Sklar Ton.

"Yes, there are," Sklar Ton said. "The King of
Bierecia's son is being given in marriage to the
King of Lustan's daughter, so all the other cities of
the Delta must gift Bierecia."

"Is that why the Pink-Eyed wanted me to make
vases?" Moth asked.

"Undoubtedly," Sklar Ton said.

"You've got them here?"

"Behind you, in the hamper you're leaning on.
But don't try to look at them. I don't want the seal
broken."

"All right."

Beneath the Warriors' Bridge the Nacre rushed furiously, thick with yellow silt. "Look at the river," Moth said. "It's already up—it looks as if it's up seven bodylengths. Do either of you remember ever seeing it this high this early?"

"No," Golgin said. "It does seem too high."

"Do you think the Sil Astrologer could have miscalculated the date for the Spring Inundation?" Moth asked Sklar Ton ingenuously.

Sklar Ton glared at him. "Of course not. I have complete faith in his predictions."

"I thought you had certain reservations about astrology?"

"I may once have had some, perhaps. No longer."

He sounded sincere. A lie, or the result of what had happened to him at the Seven-Year Festival? A lie, probably. He had no reason to trust Moth, no more reason than Moth had to trust him.

The sky was gray overhead as the caravan crawled along the East Road. Moth sat in the back of the jolting cart and tried to appear relaxed.

The caravan swung left around a swampthorn marsh, and Moth saw the Nomads lined up upon their horses, the forest dark at their back. He searched the Nomad line for Casnut, did not see him.

Tell Tas Gly that when the Nomads start commending themselves to the Judge, he is to sneak away with the sack and hide himself in the swampthorn, Moth told Tas Et. Make sure he doesn't get a chance to put himself under the protection of the Fair.

And, uncle—have him gibbering by the time I come for him. But don't let him scream. We want him to remain undiscovered.

I've trained him well, nephew. He moans at my command.

Moth scanned the line of mounted Nomads, could see no sign of Casnut.

The city men's caravan was spreading out across the meadow, as men and carts took up positions facing the Nomads. A Warrior of the Voice in white and yellow, his siltunic glittering with topaz and white quartz, stepped from the city men's line.

A single Nomad dressed in red leather rode forward to meet him. The Nomad's horse was black, but he was not Casnut, not even dressed as a shaman. His voice when he spoke was a low growl, difficult to understand.

Moth found himself—what? Not disappointed —he had dreaded the idea of confronting Casnut —but not relieved, either.

Impatient. He was just impatient to get every-thingover with.

"Is he Judge this time?" Moth asked Sklar Ton. "The Nomad?"

"No. Co-Judge. Syrr Rown is Judge."

"Oh." Moth watched the Nomads surrendering their horses' reins.

"Are you a man?" he heard the Judge say some-what later, just as his attention was caught by the sight of Tas Gly sneaking away into the tangled swampthorn. No one else seemed to have noticed.

Have him put the swords just inside the tangle,

where we can find them easily, he told Tas Et. Then have him hide deeper in, where no one will hear him moaning before the proper time.

"Yes. I am a man." Something about the speaker's voice made Moth turn back to stare at him. "I am Sulthar, son of None."

Sulthar was a tall, dark-haired man with Chaldan features. He was dressed as a shaman in a black caftan covered with silver mirrors and red snake ribbons; from the caftan dangled the silver skeletons of two birds, and his hat was a tall cone of squirrel skin decorated with more silver mirrors. In his left hand he held his drum.

Moth recognized him from Lapp Wur's description as the Nomad to whom the exorcist planned to sell Alrabanas, the Nomad whom Moth would have to seek out when the time came to sell Tas Gly. But the shaman's fidelity to the exorcist's description did not explain why, as soon as Moth saw him, he felt as though he should recognize him, as though he had known him all his life.

Sulthar had been the last of the Nomads; now it was the turn of the men of Chal and the Delta to come forward and swear their oaths. Moth knelt, swore, and was accepted without incident.

No one had noticed Tas Gly's absence. Yet Moth lingered, watching as the rest of the city men swore. Merchants, warriors, traders, freemen, artisans, a prince . . . The Royal Eunuchs came last. There were three of them, their long white robes almost clinging to their slim bodies in the mist-moist air, their mouth masks splashes of vivid color.

"Are you men?"

"No. But neither are we women, or children. We

are persons of honor and responsibility, and we beg leave to take the oath of the Fair."

The eunuch's voice was the voice of Moth's dream. He stared, paralyzed, listening as the voice that spoke fear went through the formalities of commendation.

"Hurry up, Tas Moth!" Golgin said, gesturing to a Deltan merchant. "Your buyer's waiting."

"Where's Sklar Ton?"

"I don't know. He said he had to go look at some things." Golgin shrugged. "He should be back in a while."

"In there," the Deltan merchant said. Sick with the eunuch's voice, Moth followed him into the dim interior of his tent.

ᕮᕧ Chapter Thirty-Four ᕦᕤ

Tas Et! The warrior carrying you—can you make him do your bidding?

No one carries me, nephew. I am in a trunk on an oxcart. I can do nothing to free you.

Find Tas Gly! If he's free, force him to free me!

I cannot find him. He is too far away, nephew.

Find him!

Moth tripped over something and fell, dragging down both the trader in front of him and the merchant behind him. The merchant yelled at Moth; before Moth could regain his feet, the noise had attracted a stocky Deltan warrior. The Deltan's whip licked out, cut a line across Moth's bare right side even as he struggled to his feet.

Moth's body was covered with the marks from the Deltan's whips. He had not eaten for five days. He was tied to the man in front of him, and to the man behind him; like them he was barefoot, half-naked. His arms had been lashed to a pole across his shoulders, and he was returning to Kyborash.

In the dim interior of the tent into which he had

319

followed the Deltan, he had been listening with half his attention to the merchant pretending to argue prices while with the other half he concentrated on schemes for delivering the blades undetected and ridding himself of Golgin and Sklar Ton long enough to contact Sulthar, when suddenly Tas Et burst into his mind with the news that hundreds of mounted Nomads were slaughtering the city men. There had been shouts and screams outside the tent; Moth had leapt to his feet—

And been knocked unconscious with something hard, perhaps even one of his own vases. He'd awakened to a thunderstorm, found himself one of what must have been three sixties of Chaldans very efficiently tied and left by themselves in an open part of the meadow.

He tested his bonds, found them sound. The heavy rain hammered on his throbbing head. He was a captive, soon to be a slave.

For the second time. He should never have come back to the Fair.

It was late evening when he awakened. During the night the part of the meadow where he lay had flooded. A Warrior of the Voice who had been left facedown near Moth was dead; he must have drowned without ever having regained consciousness.

The sun came out briefly, and with it, the flies.

Moth had lain for three days in the meadow, given neither food nor water, though after a while he'd managed to twist his head around so as to drink some of the water in which he was lying. Around him the other captives cried out, complained, bewailed their fates.

Though the dagger housing Tas Et had been taken, Moth could still speak with the spirit. Tas Et had lost Tas Gly in the confusion of the attack.

Find him, Moth had ordered. If he is still free, we can make him release me.

But Tas Et had been unable to find him.

Neither the eunuchs nor their representatives had shown any interest in Moth. If they'd had any plans to use him as a traitor, the plans must have been abandoned.

And though it had been Nomads who had over-whelmed the Fair, it was Deltan warriors who yanked the captives to their feet, hobbled them together, and marched them off.

Moth had been three days without food or sleep when he had his first hallucination. He was ex-hausted to the point of delirium and beyond; many times only the repeated urgings of a Deltan's whip had forced him up off the ground and made him continue; but he dared not sleep.

The voice from his dream had spoken, and he had found himself a slave. So he knew at last that the dream was real, and what it meant. He dared not risk returning to it—when he slept, the dream would come to an end, and he would die.

There was no question in his mind: the eunuch with the voice of fear was waiting for him just beyond the borders of sleep, to steal what life remained to him. If he fell asleep, the eunuch would learn who he was and he would die.

"Moth," Rafti said. "Husband. I forgive you. It was all a mistake. Nothing really happened to me. I'll be waiting for you in Kyborash."

A headless body lay sprawled in the mud by the

side of the road, its siltunic of crimson shot with
gold with the eye of the King worked in gold on the
chest matted with caked blood. A small animal was
ripping at the headless neck, snarling at the Chaldan captives as they stumbled past.

Tas Gly. Another hallucination.

No, Tas Et told him. I have been in that body; I
know it. That was Tas Gly.

Moth took no joy in the knowledge. There was
only a sense of finality, of completion, almost of
pity for the little smith.

The Nacre was swollen and gleaming like an immense yellow-brown leech; its waters lapped at the
walls of Kyborash. The Warriors' Bridge was gone,
washed away by the floodwaters or destroyed by the
city's defenders.

Moth was put on a raft with seven other captives
and forced to pole his way across a shallow part of
the river.

He had drunk mud from a puddle and once, days
ago, been tossed a hunk of hard black bread. The
whip marks on his back and sides were still open,
still oozing blood and pus.

They were marched down the Avenue of King
Delanipal the Conqueror, slogging through the
thick yellow mud that covered everything, hid the
pavement beneath their feet, blurred the outlines of
the walls. The city already stank of disease, dank
rot.

Two days later, his body chilled with fever, he
was hauled from the house in which he had been
prisoned and through the drying streets to the
Great Square.

The square was filled with young captives, many sixties of them. Moth had been too long without sleep to better estimate their number. He saw faces he knew he should recognize, but knew no one.

A Royal Eunuch, its white robes spotless, was directing the Deltan warriors who were forcing the captives into a ragged line. Moth stared at the eunuch, memory and hallucination churning like boiling mud within him.

If I fall asleep it will find me, Moth thought. It will know which one I am.

Help me stay awake! he begged Tas Et.

I am too far away from you, nephew. I can do nothing.

Casnut rode into the square, past the Deltan warriors. His horse was black, gaunt and powerful like the shaman himself. Hanging from the shaman's black caftan were the golden bones of a hawk, and as Casnut rode through the square the bones jangled and clanged, rattled against one another with a sound like a soul in torment.

Tas Et! Help me!

I can do nothing, nephew. Nothing.

The shaman rode up to the Royal Eunuch, was greeted with melodious politenesses from behind the bright silk hiding its mouth.

The eunuch's voice was the voice of fear.

They were all together: Casnut, Tas Et, the eunuch with the voice that spoke fear.

"Do you have the sword?" Casnut demanded with unfeigned arrogance, looking down on the eunuch from his horse.

The eunuch beckoned to one of its warriors, who brought Casnut a long leather sack. Casnut opened it, pulled out the hilt of a broken sword. Moth recognized it: the Sword That Was Asp.

Casnut put the sword back in the sack, lashed it in place on his saddle, and only then dismounted. He stared at the line of prisoners.

"Are these all?"

"Yes," the eunuch answered.

Casnut walked up and down the line, staring into each face in turn, tapping out questions on his spirit drum as he moved.

Twice he passed Moth by without seeming to notice him, but the third time something gleamed in his eyes and he stopped. Moth tried to back away, but the shaman's gaze held him, paralyzed, and he could not make his muscles obey him.

"Is this the one?" the eunuch asked him.

"He shows many of the signs. I must ask the spirits. . . ."

The eunuch stood silent and relaxed, watching as the shaman whispered secret words to the golden hawk's skeleton and then threw it into the air. Before it could fall to the ground it had been clothed with the flesh and feathers of a great black hawk with eyes of fierce gold.

The other captives tried to back away as the hawk circled low over Moth, but their fettered ankles prevented them from moving very far.

Casnut beat out a strange, complex rhythm on his drum. The hawk replied. Another rhythm. Another scream from the hawk.

Casnut held up his arm and the hawk came to him. Moth's vision blurred. When he could see again, the shaman was restoring the golden skeleton to its place on his caftan.

"This one," the shaman said clearly, pointing to Moth. His hand went to his drum, began tapping out a slow, almost inaudible rhythm on it.

The earth shook, and Moth fell through the skin of the world. Into the dream.

❦ Chapter Thirty-Five ❧

Neither sun nor moon to light the landscape, only the stars glinting cold and hard overhead: Sartor's frozen Nighteyes, staring down at him in mindless hatred.

A limitless plain. Dead, dry grass whose brittle blades he crushes underfoot as he looks out in all directions from his high place.

A cool breeze blows steadily in his face, as though he were rushing over the grassy sea in an invisible coracle that takes its direction from his gaze.

But his gaze has no object, controls nothing. He is only compelled to stare into the wind.

The wind shifts back and forth, compelling him to keep turning with it.

The stars are building a city on the plain. Fingers of cold light reach down, and where the light strikes, a paving stone, a section of wall, a man's leg appear.

The wind shifts. Moth turns away from the city. The wind shifts again and he turns again, shifts and shifts and shifts—

He is close to the city now, approaching it from another angle, and he recognizes it. Kyborash. Above the city Sartor's Eighty-four Aspects hang like clouds of bruised shadow.

The wind dies. He is very close to the city, looking down on it. The stars' fingers of light lend the Eighty-four Aspects definition as they reach down to fill in the final details: the blue godhouse atop the ziggurat, a beggar crouching in the shadow of a wall, two men fishing from a small boat, a bird nesting in an apricot tree.

Like water over a cascade he descends the hill.

At the first house he pauses for an instant, looking back over his shoulder. The plain stretches away to infinity behind him; the high place is gone.

Invisible, he walks the streets. When he looks closely, he can see threads, ropes, chains of chill light binding the people around him to the stars.

He stops by a well where a woman is filling a widemouthed jug with water. He looks down at his reflection in the well, sees luminous chains linking his arms, body, legs, head to the sky, binding him not only to the stars but to all the city of Kyborash, to every man, bird, animal, and stone.

Everything is chained to everything else, and everything is chained to the stars. Where the stars' bright chains cross one another, light pools in radiant plexuses, and in each plexus one of the Sartor's Eight-four Aspects is limned in cold radiance.

And now he is pulled like a toy coracle on a child's string through the city to the square where Rafti lies bound on an altar of starlight.

No! he wants to scream as he sees Tas Gly leaping

and dancing with the knife in his hand. No! No!

His eyes are directed down to his own hands. He sees the luminous chains linking the goldsmith to him: he is the puppeteer, Tas Gly only the puppet. Relief washes over him: he can make Tas Gly stop before he kills Rafti.

But he cannot halt the play of his fingers as he makes Tas Gly yank up the arm holding the knife, for his fingers in turn are dancing to the commands of the chains that link him to the stars—

And all motion stops. Tas Gly is frozen suspended in midleap.

For the first time, he realizes that he has experienced all this before.

A golden hawk appears in the distance, sweeps toward him, hovers like a hummingbird in the air before him, its wings a blur of golden fire.

No chains bind it to the stars or the city. It is free: its wings are its own.

The fierce eyes stare into his as the hawk extends itself downward, becomes Casnut. Yet he feels no fear.

"Ask of me what you will, and I will grant it to you," the shaman says, and Moth can see that Casnut, like the hawk, is free.

Rafti lies frozen on the altar of starlight; her father crouches over her with his knife poised, a puppet waiting for Moth to twitch the strings, as Moth in turn awaits the impulse from the stars that will force him to do it.

"Free me of these chains!" Moth cries.

And the shaman laughs.

He gestures, and at his gesture all the chains linking Moth with the city and the stars grow taut.

For the first time Moth realizes that every chain ends in a tiny hook.

They pull the flesh from his bones.

His brain, his liver, his intestines, his nerves —everything is ripped from his skeleton, save only the eyes.

The pain is beyond imagining.

It ends. The city is gone. There are no stars.

Casnut picks up the fleshless skull, holds it so the eyes in the bare-bone sockets can see the heaped white bones.

"Do you want me to give you back your flesh?" he asks.

Moth finds he can speak. "Yes!" he cries, his cry a dusty whisper blowing across and through the bare bone of his skull.

The shaman gestures. Chains of light come writhing out of the darkness, coiling like serpents around the naked bones to bind them together, cloak them with the semblance of flesh. And only then does Moth see the stars glinting in the sky again, the city grown up all around him, Tas Gly about to plunge the knife into Rafti's heart.

"This is your own flesh, the flesh you have always known," the shaman says. "Watch: your life begins."

And the false flesh grows younger, shrinking, compressing the bone within as Moth becomes a youth, a child, an infant. The city as well is changing, altering, becoming something different.

Moth reenters his mother's womb, and that womb too is false flesh. His life begins. In an agony of impotence he reexperiences the whole of his life, the false flesh going through the motions of what he had thought was his body's reflection of, expression of, his will. Yet he is unable to change a single word or act; everything happens exactly as it had before.

At last he stands before Casnut again, weary beyond endurance, and hears the voice of his false flesh demand the shaman free him from the chains that bind it.

And again the flesh is ripped from his bones.

"Do you want me to give you back your flesh?" Casnut asks.

Moth says nothing. It is sweet to lie a pile of bones, sweet to stare out onto the empty plain and feel the wind playing through his skull.

"Good!" the shaman says. And reaches into the skull and takes from Moth his eyes.

Moth lies there, sightless, a clean pile of bones, at peace at last.

At peace? But he cannot forget Rafti, Tramu, Pyota, Tas Et's vengeance. There is no peace. There is only a flame, hungry, growing, copper-red, driving out the darkness; the flame of his anger, Tas Et's anger, Raburr's anger; and from it Moth forges burning wire with which to bind his scattered bones together.

He makes of himself a man of bone and burning, and the stars have no hold on him.

"You have initiated yourself, shaman," Casnut says. He gestures and again becomes a golden hawk. Moth sees how the golden fireflesh wraps the shaman's human skeleton. He, too, becomes a hawk.

Casnut takes flight. Moth climbs the air after him, and his eyes are burning suns as he follows the shaman over the arid plain.

Below him he can see the cities of the world: star-wrought lies, heaped falsehoods, chained to the stars. He sees the Harg, the mines at Nanlasur, festering wounds ripped in the earth's living flesh, and he pities that flesh. And his pity and anger are a flaming sword with which to assault the heavens.

"Not yet," Casnut whispers, and the wind carries his words back to Moth. "Not yet."

Ahead, the mountain spears the sky, and it is not black, but a deep, rich lapis. Casnut banks to the right, circles the mountain, ringing it with golden fire. Moth is behind him as they spiral upward, soar over the crimson fires filling the cone, dive.

Moth plunges after the lead hawk, plummeting deeper and deeper through the fires in the mountain and beneath the earth, out into the burning depths of the Mother's Inner Ocean.

Suddenly the Mother Herself is there before him, growing like a stupendous tree, mountain-tall, from the burning yellow mud of the Ocean floor, and She is beautiful beyond all human comprehension: heavy-breasted, legless, with innumerable arms, Her great black-lipped mouth filled with jagged, discolored tusks. Yet as he glides toward Her through the orange-red burning, paralyzed with absolute terror, absolute awe, unable to stop or turn aside, he sees that Her immense brown eyes are infinitely gentle.

Then the Mother is gone, the Inner Ocean is gone, and—though he knows, somehow, that he is still deep beneath the earth—he is beating upward through crisp air, spiraling up after Casnut on untiring wings around the colossal trunk of the Tree that is the Tree of All Creation, until at last they reach the Tree's flowering branches, and that flowering is the flame that is the Heartflame of the universe. . . .

. . . Yet it is at the same time a campfire burning on a gray and frozen waste, beneath an empty sky.

By the fire Casnut sits drumming, a gray hawk on his shoulder. To his left is a vase of white ice, and within it Moth can glimpse a baby struggling feebly. Across the fire from the shaman Tas Et hangs impaled on Tvil's stake; his back is to the fire and he gazes out over the frozen waste. The blood dripping from his wounds freezes before it reaches the ground.

Moth hovers above the shaman's head, warm within the flame of his anger, the anger that protects him from the cold that has trapped the baby in its vase of ice.

Casnut sees him, and laughs. He changes the rhythm of his drumming, and above them the empty sky fills with stars that stare down at them in frozen malice. Shafts of chill light radiate out from the stars, linking them to one another in a crystalline latticework that chokes the sky, that reaches down with chill fingers to the frozen plain below.

Kyborash begins to take shape around them.

Moth's double, himself as he had been before his transformation, appears in the city, eyes closed as if in sleep. The double's flesh is star-wrought mockery, chained to the city and the stars.

Casnut touches his fingers to the skin of his drum, and a great furrow opens in the frozen plain, becomes the Nacre Valley. Chill light from the stars lashes the ground at the far end of the valley, and the Royal Eunuch whose voice is fear appears.

The eunuch grasps the chains binding Moth's false semblance, begins pulling itself toward the double, sliding along the frozen ground. Moth's double's body contorts with agony as the hooks at the ends of the chains rip at its flesh. The hawk feels its human double's pain as if it were his own, yet the pain has no power over him.

The eunuch is pulling itself slowly closer. As it draws near, Moth knows it for the lie that it is, with a knowledge as direct and inescapable as his knowledge of the Earth Mother, a knowledge that has no need for reason or comprehension, and he hates it.

He is a hawk. He screams, swoops, attacks his other self, standing stupid in its agony. With beak and talons, with wings sharp as any sword, with the Fire of which he is Master, he burns away the false flesh, doing for himself what Casnut had once done for him.

His double is clean bone now: the eunuch's hooked chains no longer bind it. The jar of white ice cracks open, liberating the baby within, and the baby is Sartor-ban-i-Tresh.

The campfire flares up, explodes into brilliance, and the baby and his double's bones are gone. There is only Moth, standing taller than any giant, with muscles of fire and fury, sinews of baby's laughter. Moth stands by the fire that pulses with the beating of his heart, and laughs at the Royal Eunuch creeping slowly toward him.

Moth laughs and his laughter is a flame, is the flame of his will, and with it he drives back the eunuch, pushes it away from him, from the campfire that is the Heartflame that is the Tree of All Creation.

The eunuch is gone. With the laughter that is no different from his anger, Moth drives back the frost, frees the plain from the grip of winter, burns the city the stars were constructing to ash, and the ash to nothingness. The grass begins to grow again.

Moth climbs the air, soars over the green plain, burning the very stars from the sky as he screams his victory.

Then suddenly he is a hawk no longer, but only his human self again, standing before Casnut.

And Casnut says, "You have won nothing, defeated nothing. Look."

He gestures, directing Moth's gaze to a place far distant, where the sky has cracked open and the frozen stars are pouring through, already beginning to reach out and construct a new city on the plain. The city is peopled with eunuchs of gray ice, and from it the frost is spreading to blight the plain anew.

"They assault the Center," Casnut tells him. "Always they assault the Center. Yet here we cannot defeat them, for the Center mirrors the World, as the World mirrors the Center, and these are only their reflections. Nothing we can do against them here can destroy them; and yet they must be destroyed. Do you hate them, Moth?"

Moth sees them pouring in through the rent in the sky, the frost from their city blighting the plain, and there is no question in his mind. "Yes."

"Then remember that hatred when you awaken in the World."

Casnut begins drumming, beating out a jerky,

violent rhythm. Moth feels a wrenching, a tearing, as if something is being ripped out of him, and then he drains through the hole the drumming has torn in him, and is gone.

❦ Chapter Thirty-Six ❦

Moth awakened to the soft crackling of flames, the smell of woodsmoke. He opened his eyes, found himself lying face down on rough brown grass, a small cold stone digging into his cheek.

He sat up, brushed the stone away. His wounds were gone; there was no trace of the fever. He felt strong, healthy, vibrantly alive.

A few bodylengths away the Nomad called Sulthar was feeding dry grass and chips of wood to a small campfire. Behind him two horses, one tan, the other spotted black and cream, cropped grass.

Moth looked around. He was on a plain, surrounded by grass, but the grass was green as well as brown, and the sun was bright overhead. In the distance he could see a small clump of trees.

There was no sign of Casnut.

"You're awake," Sulthar said, looking up from the fire.

"Yes."

"Come, sit with me here." Moth hesitated. Sulthar smiled reassuringly. "You have nothing to fear from me, and there is no one else here."

Moth walked over to him, sat down by the fire. "Where are we?"

"The Nomad Plains. A few days' journey from Lake Nal."

"Casnut brought me here?"

"Yes."

"Where is Casnut?"

Sulthar shrugged. "I don't know. He left you with me, so I could teach you to live as a Nomad, and train you as a shaman. He'll return for you when you're ready."

"Why?"

"Every Great Shaman must choose someone to carry on after him, to succeed him. Casnut has chosen you."

Moth opened his mouth to say that that was ridiculous, impossible; he was a smith, not a Nomad shaman—then remembered the dream, the Center, and closed his mouth without saying anything. "Why?" he asked finally. "Why me?"

"His spirits revealed you to him long ago, and he has been testing and training you in your dreams ever since. Remember what you did in the Center, how you drove the Royal Eunuchs back and burned the stars from the sky. Only a shaman could do that."

"It was only a dream." But if it was only a dream, how did Sulthar know what had happened in it?

"It was more than a dream. The Center mirrors the World, just as the World mirrors the Center. But both are real."

"Casnut said—to remember my hatred when I woke up in the World."

"Yes."

"In Chal they say that the stars are Sartor's Nighteyes. So Casnut is fighting against Sartor?"

Sulthar shook his head. "Sartor is nothing, a puppet the stars created to delude men. Only the stars are real."

"I don't understand."

"Once all of Ashlu was green and living," Sulthar said. "There was no desert of salt and sand; the sun was forever in the sky and there was no night.

"In those days men lived in harmony with the Earth Mother. Death came to all, and though it was a time of sadness when a man died, all knew death for a transformation from which the soul was born anew.

"Yet there were those too proud to accept that transformation, the loss of all they had gathered to themselves in their long, long lives. They were men of great knowledge and power, and they sought to escape the eternal round of birth and death.

"From ice they created the Nighteyes and set them in the sky, where the Earth Mother had no power to force them to undergo death and rebirth. Yet since the heat of the sun would have destroyed the Nighteyes, they created the night, and forced the sun to take shelter in the Earth Mother's Inner Ocean while it lasted.

"They destroyed in themselves all that was warm, all that could change and die. They left of themselves only their unliving, undying vision, and that they housed in the Nighteyes. They seek eternal night, eternal frozen death, for all of Ashlu, for only in the death of all that lives and moves will they find an end to the mutability that threatens them with death and transformation. They are the enemy that Casnut fights, that his successor will have to fight."

"Another pretty story," Moth said, disgusted.

"How can you say that, when you have seen the Mother's Inner Ocean? When you have burned the stars from the sky and seen the Center as it was when all Ashlu was living and green? The Center is the heart of all potentiality: it shapes the World even as the World shapes it. The stars can be burned from the sky, and night itself destroyed."

"What does this have to do with the Royal Eunuchs, and the cities?" Moth finally asked.

"The eunuchs are those whom the sorcerers too proud to accept death left behind them to finish their work. The eunuchs, too, pass from Ashlu when they die to become stars."

"Then Casnut is fighting against the eunuchs?"

"Yes. But not only against the Royal Eunuchs. Whenever a man worships a god of the sky or consults an astrologer, whenever he builds a city and orders it in accordance with the rhythms of the heavens, then he gazes through the stars' frozen eyes and is enslaved by their vision. The Warriors of the Voice ascend the Temple ziggurats and enslave themselves to the dead stars in their godhouses; Chal, no less than the cities of the Delta, is an abomination against the Earth Mother. A plague, spread by the stars. All the cities in which men worship Sartor must be razed; the stars themselves must be destroyed, and Ashlu cleansed for the Earth Mother."

"You serve the Earth Mother?"

"No! A shaman, even a minor shaman such as myself, serves no man, no god, no goddess," Sulthar said. "Casnut asks, not your service, but your aid in the destruction of the cities, in the destruction of the stars and their worshipers. In the destruction of night, to recreate day eternal."

"And if I refuse?"

"You owe him your life. When you killed your Ri soul, you destroyed your body's ability to heal itself. Over and over again he has healed you when without his help you would have died. Yet you still cannot heal yourself, will not be able to heal yourself until you have fully mastered your powers as a shaman and can ascend the Tree of All Creation for yourself. Until then I will stay with you, to heal your body where you are incapable of healing it for yourself. Without that help, you will die."

"Either I do what Casnut wants me to do, or I die."

"Yes. Until you can learn to heal yourself again. But the stars and the Royal Eunuchs are your enemies as much as they are his. They are the enemies of all that lives."

"If I believe what you told me," said Moth.

"Even if you refuse to believe me, there is another reason why you should hate the eunuchs, and the stars they serve. Do you remember the Royal Eunuch who rescued you from Nomads at the Fair where you first saw Casnut?"

"Yes."

"The Royal Eunuch was the one who arranged to have you kidnapped, so it could question you when it pretended to rescue you. The knowledge the eunuch gained from questioning you and your cousin was what made it decide to steal the Dying and Reborn Sword."

"Nomads stole the sword."

"Nomads in the Royal Eunuchs' pay, like the Nomads who helped them conquer Kyborash. So it is to the Royal Eunuchs that you ultimately owe the death of your uncle, the enslavement of your aunt and cousin. You owe them your grandfather's death, and those of everyone else who died when Kyborash fell.

"Yet Casnut, too, knew of the eunuchs' scheme. He could have prevented the theft of the sword; he could have exposed the eunuchs' plans at the Fair. He did not, for it served his purposes to have the sword destroyed, to see the King of Chal dead. So he, too, shares that guilt for the death of your uncle, the enslavement of your aunt and cousin.

"And he aided the Taryaa to conquer Kyborash. It was Casnut who found the eunuchs the Nomad mercenaries with whom they overthrew Kyborash. Casnut admits his responsibility: you owe him vengeance also for the deaths of your grandfather and his wife."

"Why tell me this?" Moth demanded. "Why?"

"For this reason: Casnut will see that you are trained as a shaman, that you are taught to carry on his war against the stars and the cities, and during this training you will learn that which you need to know if you are ever to have any hope of defeating and killing Casnut. And Casnut promises you opportunity for your vengeance against him.

"Also, he instructed me to give you this."

The dark-haired Nomad reached into a leather sack, took from it a copper dagger.

Nephew, the dagger said.

Tas Et.

Remember your oath to me.

"Why should I trust what Casnut tells me?" Moth demanded.

"Casnut has told you that you have a reason to kill him when he had no need to tell you anything. He has placed his life in your hands."

"Not yet," Moth said.

"No. Not yet. But he will."

"So you say. But you—why should I believe you? Who are you?"

"I am a minor shaman. A healer and a speaker to animals, not a Great Shaman like Casnut. I had no part in Casnut's plans for you, nor in the destruction of your city. You owe me no vengeance."

Sulthar paused, and then continued in a different tone, "And yet you find me familiar. You feel that you should know me, but you do not." He laughed suddenly, and his laughter was like the laughter Moth had shared with Casnut in the Center, yet was something all his own.

"Who are you?" Moth demanded.

"Once I was a man of Kyborash. Spirits assailed me, and I was seized and sold to the Nomads as a madman. Casnut bought me and taught me to control my spirits, gave me a freedom I would never have known had I remained only a potter of the Ri Sil. Now I am a shaman. Do you recognize me, nephew?"

The resemblance could not be denied. "Ri Sul? My father's brother? They always said you were dead."

Sulthar shrugged. "Perhaps it was easier to think of me as dead than remember me being jeered at, or imagine me tortured in some Nomad cage. But I am Sulthar now. Your uncle. Your teacher. Perhaps even, in time, your friend."

Moth got to his feet. The air was cold, almost as cold as the air in his dream had been before the dream changed, though the day was bright.

With his potter's soul dead and lost to him, he was as cold and empty inside as the stars themselves. But he had no love for what he had become, only the same loathing he had felt at the Harg, the hatred and anger with which he had burned the stars from the sky.

He stretched out his hands, warmed them at the campfire. Summoning his hassa, he reached out to the fire and twisted the flames into the shapes of memory, saw Rafti there dead and Kyborash destroyed, Tramu and Pyota enslaved. He had vowed that he would free Tramu and Pyota if he could, vowed to avenge Rafti and Tas Et. A shaman might be able to rescue Tramu and Pyota, carry out Tas Et's and Moth's own vengeance, where a smith without a city would be doomed to failure.

"I will try it, uncle," he said.

A Selection of Legend Titles